Christmas CHEMISTRY

Coleman Creek Christmas Book One

Rory London

Five Hearts
PRESS

This one is for my mom. I always miss you a little more at Christmas.

Christmas
CHEMISTRY

Playlist

"Kiss Me It's Christmas"
Leona Lewis feat. Ne-Yo

"Rockin' Around the Christmas Tree"
Brenda Lee

"Run Rudolph Run"
Chuck Berry

"All I Want for Christmas Is You"
Mariah Carey

"Last Christmas"
Wham!

"Greensleeves"
Pentatonix

"Snow"
Bing Crosby, Peggy Lee & Danny Kaye

"Underneath the Tree"
Kelly Clarkson

Chapter One

Marley

All the teachers crammed into one of the science labs for the mandatory faculty meeting. Sitting on the tall stool next to posters of Marie Curie and the periodic table felt surreal. I hadn't been in this room for at least twelve years. Not since I'd been a junior taking advanced chemistry.

Coach Hurley, the school's shorts-in-November-wearing ex-Marine athletic director, sat in the corner with his arms folded, complaining half-heartedly about having a staff meeting right before the holiday. A few others pretended to agree, but they didn't fool me. As much as we might be looking forward to the long weekend, we all wanted to be here.

Our group of teachers was close-knit. A small faculty for a small school. And because it was the only high school in the district, we didn't have the constant change-up and churn of staff many larger districts experienced. Seven of those present had been teaching at Coleman Creek High when I'd attended, including Mrs. Allen. She'd been my favorite teacher back in the day. Now, she was a trusted mentor.

I chuckled quietly as she finished her analysis of last night's episode of *The Bachelor* from the table next to mine, "...and that Bryan is a total smoke show, as the kids would say. I'd climb that man like a tree."

"Mrs. Allen!" exclaimed grumpy old Mr. Bailey.

"What?" Her eyes twinkled. "There are no students."

He hmphed, and I smiled. Even though I'd been working at the school for over four years, I had trouble viewing Mr. Bailey as a colleague. As far as I was concerned, he was still the history teacher who'd once given me a C on a paper about the Civil War.

Principal Nadal stabbed angrily at his computer, muttering about PowerPoint. This meeting would clearly not be starting on time.

I checked my watch, wondering why James hadn't shown up yet.

Just as I was about to text, his large frame slid into the seat next to mine.

"Hey," he said, slightly out of breath, reaching up to adjust the slouchy beanie on his head. I knew there was a messy man bun underneath. He almost always wore it that way, although occasionally it was down or in a ponytail.

"Hi." I tilted my head. "In a rush?"

His face reddened slightly beneath his neat brown beard. "Nah. Just annoyed. Fel Torres wanted to talk to me about an assignment. Apparently, if he gets anything less than an A, I'm under some sort of magical obligation to let him re-do it."

"Hmm. I know he's tough, but the parents are ten times worse. Hopefully they won't start calling."

James had only been at the school since August, when he'd moved to our small town in eastern Washington from Seattle. It was his first teaching job, so he was still learning the ins and outs of parent/teacher politics. At twenty-eight, he was also the youngest faculty member, since his birthday came one month after mine.

But he appeared unfazed by Fel's antics. "As it happens, I was planning to offer all the students the opportunity for a make-up, so it works out."

"Good news for them."

I turned my eyes toward the front of the room, keeping my expression neutral. I didn't want to give my colleagues a reason to suspect anything. Since James and I both taught in the humanities—language arts for me, social studies for him—we often worked together. Plus, in a town this small, it was impossible to hide how much time we'd been spending together outside school. Coach Hurley caught my gaze and raised an eyebrow in James's direction. I ignored him.

My own thoughts were jumbled enough without adding meddling co-workers to the mix. Luckily, I excelled at projecting calm—even though my mind had been topsy-turvy since lunch today. I couldn't stop dissecting every interaction I'd ever had with James. Starting with the first one.

Mrs. Allen had introduced us during the prep week before classes started. I'd registered that I found the new hire attractive, but only in a casual way—like how I'd notice a movie star or a good-looking neighbor. Those first weeks, I'd given him a few upnods in the hallway, and a wave at an assembly, but that was all.

My mother had died the previous October, so there had been other things on my mind then. Mainly navigating my first beginning of the school year without her. I'd been doing well enough, focusing on happier memories of the years she'd been able to help buy classroom supplies and listen to me talk about my lesson plans. But there's no such thing as a constant upward trajectory with grieving.

And when my first truly *down* day of the new school year came, James had been the one to find me.

It had been after the last bell, on the third Friday of the school year. I'd stayed late to decorate and organize my classroom. Except he hadn't caught me stapling trim onto bulletin boards or cataloging copies of *The Great Gatsby*. A sad song had come through my ear buds. Since I'd been alone, I'd allowed myself to close my eyes and give in to the melancholy, a moment of catharsis.

"*Ms. Davis, are you okay? I heard*—" *James paused in the doorway.* "*Oh, shit.*" *Crooking his elbow, he rubbed the back of his neck.* "*I...uh...heard crying, and I thought maybe someone was hurt.*"

Feeling my face heat, I peered up from my chair. After pulling my Air Pods from my ears, I ran a quick hand over my wet cheeks. I must have been so wrapped up in the music I hadn't realized I'd been making noise. "*No. It's just me. Having a moment,*" *I sniffed before giving a self-conscious huff.* "*Sorry. I didn't know anyone else was here.*"

"*Don't be sorry. It's me who's intruding. I left a book I needed on my desk, so I came back. I'll leave you alone now.*" *He began backing out into the hallway.*

"*Wait!*" *I called after him.* "*I'm a little embarrassed you caught me, Mr. Wymack, but I also don't want you to leave thinking I'm the teacher who sobs in her classroom every day after the students leave. I mean, they're a handful, but not quite enough to break me.*"

He fought a smile, his efforts causing both of us to do so. "*It's okay, Ms. Davis. I wasn't thinking that. You have nothing to be embarrassed about.*" *He glanced around. Spotting a Kleenex box on the entry desk, he gave it to me.* "*Also, feel free to call me James.*"

I took a tissue and rubbed my nose. "*Okay... James. I'm Marley.*"

We'd known each other's first names already, of course, but hadn't had occasion to use them until now.

"*Thanks,*" *he said.* "*And since we're now on a first name basis, I hope it's alright for me to ask. Are you sure you're okay?*"

"*I'm fine.*" *I appreciated his concern. And because the rest of the faculty knew my story, it made sense to share it with him.* "*It's just that my mom passed away almost a year ago. She used to help me set up my classroom every year.*" *I breathed out thickly.* "*A few minutes ago, I was collecting the students' daily writing prompts, and one of them wrote what amounted to a love letter to her mother. So, everything just kind of hit me out of the blue.*"

A compassionate expression took over his face. He paused before saying, "*That's rough. I take it you and your mom were close?*"

"*The closest.*"

"*I'm sorry.*"

"*Thank you. And I promise you I'm okay, just normal sad.*" *I stood up and extended my arm to him.* "*Maybe we should start over. Under typical circumstances, I'd have done much more to welcome a new teacher, especially one in my department.*"

He shook my offered hand. "*No apology necessary. Sorry again for interrupting your moment.*"

I laughed. "*It's fine. Sometimes it helps to be nudged out of it. I'm honestly not much of a wallower. And listen, as far as work goes, please know that you can come to me with anything you need, any questions. This is my fifth year here, and I'm pretty sure I've got all the most important data points you need about Coleman Creek High.*"

"*Data points, huh? Like what?*"

"*Well, for starters, there are three Keurigs in the teachers' lounge. Only one of them makes coffee that doesn't taste like vinegar and dirty dishwater had a baby.*"

He barked out a laugh as he let go of my hand. "*I'll keep that in mind.*" *A hesitant smile crossed his face.* "*Everyone's been great, but I'm still feeling a bit like the new guy around here. I wouldn't mind having someone show me the ropes. I hope we can be friends...Marley."*

With my name on his lips, the last vestige of my embarrassment had eased. He'd looked at me, brown eyes bright, and I'd sensed the beginning of a real connection. His kindness made me want to know him better.

At first, our friendship had been tentative. We talked about students at school, sent each other funny memes, drank coffee in the teachers' lounge. This had led to spending our lunch period together, and eventually, to hanging out outside of school. We'd watched my favorite Hugh Grant rom-coms, and he'd introduced me to obscure 1960s science fiction films. One Saturday we went apple picking, something he'd never done before. Another weekend he drove me to Spokane to try Ethiopian food, a first for me. A shared love of puzzles and games had resulted in daily battles of Othello and Mastermind—along with a week spent in my dining room working a 2000-piece jigsaw puzzle. I'd cooked him dinner. He'd brought me take out. Even our dogs liked each other. And although everything we'd done had been strictly platonic, the lines were feeling blurry.

Today at lunch, they'd shifted further.

We'd been sitting on a bench in the hallway. James had barely kept a straight face as I'd relayed the story of my second period's heated debate over whether Taylor Swift or Beyoncé was the Shakespeare of our time. Finally, he'd burst out laughing, offering, "It's obviously Justin Bieber," before slapping his hand down playfully over mine.

That's when I'd felt it. A spark. Brief, but unmistakable.

Stunned, I'd peered over at him, his eyes vivid and laughing, and I realized the connection I'd felt when James first said my name had developed into something more. Something electric.

The knowledge had come on so gradually my initial instinct was to second-guess it. The flicker of awareness caused by the light touch of his fingers. After James had removed his hand, I'd made an excuse to head back to my classroom, needing to gather my thoughts. Knowing I'd see him at this meeting.

Principal Nadal jiggled the wires connected to his laptop and several of the teachers sighed at the continued delay. After making sure no one watched us, I stole another glance at James. He sat with his arms folded across his broad chest, grinning at something Coach Hurley said.

Another revelation hit me. Over the time we'd spent together, my objective acknowledgment of James's good looks had progressed into genuine attraction.

Imposing but soft, he stood six-three, with wide rounded shoulders and a bit of a belly—extra padding that carried over into the generous curve of his backside. Those features, along with the strength he exhibited in every movement, felt like the epitome of approachable masculinity. And, of course, there was his style, so unique compared to other men in town. He was the sole male teacher with long hair, and the only one who wore jewelry—bracelets on both wrists, rings on his thumbs, and a small stud in his right nostril.

James was different, but in the best possible way. Intriguing. With his charm and good nature, he'd quickly won over not just me, but our students and colleagues as well.

He'd even converted testy old Mr. Bailey—who'd taken one look at him at the first faculty meeting and proposed that the school ban "man accessories" for teachers. When James had arrived for the next day's assembly wearing a tiara, Mr. Bailey couldn't stop his cheek from lifting a fraction. James had given the other man a good-natured wink before taking the pink plastic headpiece off, and the two had been unlikely friends ever since.

And ultimately, it was this—his kind heart—that continued to draw me in. Made him more beautiful.

Our obvious bond was the reason I often felt the curious eyes of our co-workers on us. They'd been *shipping* us for months, as the students would say. I'd dismissed it. Now I wasn't so sure.

James reached into his bag for one of the crossword puzzle magazines he always carried, offering me a pen as he placed it in the middle of the table. Was he oblivious to the other faculty members wondering about us, or did he simply not care? I had no idea. The only real pall to our budding attachment was that I often had moments like these, where I found him incredibly hard to read. His laid-back vibe occasionally felt like more of an impenetrable wall.

I needed to spend some time with him, alone, outside of school, to see if I could diagnose my own reactions. Had that spark been a momentary lapse? An aberration? Or the start of something more significant? And what about James? Had his feelings become *complicated*? I'd spent the afternoon thinking back on the past few weeks. There had been several times I thought I'd caught him looking at me in a flirtatious way, a few brushes of his fingers against my lower back that may or may not have been accidents. But nothing definitive. He certainly hadn't said anything out loud to suggest he saw me as more than a friend. And since I knew I was bad at reading him, it was possible I'd imagined those touches and glances.

I felt certain we'd both agree protecting our friendship was the priority. James had been the brightest light in my life since my mom died, and whatever else existed between us, I didn't want to jeopardize that. No need to show my cards while I was still working things out in my mind.

Which was why, as we sat next to each other on the rickety old science lab stools, I forced myself not to look at him too long, not to encourage any attention or gossip. Just a friendly shared grin over Mrs. Allen's *Bachelor* analysis. A perfectly executed high five when he finished the crossword puzzle. Synched eye rolls regarding Principal Nadal's continued inability to get the PowerPoint started.

Until finally, the presentation lit up the whiteboard.

COLEMAN CREEK HIGH SCHOOL HOLIDAY CELEBRATIONS FINAL PLANS

Yes! Here was something much less confusing than my feelings for James. Everyone in the room sat up a tad straighter. It was time for our little school to shine.

Chapter Two

James

Maniacal.

That was the only word I could use to describe Marley's grin.

A wide beam, all brilliant white teeth and pulled back lips. Cheeks glowing. I glanced down to see her purple-painted fingernails tapping an excited rhythm on her thighs.

As usual, she looked adorable.

"Why are you smiling like that?" I leaned in to ask, just as our boss started speaking.

"My fellow educators," Principal Nadal began in his typical, oddly formal way. "I'd like to focus this meeting on firming up our plans to have a wonderful and festive season at Coleman Creek High."

"It's just a normal smile," Marley said in a hushed tone.

"Sure, if you're a killer clown."

She giggled and old Mr. Bailey leaned back to give us his disapproving eye. I gave him a big thumbs up. Double thumbs, in fact, while pumping my fists up and down. He shook his head at me as the presentation continued.

"We have the holiday dance, the food drive and the door decorating contest all happening before December seventeenth..."

Principal Nadal moved through the slides but I didn't follow too closely. It sounded straightforward. He wanted to ensure we were honoring the traditions of all our students, and he encouraged faculty members to be a part of the festivities. We spent the rest of the time on teachers volunteering for various assignments, in addition to the ones we'd been given weeks ago when planning began. Since I was new to the school, I raised my hand a few times, wanting to do my part. I got the impression Coleman Creek High went big for the holidays, and the teachers all seemed excited to help.

Marley confirmed as much as we walked toward the parking lot after the meeting. A groundskeeping crew nearby blew the last of the coppery orange maple leaves into piles, working against the nipping breeze that had me pulling my beanie over my ears.

"I love this time of year. It's great we're getting an extra weekend with the Christmas tree lot," she said, swinging her arms as her hair bobbed against her shoulders.

"Yeah, everyone seemed weirdly enthusiastic about the tree lot."

"Because it's a big fundraiser for the PTSA."

I scrunched my forehead. "Maybe this is a dumb question coming from the newbie, but how come the staff is so concerned with how much the PTSA raises? I get it's important for the parents to be involved and all, but that money is just for, like, dance decorations and the grad night party, right?"

Marley huffed. "Those things are just the beginning. I don't know how much information they gave you about the budget when you got hired, but trust me when I say the school is on a shoestring."

"I know a little. It's one reason I got brought on so late in the summer. Even though enrollments were up slightly, it took a while to get the emergency funding to hire someone." In the end, that had worked in my favor. Since circumstances had forced Principal Nadal to decide quickly at a time when most teachers already had assignments, he'd been willing to take a chance on a new-to-teaching Seattle transplant with a nose piercing.

"Yeah, that tracks. The district barely gives us enough to cover the basics," Marley continued. "Without the PTSA and the athletic boosters, we wouldn't have extra for anything fun. Deejays for the dances, props for the drama department, a new sound system for the stadium. The list never ends."

I'd done my student teaching in a wealthier district outside Seattle. If it had had those types of budget constraints, I hadn't known about them.

"That's why an extra weekend for the lot is so handy," she continued. "More chances to sell. Plus, as far as money-making ventures go, a Christmas tree lot is fun. Much better than forcing the kids to sell things or take part in anything that ends in '-a-thon.'"

"Fair." I smiled, appreciating Marley's insight. She'd been helping me learn about the school and the town since we'd first started talking.

My first few weeks in Coleman Creek, I'd stuck out like a sore thumb. Trucks and SUVs surrounded my little blue commuter car in the teacher lot. I'd once made myself the target of friendly guffaws when I'd asked where the best Thai food in town was, and another time when I'd tried to use my Uber app. And even though I'd maintained a laid-back *in on the joke* vibe as the other faculty members had ribbed me good-naturedly, I'd wanted very much to fit in.

I really liked the nondescript, workaday town with its one four-lane main street. Nothing felt artificial. Most of the residents worked at the factories and warehouses up the highway. There were a few bars and a bowling alley, a handful of churches, a one-screen movie theater, and a tiny library. Two city parks. Little storefronts for buying insurance, pet supplies, and cell phone plans at one end of town. At the other, a dirt lot where you could get your car fixed or pull spare parts. In between were fast-food joints, a bank, a gym, a nail salon. The Walmart just outside city limits covered most everything else.

I wanted to find my place here, without having to cut my hair or buy Wranglers—to still be myself, just myself living in Coleman Creek. That first month, no one had been rude or unfriendly. They just hadn't seemed to know what to make of me.

Enter Marley. After the day I caught her reminiscing about her mother in her classroom, everything changed. We'd become friends, and I'd been able to relax some.

A month into the school year, she'd asked me to help her plan a scavenger hunt for the families at Back-to-School Night, since we'd recently discovered how much we both enjoyed word games. Together, we had devised clues meant to encourage attendees to check out places like the library and student resource center. Throughout the process, she'd shown me things that helped me feel like I was more a part of the school.

"See this sculpture," Marley said, pointing to a large metallic structure outside the back entrance. I could have best described its shape as a human/giraffe hybrid. "Everyone calls it 'Horsie.' It's had that name since before I was a student here. Supposedly, back in the seventies, there were some seniors who came to school wasted. They

hopped up on top and kept shouting, 'giddy up!' until a teacher pulled them off. Now it's a tradition for all the seniors to do the same thing at one point or another, except with cell phones, there's more evidence."

"Did you do it?"

"I will neither confirm nor deny." She winked.

Our next stop was a wall outside the gym listing the names of former students who had given their lives in military service, starting with World War Two. "There are so many," I remarked, "considering how small Coleman Creek is." I knew from my pre-move research there were only about five thousand residents.

"Lots of kids go into the military here. It was actually a pretty big deal for my mom that all three of her daughters went to college. The VA sponsors big parades on Veterans Day and the Fourth of July, and everyone comes out." She pointed to a name listed under the memorial for the Vietnam War. "My great uncle," she said. Her finger continued its journey to one of the three names under the Iraq War. "I went to school with Garth Tomlin. He was two years above me."

I thought of my own high school graduating class in Seattle. To the best of my knowledge, no one had gone into the military.

"It's awesome that you honor them this way."

"Yeah. Small town life, I guess. Part of the deal is we are always finding ways to notice one another. Not only memorials and parades and other traditions, but just caring. And being nosy, of course." Her fingers brushed the names again. "I'm not sure if I told you this, but I actually lived in Portland for five years. I sort of resented the anonymity. Not even meeting my neighbors, you know? I was never so lonely as when I was surrounded by a hundred thousand people."

I'd gone to college in Oregon but had lived in Seattle most of my life. I recognized the feeling she'd described.

"I think I understand."

"There's no right way to live, obviously. Small town or big city. Coleman Creek just has its own culture, I guess, the same way anyplace else does." She tucked a strand of hair behind her ear. "I like that you're curious, that you ask questions about it."

"Well, I like that you answer them without making me feel like a dumbass for asking."

She laughed heartily. "They mean well," she said, referring to our colleagues, who actually had attempted to be welcoming.

Standing in the hallway, trying to come up with a respectful scavenger hunt clue for the memorial wall, I realized that, with Marley, I didn't feel like the new guy. I felt comfortable, an unfamiliar sensation.

We finished up our tour. She pointed out which of the bathrooms the students insisted was haunted, and the cafeteria table that had once collapsed under the weight of Coach Hurley's lunch cooler. As we walked the corridors, she talked about upcoming school events. An annual roller-skating fundraiser in the gym. The marching band's rummage sale. A spring carnival where all the teachers would take a turn in the dunk tank.

We ended near a supply closet. Marley didn't open the door but warned me it held loads of holiday lights and decorations. "We go all out in December, James. You'll see."

She'd smirked, and now I understood why.

As we reached our cars, I felt the buzz of a text come through.

I checked to make sure it wasn't anything important, but nope, it was just the same stupid notification I'd been receiving for the past few weeks. The edge of a headache threatened as I frowned.

"Everything okay?" Marley asked.

"Oh, um, yeah." I sighed. "I'm not even sure how they got this number, but I keep getting messages from my old high school about our reunion."

"Ooh fun. My ten-year happened this past summer. It was a blast."

I grimaced. "I doubt mine will be. Since I haven't exactly kept up with anyone. Plus, having a reunion in December is just wrong. Isn't this time of year busy enough?"

"It's next month?"

"Um hmm. I assume whoever's doing the planning thought it would be fun to have it holiday themed. So, it's the third Saturday in December. I guess I just need to tell them *no* definitively and block this number."

I hadn't wanted to engage at all with whoever was on the other end of those texts and had hoped ignoring the messages would be enough. But the constant reminders were making me itch. I didn't want to think about high school or this reunion, let alone spend an evening catching up with my old classmates.

"You don't want to go?"

I did not want to go.

For a variety of reasons, none of which I'd be proud to tell Marley.

I settled for giving her the easiest of my excuses. "I don't want to travel back to Seattle that weekend just to go to the reunion, come back here for the last week of school before break, and then go back to the city again to spend the holidays with my family. Besides, I'm sure no one will miss me."

"No way. Of course they'd miss you."

It wasn't surprising Marley couldn't conceive of a scenario where people weren't excited to see old friends and classmates. She had a big, open heart. Making people feel welcome and wanted was in her DNA.

I felt so grateful we'd become friends. After I'd gotten the Marley seal of approval, and especially after we'd planned the scavenger hunt, my place in the Coleman Creek community solidified. Students seemed more open to accepting me. The rest of the faculty looked at my long hair and nose piercing with indulgence rather than suspicion. I doubted Marley realized how much she'd helped pave my way.

She looked like she might try to argue with me about the reunion, so I decided a subject change was in order. "Hey, is there a particular reason everyone is so into the holidays? Or is it just a small-town thing?"

The enthusiasm expressed by my fellow teachers contrasted with my own recent history of viewing the season as something to be endured, not celebrated. Last year, I'd been signing divorce papers around this time, but even before that, I couldn't remember a year where I'd felt festive. Not since childhood.

"Kind of both," Marley explained. "You've been here a while, so you understand Coleman Creek isn't the charming kind of small town with, like, kitschy gift shops and B and Bs."

"I think it's charming in its own way." I smiled, leaning my elbows back against my Mazda and crossing one ankle over the other.

She rolled her eyes. "Well, *obviously*—But what I mean is, we may not be a cute, touristy place, but we are a tight community, and the holidays are a chance to really lean into that. Once the lights and decorations go up, you won't even recognize this place. And the high school is a big part of that. Lots of folks in town will come out to watch our talent show and buy their trees from our lot. Teachers take pride in that. And the students might pretend to be too cool, but secretly they love the cookie swap and the door decorating contest, the way Principal Nadal gives out candy canes to each individual student on the last day before break."

I thought about the school I'd completed my training at last year. The administration hadn't wanted to risk any parent complaints about which holidays were being acknowledged, so they'd opted out of any celebrations or decorations at all.

"That actually sounds...really fun," I stammered, meaning it. "I signed up for the tree lot and to chaperone the dance. Maybe I'll do more." I lifted an eyebrow at her. "I don't want to look lazy since you volunteered for basically everything."

She released a small laugh. "Yeah. I love all of it—the decorating, the presents, the parties, the food. I'm looking forward to getting back in the swing of celebrating since I limited myself last year."

"Because of your mom?" I ventured carefully.

Marley nodded. "The part of me that loves the season comes from her, too. She was always Christmas crazy. So, last year, just a few months after she died... I wasn't feeling it."

She turned and tossed her purse into the passenger seat of her old red Ford F150, parked behind my car. I hadn't missed the catch in her voice. I thought about how we'd both had crappy holidays last year. Not that my split from Cindy compared to her first Christmas without her mom, but still. I almost opened my mouth to tell her, but then stopped short. Other than once mentioning I was divorced—and then quickly changing the topic—I hadn't shared anything about it with Marley. Why make things heavy?

"Hopefully, you can enjoy it this year," I said.

"I think I'm in the place now where I can be happy remembering the good times." Marley raised a hand to shield her eyes from the improbable November sun as she peered up at me. "That's why I'll be giving you a taste of my mom's fantastic holiday wardrobe. Alice Davis was famous for her impressive collection of Christmas sweaters—not to mention headbands, hats, and brooches—that yours truly has now inherited."

I grinned, imagining Marley wearing a reindeer headband or light-up tree pin. "I'll look forward to that."

"Trust me, nothing can prepare you for the sweater with the Elf on the Shelf stitched to the shoulder. It has bells, James. *Bells.*" Her tone deepened. "Honestly, skipping the festivities last year made it worse. Too much time to think about what was missing. I'm still figuring out what life looks like without my mom. Part of the process, I guess."

"Well, that may be true, but it doesn't mean it's easy. Let me know if there's anything I can do to help."

Marley angled her head to the side as she sucked on her bottom lip, expression unreadable.

"Do you really mean that, James?"

"Of course."

"Well, there actually is something." She whooshed out a breath. "As much as I've decided to get back into the holiday spirit, I've also been sort of overwhelmed with getting started. I wouldn't mind an assist with some of the decorating at my house, pulling out boxes and putting things on display and whatnot. My sisters leave Thanksgiving night. I could ask some of my other friends, but... I don't know. I just feel like it's been fun hanging out these past few months, getting to know you, talking about stupid stuff. Feeling normal. If you're willing, of course. I get that tacking up lights and tinsel isn't exactly an exciting offer."

I pretended to think about it a moment, even though I already knew my answer. "Actually, it sounds nice. I haven't done any Christmas decorating in years. I'd love to help."

"Really? I know we've hung out at my place before, but asking you to get up on the ladder and tote heavy boxes seems a lot less fun than me kicking your ass at Scrabble."

"We're friends, aren't we? I don't mind a little labor. Also, the only reason you beat me at Scrabble—once—is because you cheated."

"I didn't cheat. Proper nouns are acceptable in twenty-first century Scrabble."

"That's not a thing."

"Agree to disagree." She chortled. "But seriously, you shouldn't feel obligated if it's a bad time. I don't want to interrupt if you've already made plans for the long weekend."

I didn't want Marley to think I was a pathetic loser, so I didn't let on that I'd been hoping to figure out a way to hang out with her this weekend. I would FaceTime with my family on Thanksgiving Day and watch football, but I hadn't made any plans for the days after. In truth, spending time with Marley had been most of my social life since I'd moved to Coleman Creek. I'd had drinks with a few of the other teachers and explored a bit on my own, but I wasn't at the point yet where I had a lot of weekend options. She'd mentioned previously that her sisters would be visiting, but I hadn't realized until she'd said it just now that they weren't staying for the entire weekend.

"I don't have plans other than hanging out, maybe buying a rug or something for my apartment. I'll be there."

"Friday? Noon?"

"Works for me. And I can do Saturday and Sunday if it takes longer."

"Thanks so much. Have a great Thanksgiving, James," she said. "And I'm saving you some leftovers."

She stood on the balls of her feet to give me an impromptu hug. Even though she wasn't overly petite, I had at least eight inches on her, so I had to lean down to accept the embrace. I thought I felt her hand squeeze my hip as she pulled away, but I might have imagined it. Maybe even wished it.

I waved as she got into her truck and drove off. Not for the first time, I marveled at just how refreshing she was. Simply asking for help.

In Seattle, before, during, and after my marriage, I'd gotten accustomed to playing games with women—speaking in code, exhausting myself trying to be witty, reading into the subtext of the subtext of messages. Cindy had often complained I didn't give her what she needed. When I'd asked what that was, her reply had always been, "you should know." But I hadn't known, and within a few months of our marriage, I'd been unable to cultivate much more than her indifference. The few dates I'd had since my divorce had been the same, what with my inability to interpret the fifteen different meanings of the word "hey."

Meanwhile, Marley had one mode. Honesty and directness.

She was so different from anyone else I'd spent time with. Cute in a fresh, rosy-cheeked way, her makeup routine seemed to consist of only lip balm. She carried the same bag every day. Wore sensible boots. I didn't think I'd ever heard her swear. Smart as a whip, but never mean or condescending.

I'd thought about asking her out. In Seattle, it would have been an easy decision, considering my attraction to her on so many levels. But in this world, there was a lot more at stake. And nowhere to hide if things went south. I also had a suspicion she'd caught on that there was more going on beneath my laid-back surface than I projected.

Not to mention I didn't know what type of guys she was into, if asking her out at some point would even be an option. My infatuation could all be a moot point.

I wasn't exactly a ten. There was some muscle under my chub, but no one was going to accuse me of having abs. My ex had certainly made a point of letting me know she was leaving me for "someone who does Cross Fit." I was wide, built like a linebacker. No matter how much I slouched or kept my head down, I still felt like a giant next to most people. There were times I'd thought Marley might have been considering me in a non-friends way. But I couldn't tell if they were *I'm maybe into this guy* looks, or *I wonder how James stacks up next to Bigfoot* looks.

So, I'd kept it platonic. The smartest move in the scheme of things. I'd come to Coleman Creek for a fresh start, and as much as I liked the town's main street and the people and the school, it was mostly Marley—and the way she crossed her eyes and made funny faces at me each time we passed each other in the hallway—that was making it feel like home.

Chapter Three

Marley

My younger sister, Miranda, made a yuck face as I added sautéed baby portabellas to the green bean casserole mixture.

"What?" I threw back at her. "I'm trying something new. We agreed to mix it up a little, right?"

"I guess." She curled her lip, eyeing the Dutch oven suspiciously. I smoothed out the casserole and sprinkled a can of fried onions on top.

Mom had never added mushrooms to this recipe, but we were cooking it in one of the Le Creuset pieces she had scored at Goodwill when I was six. My mother had been a champion secondhand shopper.

At the sound of the oven door opening, my Labrador dashed into the kitchen to investigate. I hadn't dropped anything, but that didn't stop Oscar from sniffing furiously underneath the cabinets. I ruffled his ears and threw the extra pieces of bacon I'd fried into his bowl.

We hadn't cooked last year, only a month after Mom's death. My older sister Maureen had ordered a fancy pre-fab meal from a specialty grocer instead. But this year, we'd agreed to try. After all, the three of us had spent most Thanksgivings of our lives helping prepare the food. We knew what to do.

Miranda placed the stuffing alongside the casserole to bake and popped the rolls in the microwave. The turkey had just come out of the oven and was resting on the counter. It would be ready to carve around the time the side dishes finished cooking. A semi-decent cranberry chutney, courtesy of a Pinterest recipe, chilled in the fridge. In a nod to our childhood, we'd also sliced up some of the canned stuff. We had, however, forgone making the hideous whipped cream/pistachio/marshmallow/grape "salad" only Mom had ever eaten.

It was definitely different with just the three of us, but our mother would have been glad we'd made the effort to spend the holiday together, in the home we'd grown up in.

I yawned as I rinsed some mixing spoons before putting them in the dishwasher. Even though it was only two o'clock, I'd gotten up before five to put the turkey in the oven. We planned to eat early since both my sisters had to leave that evening.

Miranda had plans to spend the weekend with a friend in San Diego before returning to the Los Angeles university where she attended graduate school. She needed to stay in the city tonight to catch an early morning flight. I was disappointed because she'd only gotten in yesterday, but I'd long since resigned myself to her wanderlust.

Maureen had to head back to Seattle tonight as well. Because of work. She managed a high-end department store and it would be all hands on deck for Black Friday tomorrow.

Brief as our sister time was, we tried to make the most of it.

Unfortunately, during our pajamas and chocolate popcorn movie marathon last night, I'd made the mistake of telling them James would be coming over tomorrow.

I'd only mentioned it because they'd admitted to feeling bad about not being able to stay longer. I'd let them stew a minute before assuring them it was all good. They were off the hook because I had a friend coming over the next day to help decorate.

But in my attempt to relieve my sisters of their guilt, I'd inadvertently opened up a whole new line of questioning. I thought I'd dropped the information casually, but they must have heard something in my voice because the interrogation that had started last night continued today.

My sisters would apparently never run out of questions about my new *friend*.

Oscar weaved between my legs as I went to the refrigerator to pull out the butter dish, nearly knocking me over. I steadied myself against the countertop as he sat and tilted his head endearingly, like he hadn't just tried to take me out. My older sister used the tip of her ballet flat to rub under the dog's chin as she brought up James yet again.

"Okay, so let me get this straight..." Maureen licked the mixer paddle clean of chocolate mousse. "You've known him for three months, and you've basically been spending all your time together?"

"I mean, that's a bit of an overstatement—"

"And he doesn't have anywhere to go on this holiday weekend—no family or anything—so spending time with you is his default?"

"I already told you. His family's in Seattle. And he's divorced, no kids, plus new to town. Don't read too much into him coming over. He just didn't have anything else to do."

"You keep trying to play it off, but I'm calling bullshit. You must really like him if you trust him to help you go through mom's Christmas decorations."

It was bad enough that my own feelings about James had gotten muddled the past twenty-four hours. Maureen's cross-examination wasn't helping. "Look—we click, okay? And he makes me laugh. So, I know if he's here with me when I open the boxes, it won't be just about me remembering mom. It'll also be about me having fun with James."

Miranda had been letting me and Maureen spar, but at that, she hoisted herself on the counter and sat facing us. "Yeah. Pretty sure we can guess exactly what type of *fun* you'll be having."

"Oh my god. I told you it's not like that!"

"But why not? If he's so great?" Maureen jumped in. "Is he a troll or something?"

I laughed. "No. Definitely not. He's cute. Big guy cute. You know, like a football player."

"Well, now I'm really bummed I can't stay around to meet him," Maureen said. "I'll admit you've got me curious."

"For goodness' sake. He's just a new teacher at the school, and we get along and have become friends. End of story."

At least, it was the end of the story until I figured out how I wanted to spin the narrative. My sisters were as bad as my meddling co-workers.

"If you say so." Maureen didn't sound convinced, but the beeping of the oven saved me from further analysis.

Getting up before the sun had given me plenty of time to reflect on that moment in the hallway with James yesterday. I thought about how he'd been wearing what I knew to be one of his favorite t-shirts—a tan long sleeve from the South by Southwest festival ten years ago. He had an extensive collection of shirts from places he'd been. The furthest I'd ever traveled from home was a trip to Disneyland at age eleven. James had told me once he'd learned to surf in Australia during a semester studying abroad. I'd only seen the ocean a handful of times. Even if I felt something more than platonic toward James, it was difficult to envision a scenario where he returned my interest.

I was kind of a case study in not being able to hold someone's attention.

I knew James respected me. He'd shown me in every way possible that he appreciated my friendship and enjoyed spending time with me. But I reasoned that the novelty of the small-town girl would wear off. I could only imagine the type of sexy, exciting women he'd dated in the past. Meanwhile, everything about me was mid—medium build, medium height, medium brown hair. I'd never bought makeup from anyplace other than the drugstore, never worn eyelashes or gotten anything waxed. Even when I'd lived in Portland, I hadn't had much interest in festivals and museums and farmers' markets. I'd always been the person who was perfectly happy to grab beers at the same bar every weekend. What did I have to offer someone like James?

Friendship, that was what. And when he inevitably expanded his social circle, I'd be happy for him too. That was, if he even lasted in Coleman Creek. He seemed content to be here, and often said so. But I still wondered if the luster would fade. Maybe he'd get tired of sticking out.

There was no way to predict the future. Somewhere between basting the turkey for the dozenth time and peeling the potatoes, I'd decided I would simply enjoy my friendship with James for as long as it lasted. And if I felt more sparks, I could ignore them.

"I'll pull the casseroles out and slice the turkey so we can eat," I said to my sisters.

"I'll finish setting the table," Miranda said. "It smells delicious."

When things were ready, I gave Oscar a Kong with frozen pumpkin puree inside. He trotted toward his bed to huddle with it. I'd had the red fox lab for over four years, since he was a puppy. I'd grown used to his big, pleading eyes. But my sisters were still suckers and had been sneaking him bread cubes and bits of turkey all afternoon. No doubt the reason his doggy expression bordered on smug.

As we took our seats, I giggled at Miranda's crane-folding attempts with the napkins. Another remnant of our childhood.

"A for effort," I smiled at her, unfolding a cloth into my lap.

Conversation flowed easily. Maureen detailed the new personal shopping and styling service her store was providing, as well as some upcoming trips she had planned to meet with designers. Miranda talked about finally getting a coveted slot on a rafting trip through the Grand Canyon next summer, and about the four different men she'd been on dates with recently, including a moderately well-known influencer she'd had to sign an NDA for.

I wondered idly what our little trio might look like from an outside perspective. Miranda's life overflowed with travel and adventure. She was getting a degree, but also went whichever way the wind blew her. While Maureen's life wasn't entirely glamourous, it included some great parties and some very enviable outfits. Even today, for Thanksgiving in our little town, she wore a tailored pantsuit that looked straight out of a magazine. I had on my favorite "dressy" sweater I'd bought during my last trip to the Target outside Spokane.

Maybe some folks would see me as the sad sister. The boring one. But I'd tried leaving. I'd gone to college in Oregon and lived there until my mom got sick. And from the moment I'd put my suitcase back down in Coleman Creek, I'd known it was sprouting permanent roots. I belonged here.

AFTER FINISHING OUR DINNER, we sat in the dining room taking a digestion break before dessert. There was a lull in the conversation. The silence was pleasant at first, but as it stretched, I noticed my sisters trading some very strange glances across the table. Both looked as though they were daring the other to speak first.

"Alright, you two," I said. "What's up with the weird looks? I hope this isn't more about James, because I've got to say I'm getting pretty irritated with—"

"It's not about that," Maureen interrupted, frowning slightly. "We have something to tell you, only we decided earlier to wait until after dinner. I'm not sure if it's a big deal or not, but we didn't want to risk upsetting you before we got through the meal."

There had been a not-statistically insignificant chance this dinner could have gone sideways, or that we'd end up too sad to enjoy it. I could see the logic behind waiting. But since they both had to leave in an hour, they needed to get to the point.

"Alright," I said. "I'm listening."

Miranda straightened before jumping in. "So, when Maur and I drove in, I realized I'd forgotten the whipped cream. And obviously you can't have chocolate mousse without that, so we stopped off to get some..." Her words trailed off as she chewed her bottom lip.

"And?" I prompted.

"And we ran into Kasen."

I startled, before releasing a strangled sound. "My Kasen?"

"Is there another?" Maureen interjected, lips remaining downturned. "Yeah, it was your Kasen, just hanging out in the dairy aisle looking for sour cream. Don't ask me why the hell you need sour cream on Thanksgiving."

Obviously, he could have been buying it for anything. Lots of recipes called for sour cream. And while I appreciated my big sister thinking she needed to maintain a low-key grudge against my ex, it wasn't necessary. It had certainly surprised me to hear his name, but I realized with some shock that I'd gone months without thinking about him. How had that happened? There had been a time when my thoughts had drifted to Kasen every day.

"It's for mashed potatoes," I said absently, thinking of the Thanksgivings I'd spent with his family. "His mom likes to whip them with sour cream."

"Gross," Maureen sneered, and I didn't bother telling her it was delicious. I could tell her disdain was half-hearted. When Kasen and I had been together, he'd been a part of our family, close with both my sisters.

"Anyway," Miranda cut in, "He saw us before we could hide in the cereal aisle. Came right over, chill as you please. We made small talk, because what else are we gonna do? It took him a few minutes to get there, but eventually it became clear he just wanted to ask about you, how you were doing and all that. He told us you stopped answering his texts when you broke up."

"Yeah," I intoned. "I blocked him. I guess I just...didn't see the point."

"Good." Maureen hmphed. "After what he did to you—"

"Alright, alright," Miranda chimed in, ever the peacemaker. "He wanted us to tell you he's back in town through Christmas, staying with his parents, and he'd love to see you. Or just text with you. We almost weren't going to say anything, but that didn't seem right, so we compromised by deciding to do it after dinner."

"It's fine," I assured her. "I have no idea why he'd want to see me, but it makes sense he's in town for the holidays. Especially since he didn't come back last summer for our high school reunion."

"I wonder what he wants," Miranda said.

"It doesn't matter," Maureen grumped. "After breaking my sister's heart, he doesn't get to ask for things."

"Now wait a minute," I said. "Let's be real. He didn't exactly do that. We had different priorities. I'll admit it hurt when he stayed in Oregon, but in the end, I just wanted a clean break. He wanted to stay friends."

"Is that so bad?" Miranda had such a soft heart.

"It's not bad," I conceded. "Staying friends with Kasen just wasn't what I wanted. We were together for a long time. I didn't think I could move past our relationship if we stayed in each other's lives. Or at least, it would have made it harder."

"Ugh. You're always so pragmatic. Handling your business. Didn't you ever just want to scream at Kasen or anything?" Miranda asked, leaning back in her chair. "When I broke up with my last boyfriend, I stayed in bed eating cookies and watching slasher movies for two days. And our relationship had only lasted four months!"

I reached out to steady my baby sister, who was a quarter inch away from tipping over backward. "We're different. Besides, I told you I blocked his texts and stopped speaking to him. That honestly feels pretty harsh now that I think of it."

"Harsh, maybe. But not *messy*. Cutting off contact so you can move on and take care of yourself is, like, the literal definition of a *clean* break," Miranda asserted.

"So, you and Kasen haven't communicated in years. What do you think he wants now?" Maureen cut in.

"Probably nothing. Or maybe he just saw you two in the store and was trying to be polite."

"It really didn't sound like that," she conceded. "He seemed like he'd be thrilled to hear from you again."

"I'll consider texting him." I squeezed the napkin in my lap as my knee bounced. "Enough time has passed. It's probably okay to let some air out of this situation. I'm a hundred percent certain I'm over the break-up, so maybe it wouldn't hurt to find out what he wants."

The tone of my voice must have awakened Oscar's *good boy* instincts because he came over to curl up by my feet, rubbing his nose against my ankles. I reached down to scratch his back before sinking further into my chair.

Kasen and I had dated for eight years. I'd loved him, but that had long since faded into something between mild curiosity and indifference. Unfortunately, I hadn't been nearly as sanguine when we'd broken up, and I felt the consequences of the choices I'd made then keenly now. Him staying away from our reunion had been my first clue. I'd wanted a clean break, not to make Kasen feel uncomfortable in the town he'd grown up in.

"Okay." Maureen's voice was monotone. "Just let us know if you need anything."

"For sure," Miranda agreed. "Besides, who needs to worry about Kasen when you've got new guy, football player-adjacent hottie Jaaaaaaames coming over tomorrow?" She made kissy noises into the air.

I whacked her with a napkin and laughed. "Leave it alone. Let's eat some chocolate mousse."

We retreated to the living room for dessert. When Miranda went into the kitchen, Maureen pulled me aside. "You sure you're okay? The stuff with Kasen?"

"Peachy," I assured her. She gave me another once over before nodding sagely.

After my sisters left, I unblocked Kasen's number. I'd decide about texting him in a few days. For now, I wanted to spend this weekend getting into the spirit of the season. With James.

Chapter Four

James

The day after Thanksgiving, I set out for Marley's house with a case of the blackberry sparkling water we both liked. I only lived a few miles away. But in just that short distance, I discovered the town had transformed overnight. Every storefront already sported a tree or a snowman, and there were long lines of garland strung over each block of Main Street. The nail salon advertised Christmas or Hanukkah-themed acrylics, and a kitschy Hawaiian shirt-wearing Santa greeted everyone coming into the bowling alley. Everywhere I drove I could see people on ladders tacking up lights.

As I rounded the corner into Marley's neighborhood, there were folks in their front yards planning décor campaigns worthy of Clark Griswold. Along with traditional lights and wreaths, I saw two giant menorahs, a blow-up Darth Vader in a Christmas scarf, a reindeer made of candy canes, and cardboard cutouts of The Grinch, Buddy the Elf, Charlie Brown, and Jack Skellington, not to mention a rather terrifying Krampus. Nothing was elegant. The only unifying themes seemed to be *unrepentant enthusiasm* and *more, more, more.* I could see why Marley loved it so much.

I'd been to her home often enough that one of her neighbors waved at me as I pulled into the driveway. She lived in the same house she'd grown up in. I knew from past conversations that she'd bought out her sisters after they'd inherited their mother's estate. Alice had apparently been a prodigious saver, leaving a nice nest egg for each of her girls.

Patchy bushes bracketed the asphalt driveway on either side. The home's split-level design matched six others on the block, although its lavender paint job stood out. Unlike her neighbors, Marley had yet to re-create the North Pole on her lawn, but I noticed a wreath on the door that hadn't been there last week.

My dog Bambi whined impatiently in the back seat as we pulled in. Marley and I had met up with our pooches a few times at the park so they could play together. Bambi was a labradoodle, so he and Oscar had become fast friends. Kind of like their owners.

In addition to the wreath, I noticed a new HO-HO-HO doormat. I stepped on it when I knocked, and a few freakishly loud notes of "Rockin' Around the Christmas Tree" played. Bambi startled and jumped back, barking.

I chuckled as he crouched down into attack mode. He was inching toward the HO-HO-HO in a belly crawl when the door opened.

"Hiya!" Marley said brightly. She eyed my dog before smirking up at me. "Oscar likes the doormat too."

On cue, Oscar came bounding into the doorway, launching himself at Bambi. They tumbled into the house. Baring their teeth and pressing their faces together, they nipped and bit as they play-fought. It looked vicious, but in actuality, both doggos were big, dopey sweethearts.

After the excitement of the epic canine reunion, I registered Marley's outfit, then wondered how I hadn't noticed it immediately. Apparently, she'd dug into that holiday clothing collection she'd mentioned. Her jeans were fine, but the top—yikes. The neon green sweater almost glowed. It wasn't even a Christmasy green but more of a nuclear lime, with a giant decorated palm tree across the front. If tacky lights and ornaments hadn't covered the tree, it wouldn't have looked like a holiday sweater at all.

Eyebrow raised, she practically dared me to say something as I followed her to the living room. I sealed my lips together, fighting a smile. She placed the sparkling water on the counter in the galley-style kitchen as we walked by. I loved visiting her house because it always felt so lived in. We rarely spent time in my rental apartment because I still hadn't done much with it.

Marley's living room was pleasantly haphazard. Pieces that appeared old and well-made mixed with IKEA stuff that wouldn't last five years. Bookshelves stuffed with YA fantasy novels, colorful throw blankets on the couch and modern paintings on the walls—not to mention a dining room table littered with student essays and sharpies—made it clear this was Marley's home as an adult, not a shrine to her childhood.

"How long have you had Bambi?" she asked. "I don't think you've ever told me."

I'd adopted Bambi as a puppy right around the same time I'd gotten married. After the divorce, I'd asked to keep him, and Cindy hadn't fought me. He'd always been my dog anyway. The end of my marriage and my emergency need for a career change had all happened within a few years. Bambi had kept me sane, the one constant source of calm and consistency through it all. But I didn't think Marley needed that level of detail. And I'd gone this long without laying anything on her about my ex or my old job.

"I got him as a puppy about four years ago."

"Cool. I know he and Oscar are the same age, but I wasn't sure if you'd had him his whole life."

"Yep. I was front and center for Bambi's whole pissing in the house and destroying shoes phase."

Marley guffawed. "For Oscar it was cords. We couldn't leave anything out—phone chargers, floor lamp connectors, cable lines—it all had to be hidden or tacked to the walls because he would chew it to pieces. Luckily, he grew out of that phase by the time my mom got really sick and needed to be hooked up to monitors. Lots of cords then."

We sat down on the couch and watched the dogs rumble for a minute. "So you've had Oscar since your mom...lived here?"

"Yeah. Same as you. Got him as a puppy. In the beginning, Mom was pretty sick but could go outside and sit in a chair, sometimes even take a drive. I could still work and not have to worry too much. Eventually, she started needing more visits from the home health aide. Oscar learned to be gentle and stayed near her. He was also good company for me because, as you can imagine, it got a little lonely taking care of her. In the end, the hospice nurse said Oscar was one of the best patient dogs she'd ever seen."

"It's great you both had him." A few months ago, when I'd first been to her house, she'd pointed out the room her mother had used, clearly the home's largest. I'd gotten the sense Marley rarely went in there.

Marley's lip pulled up in a sad half-smile. "We were lucky my mom had good insurance. All that time at the plant. The union. Especially since she'd been adamant about wanting to stay in her own home as things progressed. Until she died, Oscar was always with her. Since then, he's always with me."

I looked again at the two dogs wrestling together on the carpet, playing tug-of-war with a stuffed bunny. Oscar gave up, his thick tongue lolling out the side of his mouth as he watched Bambi roll to the floor with the toy.

"Is it wrong that I sort of want to hug your dog?" I asked.

"Nope. That's pretty much me every day. So grateful for him. That's why he gets away with murder." She smiled wryly. "I'm sure Bambi takes good care of you, too."

I thought about how my dog had taken over the empty side of the bed after Cindy had packed up all her stuff and left, leaving me a note saying she was moving in with her new boyfriend. I thought about Oliver stabbing me in the back, Bambi's wet nose on my cheek as I lay under the covers, shaking with fear and asking myself what the hell I was going to do.

But I didn't tell Marley any of that, settling for a nod of agreement.

Part of me wanted to open up more. I *knew* she felt my reticence. But what if I messed up what we had? I hadn't had much luck putting myself out there. I hadn't been good enough for Cindy. Not fit enough or ambitious enough. I hadn't been enough of a bulldog to satisfy Oliver.

Marley liked easygoing James. Teacher James. Cool new guy in town James. The James who made her laugh and eased her mind about grieving for her mother. Was it wrong that I wanted to be that guy for a bit longer before I introduced her to James the undesirable? James the fuck-up?

"My sisters helped me pull out some of the stuff from storage yesterday and put it downstairs in the rec room. The inside decorations. We left the outside decorations in the garage." Marley stood at the top of the interior stairs.

"Did you want to dive right in and get started?" I asked.

"Yeah. My plan is to knock it out as quick as I can. It would be a huge help if you could bring the boxes upstairs to the living room. I don't do any decorating downstairs other than putting up a second tree, so I figure we should work from here. I tried moving them myself, but they're too heavy for me to carry alone." She smirked. "But I'm betting it'll be no problem for you."

I blushed, feeling gigantic. But also, useful. "Me. Big. Strong. Man."

I still had to carry one at a time, since they were ridiculously heavy. Six trips to bring three large cardboard boxes and three fifty-five-gallon storage tubs upstairs.

"With as much as you say you enjoy Christmas, I'm surprised you waited this long to do this," I said, slightly out of breath as I set the last bin on the carpet. "I mean, some of your neighbors are practically ready to charge admission to their winter wonderlands."

"Fair point. But it's not procrastination. It's tradition. My mom may have loved Christmas, but she was also the type of person who wanted to give each holiday its due. In our household, the Christmas stuff didn't come out until the Thanksgiving dishes were done."

I grinned. "I think your mom and my mom would have gotten along."

The two heaviest boxes held the makings of a ceramic Victorian village. Marley brought out four folding tables from a hall closet, along with a "snow blanket" she'd picked up at Walmart. Once we spread the blanket out, she set up an entire scene. There were finely detailed schoolhouses, churches, and cottages, with enough ceramic people of all types to create vignettes across the table—men in top hats carrying presents, children ice skating on a frozen pond, jugglers and peddlers in the town square.

"It took my mom years to collect this," she said proudly. "Alice Davis excelled in many things, and two of them were thrifting and eBay."

I chuckled as other items began filling the living room surfaces. A nutcracker dressed as a chef. A snow globe with Rudolph inside. A plug-in nightlight of the leg lamp from *A Christmas Story*.

Sometimes Marley would happily recite an item's history. With other things, she'd pause for a moment, turning the object over in her palms quietly before placing it. When she got stuck on her mom's homemade Advent calendar, I laid my hand over hers until she felt ready to tell me about the time her sister Miranda methodically stuffed each of its 25 nooks with used chewing gum.

There were dozens of photos in Christmas-themed frames. I saw so many that eventually Marley, Alice, Maureen, and Miranda became easily identifiable, even at different ages and stages. At the bottom of one bin was a frame wrapped carefully in tissue paper and newsprint, taped tightly.

I held it up to Marley. "Should I unwrap this? I don't want to presume, since it's sealed."

"Oh my goodness." She made a tiny stuttering noise. "I'd almost forgotten about that. Yes, please unwrap it."

I carefully slid my finger under the tape to unfold the paper edges. The frame held a photo of a man and a woman at a Christmas party, drinks in hand and making silly faces at the camera as folks behind them smiled. Based on their clothing, I guessed it was from the early eighties. The woman in the photo was a young Alice, looking similar to Marley now. The man appeared much older, with a guarded smile and knowing eyes behind thick black horn-rims.

"My parents," Marley said. "My dad was in his mid-forties when my mom started working at the factory. This was taken at a Christmas party there. He died of a heart attack when Miranda was a baby, so I don't remember him much. But my mom always talked about them having an epic love story—once he got over worrying about people thinking he was a dirty old man for marrying such a young woman."

I laughed as Marley took the frame and placed it prominently on a bookshelf.

Even though I'd decided falling for Marley was a terrible idea, I could sense myself drawing closer to her as she shared stories about her past. I couldn't help but be in awe of the way she approached everything with dignity and humor. Which made the interrupting text that came through around two o'clock that much more annoying.

UNKNOWN: Hi James! We haven't heard back from you about the Seattle Elite High School reunion. It's coming up soon, so please get your RSVP in now. Can't wait to see you!

UNKNOWN: It'll be a holly, jolly good time! All graduates may attend with one guest at no cost!

That was a lot of exclamation points. What was with these people? Who was on the other side of these messages? There was no way anyone from my high school cared if I went to the reunion or not.

I'd spent a decade with high school happily in the rearview. And it wasn't until these stupid texts had come through that I'd realized I might not have left it behind as completely as I'd assumed. It was hard to pin down the emotion that surfaced at the thought of those years. Sometimes it felt like a shot of adrenaline. Sometimes more like shame.

I'd been standing, putting removable hooks above the fireplace to hang stockings, but the weight of the phone I held had me dropping heavily into the recliner. I steepled my fingers, pushing them against my forehead until the tips turned bright pink.

"Everything okay?" Marley eyed me with concern from where she'd been cleaning off the dining table in preparation for a plaid tablecloth.

"Oh...yeah. Just my old school again. The reunion."

She nodded before coming over, sitting on the arm of the chair. "I don't want to push, James, but judging by the way you're trying to get swallowed up by that cushion, this seems like more than just an issue with making the long drive to Seattle twice in a month."

I reached back to massage my neck. "Sure. I mean...I guess it's annoying because I haven't thought about Seattle Elite in a long time. Haven't wanted to. Then these texts started coming through."

"It's funny how texts can hit you out of nowhere."

"Right. I wasn't exactly jonesing for any reminders about my teenage years—" I stopped myself before saying too much.

She waited a moment for me to elaborate. When I didn't, she asked, "It was bad?"

I glanced over at her. "Bad might not be the right word." Hellacious would be closer. "It's just that I'm...not proud of who I was back then. And these messages have me thinking maybe I didn't move past it as thoroughly as I thought I did."

"James, I'd never presume to tell you how to live your life, and of course I don't know what happened back then, but I do know a little something about trying to move on from the past by shutting the door on it." She glanced down the hall toward her mother's bedroom, but I also got the distinct sense she had something else on her mind. "The bottom line is that—whatever it is—it's obviously really gnawing at you. And ignoring the messages doesn't seem to be putting the genie back in the bottle."

"I'll just RSVP *no*. Once the texts stop coming, I'll be okay."

"Maybe." She placed her hand gently over mine. "Or maybe not. And the thing is, reunions don't come around all that often. If you decide you need to face whatever's bothering you head-on, you may not get another opportunity."

I sighed. "I hadn't thought about that."

She was right. It wasn't a guarantee I'd be able to put high school out of my mind again, even if I skipped the reunion. If I woke up a year from now and decided I needed to see my old classmates in order to get closure or whatever, it wasn't as though I could ask a hundred people to assemble in Coleman Creek.

"Like I said, I don't want to push you. But if you ever want to talk it through, I'm here." She kept her warm palm on my skin.

"Honestly, Marley, I appreciate that so much, but even considering this is making my head spin. Do you think we can...um...change the subject? At least for now?"

Was I seriously contemplating going to my reunion? Stupid, stupid texts. I just wanted to listen to Marley tell me stories about her family, and for her to keep touching my hand.

She seemed sympathetic that I'd reached my limit. "Sure. What do you want to talk about? The weather? Favorite cookie? Saddest on-screen character death?"

I laughed. "Let's see. It's a little warm for me, chocolate chip because I'm basic like that, and Grey Wind, Robb Stark's direwolf." She grinned and shook her head, and I felt the worst of the tension leaving me as I cleared my throat. "Also, Marley, I need you to answer another very important question."

"What's that?"

"Why the heck does your sweater have a battery pack?" I reached out to place my index finger on the little pouch I'd just noticed.

She stood up excitedly and began shaking her arms and legs out like a runner before a race. "I was waiting for you to figure that out!" Reaching into the tiny pocket of her top, she pulled out a plastic switch, flicking it to "on." The palm tree lit up, glowing with clear-colored lights from her chest to her belly. She raised her eyebrows. "It gets even better." With another tap of her finger, the switch flipped to "show mode," and the white lights morphed into a rainbow of colors that danced and changed every few seconds.

It was tacky AF.

But the woman twirling and cackling at me—she wore it well.

Chapter Five

Marley

After going through more than half the bins and boxes, James and I decided to take a snack break before tackling the outside.

We wouldn't finish today, that much was clear. We'd lose the light in a few hours. It probably would have been smarter to start with the exterior, but as I looked over the explosion of treasured decorations and photos dotting my living room, kitchen, and bathroom, I couldn't be sorry. I loved this time of year, and with each happy memory these items evoked, I couldn't help but feel like Christmas loved me back.

Thanksgiving leftovers weren't appealing, so I put out the last of the chocolate popcorn, along with chips and salsa, baby carrots and ranch, mixed nuts, and microwaved taquitos.

We hadn't stopped to eat lunch, so I attacked the food ravenously. James was more subdued, putting a small portion of everything on his plate.

I'd noticed before that he often ate this way. Like a picky kindergartener. At school, we usually shared our lunches and both of us brown-bagged it. Somehow, even though James stood over six feet, he always brought less than I did. And when we went to The Landslide for happy hour, he would drink a beer, but rarely ordered food. I'd always assumed he ate bigger breakfasts and dinners or preferred to cook at home. But now I wondered.

"Hey James, feel free to eat all this stuff up. I have a ton of leftovers to go through and appreciate the help getting rid of everything."

He stopped halfway through the process of lifting a taquito to his mouth, lowering it back onto his plate. "I'm not too hungry, actually." An expression I couldn't read passed over his face before he leaned back onto the couch to pat his stomach. "Besides, you know I need to maintain my svelte physique." He peppered that last word with a strained little laugh.

Oh. Oh my. Now I understood.

James was self-conscious about his body.

I hadn't registered the signs before, but as he sat on my couch, appearing to force a smile, it came together quickly in my mind.

I recalled a morning in late October. It had been before school, and I'd noticed James's car in the lot. I'd gone to find him to say hello, but he hadn't been in his classroom. Heading to my room, I'd stopped short upon hearing faint sounds of exertion while passing the gym. Since it was Friday, none of the teams had early practice, so I figured it had to be James. I'd found him in the small weight room, sitting on a bench with his back to the door doing bicep curls. Looking back, my reaction then should have been my first clue as to my growing physical attraction to him.

With each raise of his arm, he'd admitted a small grunt, and I'd felt each of those syllables to my core. He'd gathered his hair up in a haphazard bun, and he wore a white tank top and purple track pants. A sheen of sweat highlighted the definition in his shoulders and neck as he'd worked. Above his waistband, his top had ridden up, and my eyes fixated on that small strip of exposed skin, the twin dimples on his lower back like little bullseyes above his perfectly round butt.

While counting off his twentieth rep, his eyes had raised, and he'd seen me gazing at him in the mirror. Almost dropping the dumbbell, he'd jumped up. "Oh...uh...hey, Marley." His face had reddened further as he'd looked anywhere but at me. He'd tugged on his top like it was trying to strangle him. "Yeah...so...I'm gonna hit the showers before the kids get here." And then he'd rushed out before I could say anything.

That had been over a month ago, and neither of us had mentioned it since. I'd thought he'd hurried away because he'd been sweaty and gross. But now I was unsure.

He was one of the most attractive men I'd ever met. Moms at school were always checking him out, and they weren't subtle about it. It had never occurred to me until this moment that James wouldn't understand how desirable he was. Maybe not to everyone. But to lots of people. And definitely to me.

I loved how big he was. Every time I heard the heavy footfall of his Doc Martens in the hallways at school, it reminded me of his strength. Then there were his hands, the way he gripped everything just a little too tightly—car steering wheel, water bottle, phone, door handles—almost like he didn't know his own power, the current running just below his fingertips.

To me, James personified masculine perfection. But now I saw the hunched-over way he walked and the oversized coats he sometimes wore in a new light.

He came back out and picked up some of the kitchen items we'd put aside on the dining table. I took a deep breath, hoping none of my concerns showed in my features, and smiled at him.

"Do you want me to put these holiday plates in the dishwasher?" he asked.

"That would be super helpful. We may have to do two loads since I also have a bunch of bowls and serving dishes to wash as well."

James went over to examine the stack of glass and ceramic I pointed at.

"This is quite the assortment," he said, picking up a snowman-shaped platter and eyeballing the winking snowman decorated with block letters reading *Frisky Frosty*.

"Rivaled only by the sweater collection."

"That's saying something." James picked up a nutcracker that looked as though it had been split down the middle, right through its nutcracker crotch, and held it up to me. "I think this guy has had an accident. No more nuts for him."

"That's okay," I laughed. "Because he is salad tongs."

James turned it sideways. "Ahh."

He carried the first load of plates into the kitchen, placing them carefully in the dishwasher while Oscar and Bambi guarded the operation. I took the Christmas dish towels into the garage and stuck them in the laundry machine.

Coming back, I found James laughing and playing keep-away with the dogs, taunting them with a carrot. It was no mystery why I hadn't registered his self-consciousness. It was subtle. And I hadn't been looking.

But, of course, everyone's insecurities and coping methods were unique. I didn't know a single person who didn't have some sort of *feelings* about their body.

I'd once told Miranda how I thought I was "a solid five, a six when I made the effort," and she'd given me a twenty-minute lecture on self-love. What I saw as being realistic and managing expectations, she saw as self-flagellation. "You're somebody's ten, Marley," she'd said to me. "That makes you a ten."

As a teacher, I'd been through enough training to know my best course of action with James was to simply keep an eye out for patterns that seemed more serious. No good could come of making him aware of my suspicions. Ditto trying to tell him how beautiful he was. It was his journey. As much as it pained me to see James uncomfortable, I resolved to be as good of friend to him as I could, to show him how much I liked and admired him.

WE WENT OUTSIDE to put up the exterior decorations. As we worked, I attempted to ask James more questions about himself. After my revelation about his body-consciousness, I realized there was still so much I wanted to learn about him. But every time I tried to ask about his history or his experiences, he answered vaguely. Or he'd turn the conversation around to safer subjects, like school events and whether he should join the bowling league.

Slightly frustrated, I let the silence reign for a moment while we concentrated on getting the lights up on the roof edges. James insisted on being the one to climb the ladder while I held it steady beneath him. I took advantage of the opportunity to admire his perfect backside until a familiar white Chevy pulling up to the curb interrupted me.

"Hey, Marley," Coach Hurley called out as he stepped from the driver's seat.

"Hi Coach," I replied. "What brings you out here?"

"I'm on my way back into town. Went out to my son's place in Post Falls for dinner yesterday. Thought I'd stop by and check on you." He looked down at my sweater and threw an arm over his face. "My eyes! Too bright! Make it stop."

I laughed. Like most of my colleagues, Coach Hurley had been very solicitous since my mom passed away. I wanted to be annoyed with him for intruding on my butt-ogling, but how could I honestly be mad about someone caring? It's like I'd been saying to James for months about small towns. People were going to be in your business, and you kind of just had to be okay with it.

"Well, thanks for stopping by, but as you can see, I'm doing great. James is here." I pointed up to the top of the ladder.

"Yes. I saw Mr. Wymack when I pulled up." Coach glanced up and shouted, "Hello!"

James made a quick descent to the ground before reaching out to shake the other man's hand. Coach made wide eyes over James's fitted maroon track pants, beaded hematite bracelets, and vintage Joy Division t-shirt before shrugging his shoulders and saying, "I knew you guys were *friends*. But I didn't realize you were already the Thanksgiving and decorating for Christmas together type of friends." He darted his eyes back and forth between us.

Good lord. It was one thing to get questioning glances because we sat together in faculty meetings. The last thing I needed was for other teachers in the school to read too much into James and me hanging out over the weekend. I'd spent the last five years fending off my colleagues' well-intended introductions to their nephews and neighbors' little brothers. I knew it was because they worried about me and wanted me to be happy. But still. This needed to be nipped in the bud. Matchmaking was not on the approved list of planned Christmas activities for the Coleman Creek staff.

"Don't go starting rumors," I admonished. "James didn't come here for Thanksgiving dinner, and he's helping put up lights since my sisters couldn't stay. It's not like I could have held the ladder for myself."

"I didn't have anywhere else to be," James chimed in. "Marley's doing me a favor, giving me an excuse to do something fun. I would have spent the entire weekend watching TV and reading eleventh graders' thoughts on the legacy of Manifest Destiny."

"You didn't go see your family?"

"We FaceTimed. I'll go home for Christmas."

I saw the moment Coach's nosy interest morphed into true concern for James.

"You're doing okay in town, though, right son?" he asked. "I don't like to think of a new teacher being alone for the holidays when there are plenty of friendly folks around here."

"I'm grateful," James replied sincerely. "Marley offered for Thanksgiving. So did Travis—um, Mr. Bloxham—but I'm really fine. I feel very welcome." He looked over at me before continuing, "Besides, it all worked out. I can't think of anyplace I'd rather be right now."

At that, Coach volleyed his eyes between us again. *Not helping, James.* Coach looked like he was about to say more, so I played my best hand.

"C'mon, Coach. James and I are both adults and can manage ourselves. Leave it be. Or I'm going to tell Principal Nadal the truth about who covered every item in his office with aluminum foil for Halloween."

"You wouldn't dare."

"Wouldn't I?"

"It was a bonding experience for the team!"

"Which led to a bonding experience for the custodian and the district maintenance guy."

"Alright, alright. Don't worry. My lips are sealed about this." He moved his finger back and forth between me and James.

"There's nothing to seal them about but thank you," I said.

Coach made a disbelieving tsking noise before pointing upwards. "James, that strand up there is hanging funny. Looks crooked."

I lifted my eyes. "It is not! It's totally straight."

James grinned and scurried back up the ladder. "Let me make sure it's just right."

Coach spoke once James was out of earshot. "I'm only looking out for you, kiddo." He raised his chin and glanced at the top of the ladder. "You deserve it to be 'just right.' Don't settle for anything less."

With that, he spun around and got back in his car.

James came back down. "It's getting too dark to put everything up," he said. "But I think we got far enough that it looks pretty decent, even if it's not quite done."

I smiled and went over to the light timer by the porch, flipping it on. The basic lines were in place, strands of colored lights that traveled up and down the eaves and upper windows. We could tackle the lower windows, porch, and door tomorrow.

"What was that about, with Coach?" James asked.

"No big deal. He was on his way back into town and stopped by to check in on me."

"Nice of him."

It was nice of him. He was nice. And the friends who had texted me yesterday and today to remind me they could be called on any time to talk or hang out were also nice. Work friends. Friends I still had from childhood. People who worried about me because they'd seen me nurse my mom. Or break up with Kasen. I appreciated them all. But for now, I just wanted to enjoy my little holiday bubble with James.

We'd barely begun tackling the next load of tableware when the doorbell rang.

Opening the door, I found Mrs. Allen staring back at me. Her gaze went immediately to my palm tree—I'd turned the light show off—and she hummed approvingly.

"Mrs. Allen. This is a surprise." I felt mildly annoyed at yet another intrusion into my day with James, but I also loved this woman like family. I stepped back to invite her inside.

Oscar stayed curled up in a ball on the carpet. Mrs. Allen was old news to him. But Bambi came over to sniff out the new arrival. She patted the overeager labradoodle on his rump, and he wagged his tail excitedly as she continued into the house.

"Marley, when are you ever going to call me Eliza?"

"Probably never. Sorry." I smiled at her as we repeated the conversation we'd had many times.

She gave me an arch look as she glanced over to James in my kitchen, switching the load in the dishwasher.

I tried not to roll my eyes. "James is here to help me with my Christmas decorating. We just finished putting up lights outside."

"Finished?" James challenged, walking into the living room and giving Mrs. Allen a wave. "There are at least four more bins to go through in the garage." He placed the back of his hand against his forehead in mock distress.

"I meant finished for today, smarty-pants." I flicked my thumb and index finger against his chest. Turning to Mrs. Allen, I whispered conspiratorially, "I've been waiting for the right time to ask James to come back and help me again tomorrow. There's still a lot to do."

"I'm in," James said, pumping his fist. "Assuming my knees hold up. And you have to promise to wear another one of those sweaters."

Mrs. Allen chuckled as James excused himself to use the restroom.

"He's a charmer, that one." She grinned. "I like this development," she continued, hitching her neck in the direction James had gone. "I like this a whole lot."

"Don't get all excited. We're just friends."

"Sure."

"Good grief. Have you been talking to Coach?"

"He might have texted me ten minutes ago to say that there was something interesting going on at your place. Which might have sped up the timeline of this visit. But honestly, I was planning to come see you anyway."

"That sounds serious. Is everything okay?"

"Actually, no. I wanted to talk to you about this after the meeting on Wednesday, but then you walked out into the parking lot with Mr. Wymack, and I didn't want to interrupt your time with him—"

"We're just friends!"

"Of course. Anyway, this might concern him, too."

"What do you mean? Something at work?"

"Yep. I've heard that the emergency budget approval we got to expand the faculty is being re-considered by the district. We've had some students leave mid-year, so the enrollment numbers we relied on to get the money didn't hold."

"Okay. But why did you need to make a special trip here just to tell me that?"

"Because when it comes to staff reductions, it's first-hired, first-fired."

Oh. "James."

"Exactly," she said with concern. "I know you two have been getting close. And I wanted to tell you about it, so you're not blindsided. I wouldn't even know, except I happened to be in the career and college readiness office while Principal Nadal was on the phone."

"You were eavesdropping?"

"I was collecting papers in a crouched position behind the half-wall separating his office from the resource room." Her eyes lit mischievously. "Toe-may-toe, toe-mah-toe."

This would be a tricky situation if the information proved true. It wasn't like another high school existed in town for James to teach at. And even though I felt certain he could get a job elsewhere, I wasn't ready to lose him at Coleman Creek.

"Is there anything we can do?" I asked.

"It might help if the holiday fundraisers produce like gangbusters, especially the tree lot. But, of course, that's a totally different budget than the one that pays for faculty. I guess it can't hurt if our overall finances look strong. Just keep in mind, if we're being realistic, it's unlikely to make a difference."

"Well, this is the season for miracles...and longshots," I offered.

"I suppose. And it's good Mr. Wymack is already popular at school. Students would be upset to see him go. It's also possible we could get lucky and have a bunch of new enrollments." She didn't sound optimistic.

The sound of the bathroom faucet running echoed down the hall. James would be out soon.

"Should I warn him?" I asked.

"Principal Nadal will give him a heads-up once he knows more, I'm sure. I think it's okay if you just want to enjoy the rest of the weekend and not worry about it yet. No matter what happens, it's good to see you two together." I pursed my lips at her, and she held up her hands. "I know, I know. Just friends."

Mrs. Allen made her way to the door, pausing to scrutinize the nutcracker salad tongs as James reemerged.

"You're leaving?" he asked.

"Yep. I have two cats at home who'll start climbing the curtains if I don't feed them soon. I just needed to give Marley a heads up about something at school."

"Everything alright?"

James's palms rested lightly on my upper arms as he stepped behind me. He seemed to have made the gesture unconsciously, but my breath caught at its intimacy. His gentle touch burned into my skin.

Mrs. Allen looked between the two of us. "You know James, when I came over here, I wasn't sure if everything was alright, but now I'm thinking it will be." She wrapped her scarf around her neck. "It just might take a bit of Christmas magic."

I stepped away from James to walk Mrs. Allen to her car, causing him to look down curiously at his hands, like it surprised him to discover they'd been resting on my shoulders.

When I returned to the house, I found him sitting at the dining table, looking down at a word-search magazine he'd pulled from his satchel. I exhaled heavily, drawing his attention.

"Do you think Mr. Bailey will stop by soon?" he joked. "Or Principal Nadal? Maybe the math department?"

I chortled. "I know for a fact Mr. Bailey goes to Missoula to visit his nephew's family every Thanksgiving, so I'm pretty sure we're clear, at least on one."

James stretched his arms above his head. "I should get going. Don't want to wear out my welcome." He snapped his fingers and Bambi came over to his side. "You're cool if I come back tomorrow? To help you finish?"

I nodded. "That would be great. Noon?"

"See you then."

He grabbed his bag and the dog's leash, giving me a quick hug on his way out. Oscar whined for a minute as James closed the door behind himself, protesting their exit. I calmed the dog down with a treat and patted the cushion so he'd jump up next to me on the couch. He laid his furry head over my thigh while I scratched his ears.

The good news was that I'd had no difficulties managing my newly discovered, more-than-platonic desire for James. It had been easy enough to rely on our natural, effortless connection to avoid giving myself away. I marveled at how he clearly enjoyed helping me and hearing about my family. With Kasen, I'd always felt overshadowed. The lesser half of a whole. And that wasn't a knock on Kasen. He just hadn't inspired me to come out of my shell the way James did.

But I couldn't help feeling like I'd been so busy these past few months enjoying James's company, trying to savor every moment until he found his place outside of our friendship, that I hadn't done an adequate job of *seeing* him back. How had I missed his insecurities? Or that, while he'd given some details into his past, he was clearly afraid to share too much?

He'd mentioned being divorced, and I'd gathered it was recent-ish, but he never brought up his marriage. I knew he'd had a small business in Seattle before becoming a teacher—a game shop, he'd said once—but he'd offered no details about why he'd left. He'd talked about his childhood and his family. About friends he still had from his college days in Oregon. But I hadn't put it together until he got all weird about his reunion that he'd never spoken a word about high school—something that generally happened among teachers.

Had he been bullied? Been a bully? Dropped the winning pass in a football game? Farted in class? Played a part in a dramatic teenage love triangle? I'd worked with kids long enough to know it could be anything.

But what it couldn't be was something that would make me stop caring about James or respecting him any less. Because that was impossible.

Maybe I could help him with his reunion. I felt positive he needed to go. If he truly hadn't wanted to, deep down, he would have already sent the *no* to the RSVP-requesting texts.

I could offer to go with him. Support him. But I knew if I suggested that outright, he'd refuse. He'd think he was putting me out, especially since he knew how much I was looking forward to the Christmas activities in Coleman Creek. Or he'd assume I was offering out of pity, and he'd never allow that, since it was obvious maintaining the façade of being an uncomplicated, laid-back guy was very important to him.

He wasn't ready to open up yet about his whole life. And that was okay. I could be patient.

But the reunion wouldn't wait. He'd only get one chance to go, and the clock was ticking.

I looked down the hallway, at the door to the master, the room I still thought of as my mom's. A kernel of an idea formed in my mind. James needed an incentive to head in the direction of his reunion. And I might have just the thing to nudge him. An offer he wouldn't be able to say no to.

Chapter Six

James

When Marley opened the door the next day, she wore the Elf on the Shelf sweater she'd threatened me with at school the day of the faculty meeting. I didn't say a word, just reached out and flicked the little bells dangling from its hem, trying not to notice how perfectly the top hugged her curves.

We'd had such a good day yesterday. Being around her was like bouncing around inside a ball of joy. I'd gone home and felt the emptiness of my apartment acutely, even with Bambi next to me. Now, back with Marley, everything felt right again. I watched her lean back against a wall, tapping a finger against her lips as she contemplated the bins we hadn't tackled yesterday. She popped her hip, drawing my eyes to the soft line of her back and the full heart shape of her ass. I knew it was playing with fire to indulge in my attraction, but it was difficult not to when she was so tempting. Swallowing, I forced myself to focus on our tasks.

One of the remaining tubs contained ornaments. Marley put it aside, reasoning she wouldn't need it for a while since she always got fresh trees from the PTSA lot and didn't want to buy too early.

She told me her plan to purchase a seven-footer for upstairs and a smaller tree for the rec room—even though she almost never spent time there.

"How come you don't use the downstairs?" I asked.

"I dunno, really. There's a bunch of old retro board games down there you might be interested in checking out. Growing up, that's where we hung out, mostly because it's where the TV and comfy couch were, but now if I want to watch something, I just do it on my computer in my room. It's a lot different living in this house with just me."

I nodded as we sat on the couch untangling lights.

"Do any of the decorations go in the bedrooms?"

"No. Not this year anyway." Her voice sounded far away.

"Still no plans to use the master?" I questioned gently.

"Not firm ones."

I didn't want to pry—especially after Marley had been so careful not pushing me to talk about my reunion—but I was genuinely curious. If there was one thing I'd learned yesterday going through the Davis family Christmas kitsch, it was that Marley's grieving process for her mom was healthy—like she'd bought a book on how to handle the death of a beloved parent and was mastering the steps one at a time.

That's why it didn't track that she hadn't moved into the home's main bedroom. Was she keeping it as a monument? Or maybe she was less okay than I'd been thinking?

"I can see your big brain wondering," she said. "I can't say exactly why I haven't moved in there yet. It might be time." She exhaled heavily. "Do you want to see?"

She surprised me with the request. But I got the feeling she didn't want to go in there alone. "Only if you want to show me."

"I do."

The dogs perked up from their spot in front of the fireplace. We shook our heads at them to stay put.

I wasn't exactly sure what I'd been expecting when Marley swung open the oversized door, but it hadn't been an eerily empty room. We stepped into the large space in the center where a bed would normally be.

"I've already told you my mom died of Parkinson's. It wasn't the shaking kind people usually think of when they imagine that disease. For her, it was more like hallucinations. That last year, she was seeing people that weren't there. Talking to them. In and out of recognizing me. Insurance paid to have a hospital bed here. Easier for the nurses. Obviously, they took it back after..." she trailed off.

A clear plastic shoebox full of pill bottles, a hairbrush, and a little notepad sat atop a small dresser in one corner. Clothing still hung in the closet. Light came in harshly through the cracks in the blinds, highlighting tiny dirt specks floating in the stagnant air.

"It's nothing like how it was when she first got sick," Marley mused. "Mom used to have books and photos and lots of clutter. Over time, after she could no longer read and just wore hospital gowns every day, there was no use for anything other than whatever the nurses needed to make her comfortable. She had a TV on the dresser, but Maureen took it last time she came. Everything else looks like it did when she died. Since Mom couldn't leave the bed, it's as though that whole last terrible year all happened in this room. Like the worst part of it got contained in here. I know that sounds stupid—"

"It's not stupid at all," I assured her.

"Well, sometimes it doesn't make sense, even to me. I just know that closing the door to this room helped a bit. Like, I could save this and deal with other things. One at a time. That way, it never got to be too much."

"Like waiting until this year with the decorations?"

"Exactly like that. This bedroom is the last big thing I need to tackle."

"Do you come in here a lot?"

She reached over and clasped my hand. I expected her to give it a squeeze and let go, but she held on. "This is the first time in a long time, James. Thank you."

I stared at her in the silence. *Damn, this woman.* Making me feel like I'd accomplished something, just by standing next to her. This window she was offering into her heart. Her openness. I'd never experienced anything so incredible. I was done lying to myself. Even if it was a truly terrible idea to go there—I wanted Marley.

I did not know what to do next. She'd just told me about her mother, and I was standing there having some entirely unrelated and very inappropriate-for-the-moment thoughts. I felt the *want* like a physical force. But beyond that, there existed a soul-deep need to do something meaningful for her. To honor what she'd just given me.

I kept our hands linked as I asked, "Do you want me to move your stuff in here? Help you clean out your mother's old bedroom?"

Her eyes grew wide. A few different expressions crossed her face—each more unreadable than the last—before she surprised me by barking out a small laugh. "That's so weird."

Not the reaction I'd expected. "What's weird?"

She grinned as she let go of my hand. "I was planning to ask you to help me move my mom's things. Before you offered just now."

"Oh, nice. Glad we're on the same page." I said, my turn to smile. I took a few steps around the room, taking a mental inventory of what might need to be done. "Guess it's settled. Just let me know when you want to do it."

But her expression looked far from settled.

"How about this, James—" she paused, gazing up at me. "I accept your offer to help me do this very difficult thing I need to do, and in return, you let me do the same for you. Specifically, you let me go with you to your reunion."

It took me a beat to process her words. "My reunion? Huh? What does that have to do with this?"

She exhaled heavily before explaining. "After you left yesterday, I thought a lot about your reunion. How you reacted to those texts. Obviously, something happened back then, something you're struggling with. We both have this...stuff we're holding on to. That's why I shut the door on this room. But it's time to let in the light. I want to help you too. I'm asking you to please let me."

Wow. It felt as though Marley had just chucked a suitcase full of lead at my chest. I took a step back and rolled my shoulders. Worried my legs might give out, I dropped into a squat position, elbows resting on my knees as I laced my fingers behind my neck.

"Will you still let me help move your furniture into the master, even if I don't go to my reunion?"

Marley sighed. "Of course. But I really hope you'll consider the trade." She stepped away, running a gentle hand over the dresser. "It's still hard to imagine coming in here, clearing out these last pieces of my mom's life, but I've known for a while that I *need* to." She eyed me levelly before stating, "I don't want to force you to do something you truly do not want to do, but it seems like, in your heart, going to the reunion is something you need to do."

"You're sure you want to go with me?" I asked as I stood up.

"I'd be honored, James."

"You realize you'd have to skip one of your volunteer shifts at the Christmas tree lot, and we'd miss out on chaperoning the school dance, since the reunion is that weekend?" I felt my resolve weakening as I grasped for any excuse possible.

She released a small laugh. "James, it's okay. Of course I want to do my part for the school. But there's no question supporting you is more important. Other people can help at Coleman Creek. I don't trust anyone else to go with you to your reunion." Marley peppered that last remark with a wink.

She'd said it tongue-in-cheek, clearly unaware I held the same sentiment. There wasn't anyone else in my life I trusted not to judge or pity me if things went wrong. I'd left acquaintances behind in Seattle, but no one I thought of as a true friend. Oliver had been like a brother to me—until our friendship imploded. My family loved me, but I'd never been able to talk to them about high school.

As the idea established itself in my gut, I knew Marley was right. I tilted my chin to my chest and folded my arms. "We'll go to my reunion, and I'll help you move furniture."

"Deal." She grinned. "*Now* it's settled. Let's wait until after the holidays to switch the rooms, though. Then it will be like starting fresh for the new year."

We walked back out to the living room, Marley closing the door behind us. The dogs were still knocked out in front of the fireplace, Bambi on his back with Oscar's paw draped over his belly.

"How about I make us a snack and then we can finish up outside?" Marley asked.

"Sounds good."

"Sandwiches okay?"

"Perfect."

She disappeared into the kitchen for a few minutes before returning with two plates of leftover turkey sandwiches and sparkling water. I smiled, reaching to grab one. She seemed tense for a moment, but relaxed after I started eating.

As we ate on the couch, I glanced over to find her going through a photo album of pictures from past Christmases.

"My mom put this together after Miranda went away to college. There was a brief time when all three of us were out of the house. It's just print-outs of her favorites from holidays over the years." Marley turned the page to reveal some sepia-toned photos of her mother, yellowed further with age. "God, look at that hair. Teased to the sky."

I put my plate on the coffee table and leaned against the side of the couch, head resting against my fist. Marley sat with her feet tucked under her, laughing and pointing at the images, occasionally explaining something to me. I felt content in a way I never had been before. Not just because I knew how much she cared about me, and not because I'd finally admitted to myself how attracted I was to her. But because I'd never felt this comfortable in my own skin.

In that moment, I felt thankful she'd be coming with me to my reunion—still scared about what could happen, but thankful. Because everything else aside, I wanted Marley to know me.

The plastic sheeting covering the pictures stuck together and creaked as she turned the pages. Her glassy eyes roamed over the ancient prints, and I knew these glimpses of the past, especially her mom, were bittersweet. I couldn't help but admire her ability to find peace within the storm. That, along with my earlier realization of how she made me feel, might have made me slightly stupid.

"Marley, you are amazing."

Had I said that out loud? Shit. The air between us charged instantly.

Freezing in her perusal of the album, she turned toward me, cheeks red. "Thanks, James. Was it the sandwiches that made you realize?"

Even though she was deflecting, giving me an out, I didn't want to take it. "Seriously, Marley. I'm in awe of the way you care about the people in your life. I feel really lucky to be one of them."

Her mouth opened and closed a few times before she finally said, "I'm not so special, but thank you for saying that. I...do care about you."

She did not know. The way Marley put herself out there for the people in her life was beyond *special*. That's why Coach Hurley had shown up yesterday. And Mrs. Allen. It was why the students lobbied for her to be their advisor for every club and why even senior teachers came to her for advice on tough kids. Everyone wanted to return at least some of the love she projected so fearlessly into the world.

Had I ever been that fearless? Been so open with the people who loved me? Not by a long shot.

I wanted her to teach me. I wanted... her.

Marley untucked her legs as I scooted in closer on the couch. She hadn't tried to move away, and the certainty of my affection made me bold. I reached my palm out to place it on her knee, using my thumb to trace small circles. Feeling the slight trembling in her thigh, I murmured slowly, "When I'm with you, it's like I can breathe properly for the first time in forever."

She shuddered and peered down at my hand, raising her leg a fraction to meet my touch. "What are we doing, James?"

I leaned in closer, registering the flecks of gray in her brown eyes, the tiny beauty mark on the left side of her jawline, the pulse point beating rapidly in the hollow of her neck. "What we probably should have done months ago. What I've been dreaming about doing for days."

The weight of the physical desire I'd been keeping in check rolled over me like a wave. I itched to pull her close. To kiss her so soundly, there would be no doubt how special she was. Now that I'd finally allowed my mind to go there, I couldn't stop my head from spinning with...*images*. Marley on her back with me above her. Marley with her hands on my belt buckle. Marley biting her bottom lip while I gripped her hip. All the blood rushed south as I felt my cock growing thick.

She looked up with open eyes, unspeaking, letting me lead. But the rough swallow that moved down her throat and her widened pupils gave her away. Marley wanted me too.

I knew I had baggage, knew there were things about me she probably ought to know. Things she'd most likely find out at my reunion. But selfishly, in that moment, I didn't care. If I let myself come up for air, examine it too hard, I knew I'd find a million reasons to hold back.

Reaching my other hand out, I dragged my fingers along Marley's arm, from her wrist to the top of her non-elf shoulder. She closed her eyes as I cupped her cheek.

Releasing a contented exhale, she nuzzled into my palm, turning her head to place a soft kiss in the center. "Is this really happening?" she breathed out shallowly. "I never thought you would—"

"Marley...how can you not know? I can't get enough of you."

Her breath on my skin felt like a brand. I grabbed the stupid elf and tugged her closer, feeling the hammering of our hearts. She flinched, just barely, like she was still deciding if this was a good idea. But she didn't turn away. I began lowering my mouth to hers.

Both dogs jumped up and started barking explosively, nosing their faces through the curtains to give the delivery truck in the neighbor's driveway a piece of their minds. Oscar placed his paws on the window, banging on the glass, while Bambi complemented the move with a full chorus of growls and snarls.

I released Marley and turned my face toward the window. "Bambi! Quiet! No bark!"

The noise died quickly as the dogs offered sheepish expressions. But the damage had been done, the moment lost as effectively as if it had been bathed in ice water. My cock-blocking canine gave the truck one last pitiful "woof" before going back to the fireplace.

"Oscar! Heel!" Marley commanded. The excited lab took another second to observe outside the glass but finally laid down with his buddy.

Once the dogs settled, Marley looked back toward me. The dreamy, glazed expression she'd been wearing a minute earlier was gone. Our dog-inspired reprieve had turned that flinch of hesitancy I'd noted into a full-blown retreat. She moved farther away on the couch, putting a foot of distance between us.

"James, I think we should take a pause," she said, still slightly panting. "It's been an emotional few days, and I know the thought of going to your reunion is...a lot." She exhaled deeply and stood up. "I don't know exactly what was happening just now, but I don't want to get all caught up in a moment...and maybe make a mistake."

Marley took a few steps over to the dining table and grabbed the back of a chair. I ran a hand over my beanie and squeezed my eyes shut, willing my erection to subside. Everything in me screamed to pull her back into my arms. To find out what those lips felt like. But she had a point. These past two days had been intense. Probably not the best time to elevate this situation. Changing our dynamic—the one built over countless hours spent together as friends—was a big deal.

I'd fallen for Marley. One hundred percent. And I hoped she was right there with me, even as her wide eyes pleaded with me to understand her hesitance.

But if we were going to take this further, I also wanted to earn it. To give her more of myself.

"How about we go outside and finish the lights?" I suggested. She responded with a grateful smile.

We got through the rest of the day with minimal awkwardness. By unspoken agreement, we didn't talk about what had almost happened on the couch. There would be time for that. When I left that evening, I'd resolved to give her whatever space she needed, while also figuring out how to open up to her. I just wasn't sure where to start.

MY HOURS WITH MARLEY played on a running loop in my brain for the rest of the weekend. Not only our near-miss kiss, but realizing I trusted her enough to want to introduce her to the less flattering pieces of my past. But those careful thoughts were derailed by some very disconcerting information I received when Principal Nadal called me into his office first thing Monday morning. Information that made getting clarity with Marley much more urgent.

He gave me the heads-up that there were some budget challenges, and I might not have a teaching position at Coleman

Creek the following year. My contract lasted until June, but he didn't sound hopeful it would be extended.

It was a blow. I'd come to this town for a fresh start, because I couldn't stop feeling like a sad sack for being rejected by my ex-wife, for letting my business partner and supposed best friend get the better of me. Now I was possibly going to lose a job I loved. Would the hits ever stop coming?

Saturday, I'd been feeling fantastic. Thinking that someone as amazing as Marley might want to be with me. That I might finally be in a place where I could be honest with someone about who I was inside, that I could grow together with someone worthy of the effort. I knew she saw my insecurities—and she liked me anyway.

But if I couldn't teach, was there even a reason for me to stay in Coleman Creek? Did it make sense to start something with Marley if I was going to be forced to leave next summer? Even if I found a teaching position elsewhere, Coleman Creek was her home. She'd made that clear.

I didn't know what my next move should be. I'd already been dreading my reunion. And now I had job security to worry about. I needed to take a page out of Marley's book and take things one step at a time.

Chapter Seven

Marley

I woke up for school Monday morning still thinking about the days James and I had spent together. Initially, I'd been worried putting the brakes on being more intimate would dampen our friendship, but with fresh perspective, I'd grown even more sure going slow was the best course of action. For both of us. The important thing was, he'd almost kissed me. He was as attracted to me as I was to him. The question of what to do about it didn't need to be answered right away.

Besides, it wasn't like James and I were destined for some grand love affair. I liked knowing he desired me. My ego thrilled that I'd captured the interest of someone as fascinating as him. I definitely wanted to see where the attraction led and enjoy the ride for however long it lasted. But I wasn't delusional. I hadn't been able to hold the attention of Kasen—the type of practical small-town guy I'd always assumed I'd end up with—so I had zero chance of James falling for me long-term.

There was also the fact I still had a lot to learn about him. Something important held him back. And whatever his hangup,

I couldn't force him to deal with it. I just needed to wait and see what happened next. Be patient.

The soreness in my muscles from all the box hauling and ladder climbing made its presence known as I rolled over to face the window. I could hear Oscar's doggy snores from across the room where he lay curled up in his bed. Once he figured out I was awake, he jumped on the mattress. "What do you think will happen with James, boy?" I asked, scratching under his collar. He went back to sleep almost immediately, his snores right next to my ear. Like a rusty buzz saw. Time to get out of bed.

As I brushed my teeth and started the coffee, I could not stop reflecting on how James had become such an important person in my life in only three short months. I'd learned a lot more about him over the weekend, but in so many ways he remained a mystery.

My thoughts had been so consumed with him I completely forgot I'd unblocked Kasen's number on Thanksgiving. So, when my ex's text came through, it startled me.

KASEN: Hey Marley. I know you've blocked me but I figured it couldn't hurt to try. I saw your sisters the other day and I really hope they gave you the message that I'd love to reconnect. It's been so long since we've talked and I just really really miss you. Maybe it's selfish of me to ask when you clearly want space, but whenever you're ready, just know that I would love to see you. I don't want to be strangers.

I blinked and leaned heavily against the counter. These were the first words I'd heard from Kasen in five years. They hit like bricks on the freeway. Hard. And completely out of nowhere.

When I'd told my sisters I was over my ex, I'd absolutely meant it. But we'd been together for eight years. There was no way to tell the story of my life without including him in it. I just hadn't thought about those chapters in a long time.

Leaving Kasen on read, I headed into work. I couldn't worry about him right now. I had classes to teach.

Racing to beat my first period students, I saw James exit the principal's office wearing an agitated expression. I wondered what that look was about, but the late bell was about to ring.

Figuring he could fill me in later that morning, I went about my usual routine. The students were rowdy after the long weekend, so getting them to settle down for a discussion about iambic pentameter required all my abilities.

But when our shared free period rolled around, James didn't come to my classroom as usual. He texted an hour later to ask if I could meet him in the teacher's lounge during lunch.

I arrived first, the only one in the small room except for Mr. Bailey, who huddled in the corner with *The Washington Post*, mumbling something about wasteful government spending.

James came in a few minutes later, appearing unfocused and irritable. He and Mr. Bailey were generally friendly, but one look at James's turbulent expression had the other man hiding behind the newspaper, raising it above his forehead.

Falling heavily into the chair next to mine, James rolled his shoulders and tugged at his collar, releasing the top two buttons of his shirt.

"Can we go out tonight?" he asked suddenly. "Dinner at The Landslide?"

"Sure." I spoke gently, "Are you alright?"

He ran a palm over his face, rings on his middle finger and thumb catching the light from the fluorescents. "You know me too well. That's why I can't stop thinking—" He paused and stilled his movements.

He seemed so anxious I started to worry, a pit forming in my stomach. "You haven't changed your mind about going to the reunion, have you?"

"Huh? Oh...no, it's not that. Even though I probably should." James stared at me, and I saw a muscle in his jaw twitch. "After this weekend, we just...have a lot to talk about.

My breath stuck in my throat. Did he mean our close moment on the couch? I hoped he didn't regret it.

I was working up the courage to ask when Coach Hurley came into the lounge carrying his ancient red Igloo lunch cooler. He took off his hat and sat down at our table.

"Not surprised to see you two together," he enthused. "Evidently you got that crooked strand of lights all fixed up?" Coach winked as he spoke to James. "I'm sure there are lots of things you can help Ms. Davis with now." Another wink.

Clearly, Coach hadn't read the mood before he'd sat down. Mr. Bailey huffed from behind his newspaper, crinkling it dramatically before getting up and leaving, shaking his head at all of us.

James made no reply. I sat rigidly in my chair.

Coach hmphed. "Alright, alright. I can see you guys are trying to keep it on the down-low, as the students would say." I opened my mouth to protest, but he held up a hand. "Save it, Marley. You'll never convince me. But it's none of my business." He pulled his Coleman Creek Royals baseball cap back over his head and stood up, grabbing his cooler. "I'm going to eat on the benches outside the athletic office." Then he leaned in close to my ear and whispered, "You've been an absolute angel these past years, with your mom. And at this school. I want you to have...*lights*. We all do. No one deserves solid lights more than you."

I didn't know how to reply, so I merely dipped my chin. Coach's entrance had been ill-timed. But his presence and obvious rooting interest for me and James as a couple relieved some of the thickness in the air.

"What did he whisper to you?" James asked after Coach left.

"Nothing. He just reminded me I'm not the only one who cares about Christmas decorations."

James directed a puzzled glance my way but didn't ask for clarification. He returned to the topic Coach had interrupted. "Can we meet at seven?"

"See you there."

I ARRIVED AT The Landslide fifteen minutes early. There were some other bars in and near town, but this was the local favorite, situated just outside the business corridor and close to the highway. Its small dance floor functioned as the closest thing Coleman Creek had to a nightlife scene.

The owners had lived in town forever, and they'd plastered the walls with their love for it. Black and white photos of Main Street circa the 1950s were interspersed with team pictures of Coleman Creek High School football squads. There were copies of elementary school yearbook pages, soldiers in military dress, a framed watercolor painting of an old town diner, and corkboards full of pinned up images of patrons enjoying the bar. A faded picture of my mom and dad sitting in a corner booth had been tacked up to a wall near the restrooms for two decades.

My stomach danced with nerves as I sat down at a two-top table near the ancient jukebox. Why had James asked me to dinner? Did he want to forget our moment? Or pursue something more?

I ignored the menu I'd long-since memorized and tugged at my sweater. It was one of my most subdued. Just Rudolph's face with a giant red pom for a nose. I had a fond memory of my mother wearing it to the high school talent show the year Miranda and her friends had performed an acoustic guitar version of "Last Christmas."

I'd considered dressing to impress. But James already knew about the sweaters. He would expect nothing less—a fact confirmed when he walked in a few minutes later, took one look at me and declared, "That one is actually sort of cute."

"Wanna borrow it?"

"Don't tempt me, Marley. I already have my eye on the one you wore earlier today." He smiled, seeming much more relaxed than at lunch.

"That was just a boring Seahawks holiday sweater."

"I know." He reached down and patted his rounded belly. "Not that I could fit into your clothes."

Considering my newfound awareness of his self-consciousness, I had no ready reply to that comment. A few beats of silence passed before I decided the best course was to act the way I'd always done when we'd gone out. "Should we order an appetizer? I'm starving."

"Sure."

Katy Baumbeck, who'd been two years behind me in high school, came over to take our order. I recalled her husband was out of town for a few weeks dealing with his ailing parents in Arizona. I inquired about them and her twin toddlers before James and I ordered beers and mozzarella sticks.

"Do you know everyone in Coleman Creek?" James glanced at Katy's retreating form.

"Not *all* of them. I saw a moving van roll in yesterday, so I'll need to go introduce myself," I joked. "When you grow up here and teach at the only high school, you meet people. Also, everyone knows Katy because the whole town comes to The Landslide."

"You really don't understand the way you affect people, do you?"

I scoffed. "It's not a big deal to ask someone about their kids. Besides, I'm pretty sure the sophomores would tell you I *affected* them last week by causing boredom-induced comas during our poetry unit."

He gave me a courtesy laugh but then said, "You don't need to undercut it. You're a genuinely kind person, Marley. I've never heard you say a bad word about anyone."

I shifted in my seat. "I'm an ordinary level of friendly, James. You just have a skewed view because you've always lived in big cities where there are too many neighbors to know them all."

"You are a lot of things, Marley. 'Ordinary' is not one of them."

My face heated and I looked away, unable to respond. Did he wish I was more interesting than I actually was? At some point, he was going to have to accept I was Mid-Marley and that wouldn't change.

"We can talk about something else," he said, grabbing the menu he apparently hadn't yet memorized. "The last thing I want to do is make you uncomfortable. At least not about that."

"So you want to make me uncomfortable about other things?"

I meant those words as teasing, but James's features were serious when he replied, "Maybe." He lowered the menu and adjusted the beanie on his head. "There is something we should probably discuss."

I braced myself for whatever it was. *Let's just be friends. I don't want to go to my reunion with you. The moment on the couch was a mistake.*

But James said none of those things.

"Principal Nadal told me this morning they might cut my position after this year."

What? Oh. Right. I'd almost forgotten about that little hiccup. "Yeah. I know."

"You knew? How?" His expression transformed from confusion to hurt. "Why didn't you tell me?"

"Sorry. I mean, I didn't *know* know. When Mrs. Allen came to my house on Friday, she told me she'd heard some gossip about the budget. Nothing concrete. I didn't want to worry you unnecessarily until the administration told us more. And I would have said something. Except then we had that moment on the couch—"

"I get it," he said, nodding. "I'm not going to pretend it hasn't been on my mind too. Then Principal Nadal added this new component to the equation. Now I'm not sure if maybe it changes that conversation, since there's a chance I won't have a job here in six months."

"And there are no other high schools nearby. No reason for you to stay." I understood his dilemma. He'd told me how much he loved being a teacher, that he regretted not getting his credentials sooner.

He reached across the table to grab my hand. "Don't say it like that, Marley. I don't know what we're doing here exactly. But whatever it is, I don't want you to think it would be easy for me to walk away from you, to walk away from our..." he trailed off.

"Friendship?"

"That, and...it's more now, isn't it?" He blew out a long breath. "You're always so straightforward. It's one of the things I admire most about you. I struggle with that. But I don't want to use that as an excuse to shy away from being honest about us." A moment later he ground out, "And I want you to be honest, too, even if you think it might hurt me."

His gaze had been downcast, but he looked up then, eyes wide and seeking.

"Hurt you? What? Why would you think that?"

"I'm saying you were the one who pulled away from me. And even though I agree it was the right move, I still need to make sure I know why you did it. I understand everything is weird right now, with my reunion, with us being co-workers, and now this budget situation." He ran his thumb in circles over my wrist. "But if you put the brakes on Saturday because you think us being together is a terrible idea, and you could never see me as more than a friend, I guess I just...need to know."

I understood. "You want to know if I'm in this, because it might factor into your decision-making."

"Yes."

I felt the dilemma within myself. I wanted to argue with him that this was all a moot point, that no matter how *in this* I was, he would get bored with me soon enough. But I doubted he'd hear that now, considering he'd just tried to sell me on not being ordinary. Briefly, I contemplated if it would be kinder to lie and say I didn't want him, to nip this in the bud and make his choices that much easier. Hurt him now to save both of us from pain down the road.

But the thing was, I welcomed the pain. I wanted whatever time I could get with James before the inevitable end. He made me feel alive in a way I hadn't before, and I planned to hang onto that feeling as long as possible.

Lying about my attraction wasn't truly an option anyway, considering how clearly James telegraphed his issues. I'd never allow myself to be another person who betrayed his trust. But maybe I could split the difference. He wasn't the only one that had concerns about who was or wasn't *in this.*

"James, I'm attracted to you. And I don't regret what happened. So, set your mind at ease about that. But let's be honest about something else. I might have stopped us on Saturday, but you and I both know I'm not the only one holding back."

He was quiet a moment, pulling his arm away as he replied, "I know. It's difficult to explain. There's a part of me that's terrified of jeopardizing what we have. You've come to mean so much to me in just a short time. Obviously, I don't want to risk our friendship—or cheapen it." I read between the lines there. That some type of friends-with-benefits arrangement would not be in the cards. "But it's more than that."

"Okay." I gave him an encouraging glance.

"I wish I could explain this better, but it's like, from the first moment I met you, you've been open and honest with me. That day, you were sitting at your desk with tears on your face. You didn't try to hide them from me or make excuses. And then you joked around and made *me* feel better." He blew out a forceful breath. "What's holding me back from taking anything you're willing to offer is that I don't want to disappoint you. I've spent my whole adult life trying to prove myself, to create a version of me that people like—with mixed results, I guess—and that's meant putting up a front." He placed his elbows on the table, one fist resting inside the other palm, words spilling out tight and fast. "I don't want to hesitate or wonder if I'm doing the wrong thing with you because you haven't met my darker, sadder sides. I owe you the openness you've shown me, and—"

"Hey James?" I interjected. I knew what he was saying, and what it was costing him.

"Yeah?"

"It's okay." I reached across to grasp his clenched fist, re-joining our fingers together on the table. "It's okay."

Something had clearly hurt him—badly—and he was recovering, figuring out how to be vulnerable.

"What's okay?"

"It's okay that you don't have it all sorted out. That you don't feel ready. Or that I don't. We're good right now. It's enough to know we're on the same page, that we're not going to pretend the attraction isn't there. We can decide the rest as we go. Take steps. One thing at a time."

He smiled. "Your life philosophy."

"I suppose. We've got lots of things taking up our mental energy right now. You with your reunion and the school budget. Me with moving the last of my mom's things. Not to mention Christmas." Also, there was Kasen's potential re-entry into my life, but no need to burden James with that. "Maybe let's just...keep getting to know each other."

He nodded. Katy reappeared to bring us the drinks and take our dinner orders. Burger for me, pasta for him.

After our food arrived, we moved on to safer topics of discussion, student shenanigans and school activities.

"It feels weird saying we're still just friends now," he said.

"We don't need to put a label on it. It's no one's business but ours. No matter how much Coach and Mrs. Allen want to stick their noses in."

"Don't forget about old Mr. Bailey. He's probably put twenty down on us, too."

"Small towns." I shrugged. "We can just do what makes sense to us. Think of it as our own, unique *situationship*, or whatever the cool kids call it these days."

He chortled. "Okay. Yeah, that sounds good."

Over dinner, I noticed we were slightly more tactile than we'd been previously, brushing hands across the table, resting our ankles together underneath. We couldn't completely turn off the physical pull we'd admitted to. There had to be some allowances made for the fact that our friendship had evolved.

Still, when James walked me out to my car afterwards, he hugged me quickly, maintaining some boundaries, at least for now.

Achieving a sense of clarity with him reminded me how much I hated loose ends and inconsistent pathways. I liked things neat, not messy and open-ended.

Which is why I texted Kasen.

ME: We don't have to be strangers anymore. I think I'm okay with that now. What did you want to talk about?

Chapter Eight

James

For the next week, Marley and I made a concerted effort to get our groove back. I knew she was waiting for me to talk more about my past, and I planned to, but first I wanted to confirm that we were on solid footing.

My biggest challenge in navigating our *situationship* was the internal struggle happening in my head. Besides the mental energy involved in psyching myself up to tell Marley about my ex, my failed business, and why I didn't want to see anyone from high school, knowing she wanted me physically had stoked other doubts. I hadn't stopped to worry about them when I'd let my dick take the lead on her couch, but now those thoughts ran wild. Would she still want me when she saw my naked belly in all its glory? Did she care that I hadn't been to a real gym since I'd left Seattle? I'd never thought about waxing my ass before, but I seriously considered it now.

Battles in my head notwithstanding, our easy familiarity seemed to have returned. We spent our break and lunch periods together and had taken the dogs to the park several times since our conversation at The Landslide.

Principal Nadal's response to finding out we'd be out of town for the holiday dance to attend my reunion had been to assign us most of the pre-event grunt work. Until the Friday we left, we'd be staying after school every day with the student council to supervise plans for turning the gym into a winter wonderland.

Since Thanksgiving, the students had done a great job making the school look festive. Artificial trees lit up the common areas and paper ring chains hung from hallway ceilings. The finishing touch—and most anticipated piece—of the school's holiday aesthetic would be the doors to the classrooms.

Marley had explained to me weeks ago that each teacher decorated their door for the season. The senior class officers judged the designs, awarding first through tenth place titles. While some teachers kept it simple, many took it as a point of pride to get a placement and went full blown HGTV on their doors.

Knowing how much she loved the holidays, it hadn't surprised me when Marley then mentioned she took the competition seriously and planned to win. I'd responded by vowing to give her a run for her money. My words had been meant mostly as a joke—I could honestly care less about my classroom door—but she'd seemed so delighted by my enthusiasm, I'd felt compelled to follow through.

So, we'd made a side bet. Teachers had the option to perform in the school's holiday talent show. Most of us knew better than to submit ourselves to potential public humiliation in front of teenagers and thus avoided this *opportunity*. Coach Hurley told me the only one who ever took part was Mr. Bailey, who annually treated the student body to his rendition of "Snow."

Marley and I wagered that whichever one of us placed lower in the door decorating rankings had to participate as well.

Most of the teachers worked on their creations over the weekend. Principal Nadal didn't necessarily condone all the off-hours labor, but he didn't fight us on it either. After completing our doors, we were supposed to cover them in brown paper, with the plan being to unveil them on cue Monday morning—a fun tradition to start the first full week in December. The students would roll their eyes and call us corny, but we knew they secretly enjoyed it.

I came in Sunday afternoon to finish. At least a dozen other teachers also showed up. The expectation was to work independently, to keep our eyes on our own doors, but I couldn't help peeking at my co-workers' designs. In the classroom next to mine, Mrs. Allen appeared to have covered her door in snowflake wrapping paper and called it a day. Mr. Lemon across the hall tried a little harder, going for a forest scene centered on cut-out animals romping in cotton ball snow.

Still, if their designs indicated the caliber of the competition, I figured I was in the mix to win.

Marley met me in front of my brown paper-covered door Monday morning before school.

"Feeling cocky?" she asked, raising a brow.

"Feeling like you're going to a holiday rave?" I teased back, pointing at her metallic purple and pink candy cane sweater and matching headband.

She snorted delicately before turning toward her classroom. "You're going down, Wymack," she called as she walked away.

"We'll see," I replied, smiling at her retreating form.

Our exchange might have been a bit too loud because it attracted the attention of some of my students. They made a point of looking back and forth between me and Marley before smirking.

Great. The kids were as gossipy as the teachers. "Mind your business and get inside," I told them good-naturedly.

"What? We're not allowed to ship you and Ms. Davis?" Diane Montoya, one of my juniors, asked with a grin.

"You do realize I can produce pop quizzes on the Persian Empire at a moment's notice?"

"You wouldn't dare!" Diane brought her hand to her heart dramatically, drawing giggles from her classmates. "Not right before the holiday."

"Oh, wouldn't I? Just call me Scrooge."

"Sure, Mr. Wymack... Hey, wasn't his best friend named Jacob *Marley*?"

The students laughed and took their seats as the late bell finally rang, me shaking my head the whole time.

There was a fifteen-minute break between second and third periods. As soon as it began, Principal Nadal came over the loudspeaker to announce that it was time for the teachers to reveal their doors.

I did so slowly and carefully, making a show of it for the students hovering in the hallway.

My design was simple but eye-catching. Silver paper covered the background, and I'd put an enormous Christmas tree on top. But I hadn't just used green construction paper or felt. I'd cut the shape out of one-and-a-half-inch thick turf. So not only was the tree massive, it was also three-dimensional, puffing out proudly from my classroom doorway. Two strands of battery-powered lights outlined it. Ornaments, tinsel, and ribbons decorated the branches. It could be seen sparkling from halfway down the hall.

After pulling down the paper, I pinned on the finishing touch—a gold star tree topper. Then I leaned back to survey the result. Folding my arms, I smiled proudly. Even if I didn't win, I'd certainly made a worthy effort.

Feeling satisfied that everything looked straight and would stay tacked up, I walked around to view the other teachers' creations.

My first destination was Marley's classroom, our wager on my mind.

As soon as I reached it, I knew I'd been had.

I could only hope that the talent show audience would appreciate my juggling skills.

Ms. Allen saw me first, and she couldn't stop herself from laughing at my expression, stifling the noise with her fist. "We're sorry. When Marley and you made that bet, I should have warned you she was a ringer, but I kind of wanted to see this look on your face."

I stood there, mouth agape, lips in an O like I was sucking on a straw that wasn't there.

Because Marley's entire door was a snow globe.

Eight inches of plastic protruding roundly into the hallway put my one-and-a-half-inch turf to shame. I could hear a motor running. Behind the door, an electric pump fed air to the clear vinyl bubble via the door's inexplicably present mail slot. A charming fireplace scene provided the globe's centerpiece. Glittery paper confetti blowing within the plastic sheeting completed the picture.

"Don't feel bad," Ms. Allen said, patting me on the shoulder as I marveled at Marley's ingenuity. "She wins every year. Except last, of course. That girl loves her holiday cheer."

"I should have known," I replied, thinking of the bins I'd unloaded at her house. I took in the meticulous details in front of me. Painted plywood underneath the bubble evoked an intricate snow globe base. On the background of faux bookshelves, she'd taken the time to write in the names of holiday classics.

Students were milling about, full of "oohs" and "aahs." Many had made a beeline for Marley's classroom as soon as the paper came off. Apparently, I'd been the only person unaware of her door design dominance.

The creator herself stood proudly next to her masterpiece, winking when she saw me. I shook my head at her while mouthing, "I surrender."

"That looks really great, Ms. Davis," said Henry, one of the student council judges. "A winner for sure. I can't believe you got that motor thing to work."

"DIY YouTube," Marley said. "Saving Christmas since, well, I don't know. Early 2000s maybe." She hitched her shoulders. "All I know is you can learn anything these days. But you and your crew should look at all the entries before you decide."

"Sure Ms. Davis. We'll keep it fair." He gave her a significant look. Code for *I'll go through the motions, but we both know you've got this in the bag* before putting an arm around one of his buddies and dragging him down the hall.

Other students drifted by, widening their eyes in approval and giving Marley a thumbs up.

She approached me. "Are you mad?"

I laughed. "No. You win fair and square. I mean, it's my own fault. I should have assumed you'd be the Martha Stewart of Coleman Creek High door design."

"You're right. You should have." With that, she strolled off down the hallway.

"Where are you going?"

"To see your door, of course. Just because I'm in it to win it doesn't mean I can't appreciate whatever you did."

I followed her to my class in the next corridor, satisfied to see a few students clustered there. Even if it wasn't a freaking full-sized snow globe, I'd still made a passable showing.

Marley stopped short. "It's beautiful, James," she said, taking in my sparkling tree. "You really did try."

"Of course."

Her eyes grew glassy as she examined the tree, pondering each ornament. She smiled when she noticed the ceramic dogs labeled "Bambi" and "Oscar." Reaching out a hand to run it over the turf, Marley pinched a piece of tinsel between her thumb and index finger.

She seemed oddly emotional. Had she not expected me to put in any effort? Her next words gave me my answer.

"I know we made the bet, but you also told me how you've never been much of a holiday person, that it's not really your thing."

"But it is your thing."

"All this...was for me?"

"Not exactly. I don't think I ever consciously said to myself, 'I'm going to take the holidays seriously this year because they're important to Marley.' It's more like this is the first time I've felt inspired by the season. I like being with you and being part of this school."

As the words tumbled out, almost without thought, I felt their strength. Every step I made towards solidifying this life—being with Marley, being a member of this community—felt right. And the safer I felt, the closer I was to being able to reconcile my past.

The bell rang and students dispersed into their third period classes. Marley grabbed my hand behind our backs, mindful not to attract their attention as she leaned into me. "I like being with you too, James, and that you made this door—" She stopped, running her pinkie along the outside of mine.

I tried not to dwell on how large and cumbersome I felt. The metallic candy canes of her sweater caught the twinkling lights on my door, and I saw the glow reflected in her brown eyes. This woman might be the one to truly accept me. The thought arrived unbidden. I could show her all the parts that hadn't been good enough for others, but for her, they could be okay.

As I walked back to my classroom, feeling lighter, one of the other teachers caught my attention.

Mr. Bloxham—Travis—was the third-youngest teacher in the school. Even though he only had five years on me, our lives were very different. At thirty-three, he already had four kids and had been married a dozen years. We'd gone out for beers a few times, and he was the closest thing I had to a friend in Coleman Creek other than Marley.

"Drinks tonight?" he asked quietly, avoiding the ears of his geometry students.

It occurred to me he and I hadn't hung out since before Thanksgiving. And we'd always had a good time, usually watching the Seahawks or Kraken games. I could see us becoming even better friends, assuming I stayed in town.

"Yeah, that'd be great. Meet at The Landslide around five?"

"Can we do five-thirty? I need to grab my youngest from gymnastics."

"Sure thing."

TRAVIS RUSHED INTO the bar twenty minutes late. He apologized as he sat down across from me in a small booth.

"Sorry, we got derailed. Rylee couldn't find her water bottle and it took us twenty minutes of looking behind every mat and trampoline in the place before we realized she'd never brought it in. It was in my back seat the whole time."

I grinned.

"Don't mock my pain, dude."

"I would never." I bit my lip.

"It's exciting to have a night away." Travis unwound his scarf and caught the eye of a server. "My wife has been trying to get me to go out more, to have a life." He laughed.

"It's nice she cares about that."

I thought about Cindy, how she'd complained every time I'd tried to do something without her, accusing me of being an inattentive husband. Although there were other times she'd called me a "loser" because we didn't have any exciting plans, as though it annoyed her we weren't part of some elite Seattle society. Being married to her had always felt like playing a game I didn't know the rules to, one I couldn't win.

"Yeah, Vivienne's the best. That's why I locked that shit down after graduation." Travis laughed again, and I recalled that he and his wife had gotten married right out of college and proceeded to have four babies in a row.

"Well, I'm glad you could make it, that you asked me to go out," I said.

"For sure." He looked over at the TV. "Who's playing?"

"Green Bay and Minnesota."

We stared at the screen for a while. He ordered a beer and wings for us to share. Travis was thicker around the middle, like I was. Maybe it made me a jerk, but I felt less self-conscious around him than with trim and fit people like Coach Hurley.

The game was in the third quarter and we were on our second round when Travis asked, "So, are you and Marley dating?"

"What?" I stuttered out the word. I knew the other teachers had noticed our friendship, but I hadn't been prepared for him to ask me so bluntly.

"Sorry, man, I know it's not my business. And if you want to keep it to yourself, I totally understand." He looked me in the eye. "I mean, we're all rooting for you two, but she's been through a lot—"

"We're not together," I cut in. Technically, it was true. We might work our way there, but we certainly didn't need an audience, even if Travis and the rest of the teachers meant well.

"Oh. Hmm." He seemed confused.

"Hey, I get it. We've been spending a lot of time together. But I think she's just been taking pity on me since I'm the new guy."

Travis leaned back in his seat and tipped his bottle toward me. "Like I said, it's no one's business but yours. I guess with her taking care of her mom, plus everything that went down with Kasen, we're all just hoping she gets a little happiness."

Kasen? I nodded casually, like I knew what he was talking about, and my mind immediately went to the first day of going through Marley's Christmas boxes. Specifically, the photo albums. There had been multiple pictures that included a leanly muscled dark-haired guy with a crooked smile. He'd appeared alongside high school and college-era Marley, usually with an arm draped over her shoulders. Some pictures were of him hugging Marley's sisters or mother. When I'd asked Marley who he was, she'd said, "Kasen," with no inflection in her voice, and I hadn't pushed for more.

I mentally tucked away Travis's mention of him. Since I hadn't exactly been forthcoming with Marley about my own skeletons, I didn't have the right to ask about hers.

"If you and Marley are just friends, have you thought about dating anyone else in town? I could introduce you to some of Vivienne's friends?"

Travis's question knocked me from my reverie, and I realized how little of myself I'd offered anyone but Marley. "Oh, um, I'm actually coming off a divorce. Finalized about a year ago. I'm not a hook-up guy and not really ready to try anything serious again."

"Aww, man, that sucks."

"It's okay. To be honest, the thought of getting back out there makes me want to crawl into a coffin and bury myself." Internally, I acknowledged that this was true for the thought of dating anyone but Marley, but I didn't need to let Travis in on that qualifier. "Teaching at Coleman Creek is awesome. I have a great dog. And I'm making friends." I tipped my drink at him. "It would be nice to be with someone eventually, but I'm good for now."

"Well, we enjoy having you," Travis said genuinely, turning back to grumble at the TV showing the lowlights from the Seahawks' loss on Sunday. "Plus, I'm looking forward to seeing you perform in the talent show." I barked a laugh as he gripped a spoon like a microphone, miming hitting the high notes.

The pieces were coming together for me in Coleman Creek. Friends to have a beer with. Students to tease. People at the park who knew Bambi's name. Bartenders at The Landslide who brought me a Heineken without me having to ask. And, of course, Marley.

This felt like the first "real" life I'd ever had. I needed those budget cuts not to materialize.

I needed to stay.

Chapter Nine

Marley

The second Saturday of December I pulled my first shift at the Christmas tree lot. Snow had yet to fall this season, the afternoon chilly but clear. Rumors about the budget had spread among not just the staff, but also the student body, although no one knew the specifics.

The PTSA had gone all out to ensure we earned as much as possible. Besides trees, wreaths, and fresh garland, there were also Christmas cookies, hot chocolate, and cider available to purchase. Families donated the food items, and one well-connected parent had sourced all the greenery from a local farm at cost. If things sold at a steady clip, profits would be excellent. And even though I knew we couldn't fund a faculty position with PTSA funds, I couldn't help but feel the karmic universe would reward our efforts somehow.

I knew this shift would be slow. Most people were like me—they didn't want to buy too early and risk having a dead tree on Christmas morning. Brown needles not only looked terrible, they had the potential to keep the fire department extremely busy.

Still, a few optimistic souls always bought this weekend. The people who claimed to have an old family trick or voodoo magic to keep cut trees alive. *Misting salt water over the branches? Sure, why not? Sprite in the tree stand? Makes perfect sense to me. Christmas is the time of miracles, after all.*

The students had done their part, decorating the corner of the parking lot we used as a sales floor. Strings of colored lights crisscrossed over the space. Red and green ribbons braided into the temporary chain-link fence swayed in the crisp air.

Wooden boards covered in different wrapping papers made a festive backdrop against the side of the school. Students had designated this area as the "selfie station," encouraging families and their peers to use the #colemancreekholiday hashtag when posting the pics on social media. I appreciated this attempt to draw some customers to the lot who wouldn't otherwise have a reason to go. The idea of a designated place to take an *official* Coleman Creek holiday photo. There was even a little prop table. If folks who normally avoided the lot because they put up artificial trees came to take a photo, they might decide to buy a wreath or a cookie. It couldn't hurt to try.

As I pulled into the parking lot, my phone vibrated.

KASEN: Have you given any more thought to drinks? I'd love to see you before you go out of town next weekend. No pressure though *smiley face emoji*

I stared at the text. It had been almost two weeks since I'd unblocked Kasen's number, telling him we didn't need to be strangers anymore. We'd traded dozens of messages over the past twelve days, clumsy at first, but soon becoming a friendly exchange of information.

He still lived in the Portland apartment we'd shared five years ago. He'd been working remotely for a few years and was considering moving, since he could do his graphic design job from anywhere. I told him about teaching and Oscar. And that I had plans to go to Seattle with a friend next weekend—although I hadn't given him any details about James.

Texting with Kasen re-affirmed my belief that I'd moved on from our relationship. I'd been hurt, sure, but I hadn't been pining this whole time. However, communicating after so many years had caused some of that hurt to bubble back up to the surface, more strongly than I'd expected. Everything from his word choices to his dry humor offered the warm hint of nostalgia. It reminded me how good we'd been together, what we'd lost when he'd chosen city life over me. I didn't desire him now, but it still smarted that he hadn't wanted me then.

Kasen had asked to meet in person. "Just to catch up." I hadn't answered him yet.

Would seeing him be upsetting? Texting was a lot different than sitting across the table from someone.

And then there was James to consider.

Even though we weren't officially more than friends, I felt like I needed to at least broach the subject with him first. Not just hit him with "hey guess what—I had drinks with my ex" after the fact.

I'd been reluctant to bring up the subject of Kasen because things between James and I had been so easy since the door decorating contest.

Good-natured about coming in second place, James had refused to even hint at what he planned to do for the talent show. I'd made dinner for him twice this week. The first night, he'd told me more about his childhood in Seattle and his college days in Oregon. The second, he'd spoken briefly about his marriage. I now knew he'd been married for three years to a woman named Cindy. They'd adopted Bambi together and been generally unhappy the whole time.

"She wasn't who I thought she was, and in the end, she didn't know me either, other than she knew I disappointed her," he'd said.

I struggled to imagine anyone being disappointed in James, but my experience had taught me that trying to dissect a relationship you're not part of is pointless.

ME: How about a tentative yes to meeting up in person? I need to check on a few things.
KASEN: I'll take it. Tentative is better than a flat-out no. *fingers crossed emoji*
ME: I'll let you know by Tuesday.
KASEN: Sounds good. I hope I see you soon.
ME: *thumbs up emoji*

The thumbs up was a little weird, but it didn't feel right to reply, "you too," or anything similar. I hadn't missed Kasen. Not in any meaningful way. I'd only forgotten the magnitude of the pain I'd experienced coming back to Coleman Creek alone. Maybe seeing him in person would help me leave that last vestige of hurt in the past where it belonged. Maybe we could be friends. Or at least be something new.

But at the moment, figuring out my friendship with Kasen seemed much less important than figuring out my *friendship* with James.

Resolving not to think on it too heavily tonight, I focused instead on my volunteer duties.

I spent the first half hour helping unload the truck from the farm. After that assignment turned my arms to spaghetti, the project coordinator showed mercy and relegated me to tasks requiring less lifting.

James arrived to find me wrestling with tree netting as I attempted to arrange some garland for sale. My coat and sweater lay in a heap on the ground, casualties of my exertions. Even in nothing but my thermal in the forty-five-degree air, sweat still pooled between my shoulder blades.

"Need a hand?"

"I could be an octopus and I'd still need a hand." I blew air upwards to remove the hair plastered to my forehead and finally located the scissors I'd stuck in my back pocket. "This netting is now officially at the top of my inanimate objects enemies list." I began hacking away at the strings.

"An 'inanimate objects enemies list?' That's something I'd like to see."

"It's a short list. Uncooperative tree netting. Grocery store displays blocking the middle of the aisles. The seventy-five percent of buttons on my TV remote I have no idea what to do with."

"That's it?"

"I'm easy, James."

He laughed, helping to disentangle me before asking, "What can I do?"

After brushing myself free of stray needles and putting my unsalvageable hair under a beanie, I forced him to take a #colemancreekholiday selfie with me before putting him to work.

"Can you go check on the kids? They're over in the student parking area making signs. I'll join you in a few minutes after I get this all sorted."

"No problem."

Once I'd freed all the garland and displayed it in a reasonably attractive manner, I crossed the lot and observed James huddled with several teens near the sidewalk. I couldn't hear their conversation, but judging by his stormy expression and forceful gesturing, it didn't bode well.

Nan Tourman, president of the senior class, saw me and jogged over, waving and smiling. "Hi, Ms. Davis! Me and Penny finished the signs. We're trying to convince people they need more than one tree."

She held up two well-designed green poster boards with neat red lettering. One had a huge tree painted on it with the words, *"Like Our Trees? Why Not Buy Two?"* Another had a cartoon Santa with a caption bubble coming out of his mouth that said, *"Santa says...You need a tree for upstairs and a tree for downstairs."*

"Great work," I complimented her. "But what's going on over there?" I pointed to James and the other students.

"Oh, that." She frowned. "Fel Torres was just being an ass—I mean, a butthole to Daniel. I don't think he noticed Mr. Wymack coming up behind them."

Daniel Halls, a sophomore, had tagged along for his mother's volunteer shift and had been put to work with the rest of the students.

"What did Fel say?"

Nan bit her lip before speaking soft and fast. "He called Daniel a loser who didn't have any friends. And he said that just because Daniel was here didn't mean he could, like, talk to Fel and the other guys."

"Mr. Wymack heard him say that?"

"Yeah. But he was cool about it. Daniel would be way more embarrassed if he knew a teacher had heard. Mr. Wymack pretended he'd just walked up. Daniel still seemed pretty upset, though, so Mr. Wymack gave him his keys and asked him to go to his classroom to get some spare scissors."

I knew we didn't need more scissors. School rules also prohibited us from giving students our keys. But I couldn't fault James. He'd given Daniel a means to escape the situation without making him feel even more exposed.

"Thanks for telling me, Nan." She looked pained, so I asked, "Are *you* okay?"

"Yeah. I just...I heard what Fel was saying. So did Penny. From where we were working. I wish I would have said something. I don't know why I didn't just ask Daniel to come help us. We wouldn't have minded having him. Fel's such a jerk."

"You're a good person to feel that way, Nan," I reassured her, putting on my teacher hat. "It's a hard lesson to learn. But maybe think about how you feel right now and remember for next time."

"Definitely. And I'm going to hang with Daniel for the rest of the shift. After he comes back."

"Great idea. Will you go check up on him if he's not back within, say, ten minutes? That'd probably be easier for him than if Mr. Wymack or I did it."

She nodded and ran off to deliver the finished posters to the display lot. I walked over to where James stood, nostrils flaring, speaking vehemently to Fel while his friends stood off to the side.

"Are you seriously trying to justify bullying Daniel?" James asked.

"I wasn't bullying him!" Fel insisted. "I just told him I didn't want him to hang out with us. He kept trying to be next to us, listening to our conversations. It was annoying. I'm not under any obligation to be friends with everyone in school just because I'm on the student council."

James pinched the bridge of his nose. "Obviously, you don't have to be friends with everyone. But you know Daniel is shy. It wouldn't have hurt you to just let him stand next to you."

"We were talking about things that are none of his business. Football team stuff. Who we're going to ask to the dance. It doesn't make me a bully because I don't want Daniel to hear about that," Fel whined.

"First, you called him a 'loser.' That's beyond just asking him not to stand next to you. Second, exclusion *is* bullying. It's not just giving people swirlies and throwing them into lockers."

Fel rolled his eyes. "Mr. Wymack, am I in trouble? Are you gonna give me detention because Daniel got his feelings hurt?"

James executed a superhuman ability to remain calm as he replied, "No, Fel. Not because you don't deserve it, but because that would probably make this whole situation worse for Daniel."

"Cool." Fel started to back away.

"Fel?"

"Yeah?"

"It ends here. I don't want to find out that this situation escalated. I don't want you talking about Daniel to anyone, putting anything online, or doing anything to make him feel worse than he already does. Clear?"

"Sure, Mr. Wymack." Fel put his fists in his pockets and went back to his buddies. Their mouths moved and their arms gestured animatedly in our direction. Fel looked back to see James's narrowed gaze on him before he shrugged his shoulders at his friends and re-directed their attention to the poster boards.

I brushed James's shoulder. "Good work."

His eyes shone as he whispered, "Fel is such a little dick."

We both liked Daniel and had spoken many times about the introverted student who dealt with clinical anxiety. A late bloomer, Daniel looked like he could still be eleven years old. He ate lunch alone every day in the hallway alcove. His loneliness was palpable, painful for the faculty to watch, knowing there was little we could do.

Still, the intensity of James's tone took me aback. His arms clenched and his neck muscles flexed. He gazed at Fel with an expression bordering on contempt.

Something clarified in my mind. Since he'd come to Coleman Creek High, James had attempted to engage students who existed on the outskirts of the school's social order. Student interest clubs needed volunteer faculty advisors to be sanctioned and receive school resources. James had agreed to advise both the Dungeons & Dragons group and the Esports team, helping create social spaces on campus for pockets of students who'd previously had none. In the hallways, I'd seen him make a concerted effort to connect with the quiet kids and the loner kids and the kids who consistently got in trouble.

I pulled us to the shadows where the students couldn't see, with me facing his back. Looping my arms around his belly, I squeezed into the softness there as I rested my head between his shoulder blades.

"What happened to you, James?"

He stayed quiet at first, placing his hand over mine and leaning his tall frame back into my embrace. He tensed when Daniel exited the school, relaxing once Nan guided the shocked sophomore over to where she and Penny were working.

"I got through it."

Chapter Ten

James

I needed to talk to Marley. My reunion was next week, and after seeing how I'd reacted to Fel and Daniel, I knew she had questions that couldn't wait any longer.

Part of me worried she wouldn't understand, even if I explained.

From everything she'd told me, she'd had a decent high school experience. That's why I wondered whether she realized what we'd witnessed with Daniel might have long-term implications for him.

Those of us who'd spent our teenage years barely putting one foot in front of the other knew. That shit stung. Maybe forever.

I hadn't said much during the rest of our shift at the tree lot, but I'd asked to come over and make dinner for us at her place the next night. So we could talk. Bambi and I lived in a run-down one-bedroom—pickings for rentals were slim in Coleman Creek—and we usually ended up at Marley's. I'd gotten used to cooking in her kitchen.

At Walmart, I considered something fancier, but ultimately decided on the tried and true. I grabbed a pack of the black bean burgers Marley liked, ingredients to make a salad, and a bag of frozen waffle fries. At the holiday display near the register, I picked up new chew bones for the dogs, vaguely labeled "Christmas Flavored."

Marley zeroed in on the dog treats as soon as me and Bambi came through the door.

"What do you think that means?" she scrunched her forehead at the label. "Eggnog? Cinnamon? Or just, like, noble fir bark?"

"Call me unimaginative, but I was thinking turkey dinner. Then again, what dog would turn down a tasty eggnog bone?"

Bambi and Oscar seemed unconcerned with the flavor profile as we handed over their prizes, immediately skulking off to the corner as though we might snatch the treats back.

Marley and I shuffled into her kitchen. The fries would take the longest. I popped them onto a cookie sheet and put the pan in the oven as she watched. While I worked, her phone buzzed a few times with incoming texts. She made a quick reply and stuck it back in her pocket.

After getting a skillet out to fry the burgers, I decided to just rip the Band-Aid off. "Marley, can we talk about what happened at the tree lot?"

She hoisted herself up on the counter next to me. "Okay."

"I know you've figured out there's something personal behind how I reacted. What Fel said to Daniel bothered me more than it probably should have."

Her eyes softened. "You're right. I've put those pieces together. But you don't need to tell me things if it makes you uncomfortable. If you're not ready."

"I appreciate that. But I want you to understand why I am the way I am with our students. Since we're going to my reunion, I think it's important you at least have the basics of what it was like for me back then."

"Alright."

She regarded me so intently, I almost changed my mind. Figuring it might be easier if I kept my hands busy and my eyes down, I pulled out the salad vegetables. Marley reached behind herself on the counter to retrieve a wooden cutting board for me.

"Obviously, it's not just losing touch with classmates," I said, before taking a deep breath. "I had a...difficult...experience in high school. There were a few friendly faces, but mostly it was a daily marathon of me keeping my head down, trying not to get called names." I took a red bell pepper and gave it a quick rinse in the sink, speaking quickly as I chopped it up. "I was a scholarship kid at a private school, and all the other students had a lot more money than me. My parents bought their house back in the day, before real estate went nuts, so I lived in the same neighborhood as my classmates, but that was about all we had in common.

"All their parents worked in tech or finance or the corporate world. My dad fixed HVAC systems in office buildings. So, not only did everyone make fun of me for being a chubby nerd who was no good at sports, they laughed at my Target brand clothes and old shoes. Not to mention I had a case of acne so explosive I forgot what my face looked like without it." I attempted a humorless smile, but Marley remained stock still on her perch.

"The other kids made it clear at every turn I wasn't like them. Not just name-calling. Although there was that. They also excluded me. They'd make a point of letting me know I wasn't invited to parties, that I couldn't be in their clubs. Whenever I got assigned to a group project, they'd meet without me and not let me know. I felt like a disease. Even with my friends—other misfits who just needed someone to walk next to them—I stuck out. Because at least the other weirdos' families had money."

"James—" Marley covered her mouth with her palm.

"It went on for years, Marley. Coming home and putting on a face so my parents and brother wouldn't be worried or look at me with pity. Feeling like every day I was living in my own personal hell. The last two years were the worst. All the things I missed out on. Everything I was too scared to do. School clubs. Homecoming. Prom. I almost skipped graduation because I was afraid someone might shout out something horrible in front of my parents." I exhaled heavily. "Senior year, I thought about ending it every day. Every. Day."

I really hoped Marley didn't need more specific examples to comprehend the depth of what I'd endured. As I recited my story, I felt all the bitterness I'd shoved down for so long resurfacing.

What happened to your face, James? It looks like a connect-the-dots worksheet. Great, James is on our team. I guess that means an automatic loss with fatty bringing up the rear. Ewww. I heard Chubby James sits next to Layla in biology. We feel so bad for her.

"I'm sorry I didn't tell you sooner, Marley. You deserved the heads up in case the reunion is...bad. I guess I was embarrassed. I know you think of me as this laid-back guy, possibly even cool, but..." I trailed off, moving on from the bell pepper to shredding a carrot.

"Oh my God, James." She jumped down from the counter and came up behind me like she'd done at the tree lot. "Can I?" she asked tentatively, raising her arms. I nodded. The air whooshed out of my lungs as she grabbed me so tightly around the middle I stumbled into the counter. I felt the wetness of her tears against my back. "I'm so sorry that happened to you. You have nothing to be embarrassed about. Nothing."

I reached up to put my hand over hers. "Marley—"

"Not to be harsh, but your former classmates were clearly trash. They sound like absolute, certifiable garbage people. I hope they all grew up to be adults who get regular kidney stones. Or at least paper cuts and hangnails and incurable bad breath." She squeezed me again, this time nuzzling her cheek against my back. "And you are still the coolest guy I know. Always." She placed a closed mouth kiss right between my shoulder blades. "Their vileness says nothing about you and everything about them. Like I said, garbage people."

I'd never heard her speak so strongly before, even if—true to form—she kept her language PG. It released some of the tension in the room and, shockingly, I chuckled. "I think I like vicious attack dog, Marley. She's pretty hot."

"I am so, so sorry I pushed you into going to your reunion. It never even crossed my mind that high school would have been that rough for you."

"I got good at hiding, Marley," I said. "Pretending. Not saying much. If I were to shave this beard, you'd see some pretty gnarly acne scars. And, of course, that chubby kid never entirely went away. He just got taller." I patted my belly above my belt. "In my mind, that's who I am. On some level, it's who I'll always be."

"Let's not argue about how wonderful you are, James. It's already decided. You're a top-notch, grade A man. And we don't need to go to the reunion. You owe those people nothing. Less than nothing."

"No, you were right to give me the nudge. I need to know that I can be in a room with them and hold my head high." I released a small laugh. "Grade A, huh?"

"A-plus."

I felt calmer, Marley's reaction fortifying my resolve. While I hadn't honestly thought she would reject me outright, I'd wondered if knowing what a heinous loser I'd been in high school would affect how she saw me. I mean, it still affected how I saw myself.

"Marley, it's important you understand that I'm okay. I told you Saturday, I got through it. And I really found myself after high school. I went away to college, near enough to keep close with my family, but far enough for it to feel like a fresh start. I was wary there at first, but eventually I found my tribe. Made friends, had fun, discovered myself. My acne cleared up, and I realized I was destined to be a long-hair guy."

She finally released my waist, and I missed the soothing contact immediately. But then I felt her warm fingers against my hip, urging me to turn around.

I peered down at her beautiful face. "I'm so glad things got better for you," Marley said, moving to hug me from the front. "You're one of the best people I know, and you didn't deserve that."

I wrapped my arms around her tightly. It felt amazing. "Thank you."

"You have nothing to prove to those dummies. If they were so ignorant back then that they couldn't see how great you are, they're obviously idiots. I'd like to think that people can change. That those teenagers who were horrible to you feel some remorse and are now old enough to know how wrong they were. But if we go to that reunion and they are anything less than completely welcoming to you, we're outta there." I felt her speaking into my chest as she followed up with. "Right after I give them a piece of my mind, and maybe poison the punch bowl."

I laughed and released her, both of us turning back to the counter.

We prepared the rest of our dinner in silence, and I reveled in the sensation of relief. I'd finally opened a window to my past for Marley. She still didn't know about Cindy, or Oliver and the business, but it was a start. Plenty for one night.

Her phone buzzed a few more times while we worked, and she sighed as she contemplated the device. After a third text came through, she asked, "Can I talk to you about something over dinner?"

"Of course. Everything okay?"

"Yeah. It's no big deal. Let's get all this stuff on the table first. I'm starving."

We sat down at the corner of her large dining set. Bambi and Oscar stayed conked out in the living room, satisfied by the eggnog bones.

"Do you remember I pointed out a person named Kasen in the Christmas albums?" Marley asked.

"Uh huh." I tensed as my conversation with Travis came back to me.

"Well, Kasen and I have known each other our whole lives. Dated for a long time. Part of high school, throughout college. We lived together for a while after that."

Hmm. While I'd assumed he was Marley's ex, I hadn't realized they'd had such a lengthy relationship. "So you guys were together for..."

"Eight years," she stated flatly.

I slouched in my chair. "That's a long time. Do you mind if I ask why you split up?"

"No. It's actually not that complicated. We hit an impasse. When my mom got sick, I knew I needed to move home, that I wanted to be the one to care for her. He refused to return with me. I'd hated living in Portland anyway. I'd never really settled in. But Kasen was different. He'd made friends and had a good job, a gym membership, a favorite taco truck. When it came down to it, he liked living in a big city more than he liked being with me." She shrugged her shoulders.

Her words may have signaled acceptance, but I sensed the hurt behind the casual movement. "That sounds rough."

"It's okay. He's allowed to make that choice. Just like I made mine to stay here and take care of my mom."

Her features remained placid. Not the expression of someone feeling conflicted about the past or needing to make a confession.

Somewhat confused, I asked, "Why are you telling me this now?" I hoped Marley didn't want to go into detail about our love lives. After giving her the story of my high school days, I doubted I had it in me to talk about Cindy.

"Because he's been texting me. Since Thanksgiving. I'd blocked his number after we split up, but he's always wanted to be friends. I'm in a different place now, so I'm willing to consider it." She squirmed in her seat a little. "He's back in town for the holidays. He wants to meet up in person."

"And you haven't seen him in five years?"

"No. And I'm still not sure I want to."

I huffed. "You sound like me with my reunion."

She gave me a half smile. "Sort of. Except Kasen isn't a dragon I need to slay. He's more like another door I thought I'd shut for good. And some doors *should* stay shut. I just don't know if this one should." She exhaled. "The only thing I'm sure of is that it didn't feel right to even consider opening it again without letting you know. Because things between us are so...in flux. I don't want to add in any complications."

I considered her words. "Marley, if you want to hang out with Kasen and see if there's a chance to be friends, or even just to figure out where he fits in your life, it's fine with me. I get it."

"Really?"

"Of course. You were with this guy for eight years." I forced myself to tamp down the stab of jealousy I had no right to feel. This wasn't like with Cindy. My ex had cheated on me and gleefully told me all about it, twisting the knife when she finally left. Marley's breakup didn't sound vindictive. Merely sad. "If you've known Kasen most of your life, it makes sense there might still be a place for him in it."

"I'm not sold on being friends. But I think maybe listening to him is the right move. To try and be in the same room again. It's a small town." She nodded, as though convincing herself. "I just want to be totally transparent with you. Figuring out what you and I can be together is my main concern right now. Not Kasen."

I smiled, fascinated as always by her directness. "Okay."

We stuck to benign topics for the rest of the meal. Marley hadn't said so, but I suspected Kasen's choice of big city life over their relationship weighed on her—the fact that she hadn't been his priority. I wanted to show her just how important she was to me.

But we had to get through my reunion first.

Chapter Eleven

Marley

I spent the days before James's reunion growing even more indignant on his behalf. He'd carried so much pain with him into adulthood.

I taught high school, so I knew better than most how cruel teenagers could be. Dealing with bullying within the school walls continued to be one of the hardest parts of teaching. Teachers could provide guidance, put a stop to behaviors we witnessed, and reinforce the kinder instincts of students like Nan—who'd been looking out for Daniel since the tree lot incident. Yet there would always be kids like Fel, who validated their own self-worth by making other kids feel like poop.

But watching it happen to teenagers, versus being confronted with its long-term effects on a twenty-eight-year-old man, were two entirely different things.

James and I had both gotten subs for Friday and planned to leave early that morning so we could make it to Seattle before dark. We'd be staying with his parents. I'd offered to get a hotel room, but he'd insisted.

"It's not just to save money," he'd said. "I need you with me for moral support."

That made sense. If the reunion went poorly, he wouldn't want to spend the night alone, trying to save face in front of his parents. From what he'd told me, he hadn't exactly been forthcoming with them about all he'd endured back then.

Before we left, I met up with Kasen. I didn't want to have that looming in the background when I'd need to be fully present for James.

On Thursday, I arrived at The Landslide to find Kasen waiting in a two-person booth.

Katy looked up from taking an order on the other side of the room to raise an eyebrow at me. Like most of the town, she knew our history. She'd been the sophomore princess the year Kasen and I were on the senior prom court. I widened my eyes back at her and shook my head slightly, hoping she got the message to not read too much into the situation.

I walked over to Kasen, and he angled in like he might hug me, so I stuck out an arm to initiate a handshake. The air was uneasy at first, but as I slid into the booth and he smiled across the table from me, the familiarity of everything about him helped to fill in the awkward spaces.

He had on a blue plaid flannel and a pair of well-fitting dark Levi's. His brown hair was different. Shorter on the sides and longer on top. Sophomore year of college, I'd dyed those curls green for St. Patrick's Day. His lean physique carried more muscle than before, and I recalled a recent text exchange where he mentioned getting into strength training after hurting his knee playing basketball.

"Marley. Thank you for coming. I know this is weird, with everything that happened. But it's so good to see you." He smiled, noting my outfit. "I've missed your mom's Christmas sweaters these past few years."

I glanced down at my navy-blue cardigan with little snowmen doing breakdancing moves and grinned. "This was one of her favorites."

"I remember. And I intentionally waited until we were in person to say this to you, but I want you to know how very sorry I am for your loss. I know how close you and Alice were. She was a great lady."

There was nothing but sincerity in his voice. "Thank you."

"I stayed away from the funeral like you asked me to, but I have to be honest—it was hard. I thought about you all the time after she passed."

"Your parents told you?"

"Yeah. They showed me your letter."

When it had become evident last September that my mom's time was near, I had given his parents a letter for Kasen, letting him know I'd prefer it if he continued to stay away from me. That he not attend the service. At that point, we'd been apart for almost four years, and I'd told myself I didn't need to add seeing him to an already stressful time. I'd figured he'd be wondering, and I'd wanted to make my wishes clear. He'd respected my request, but his parents had come to the funeral—along with most of Coleman Creek—and they'd passed on his condolences. That letter had been the sum of my direct interaction with Kasen since we'd broken up. But looking back on it now, I wasn't sure I could justify the excuse for sending it. I'd been well over our breakup by that point. Why had I felt it necessary to order him to avoid the funeral?

"I appreciate you doing what I asked," I said, still questioning my motivations internally. "I'm sure it wasn't easy."

"It wasn't. I felt like a real dick, honestly, after we'd been together so long. And I know it's nothing compared to what you endured, but I hope you realize how much I loved Alice."

His point was well made. Kasen and my mom had had a great relationship. "Sorry."

"It's okay. I made my decision when I stayed in Portland. I know that."

Katy came by, and wc placed an order for beers and burgers.

"It's nice coming here," Kasen said. "Hasn't changed a bit."

Strange. Kasen had been so adamant that he didn't want to live in Coleman Creek because it was "boring" and "nothing ever happened." Now, he sat across from me, apparently nostalgic about a place that epitomized the town's slow pace and everybody-knows-everybody aesthetic.

"How long are you in town for? You're staying through Christmas, right?"

"It's open-ended. I can work remotely with my job, so I'm lucky there."

"Yeah, it was a surprise when you texted that you're doing that now. I'm shocked Myerson lets you work at home." When we'd lived in Portland, Kasen had worked as an artist for a demanding graphic design firm that provided lots of opportunities for advancement but almost none for work-life balance.

"Um, I actually left Myerson a while back. Couldn't keep doing the hours. I've been working for myself about three years now."

"Oh." This news drove home the point. I didn't know Kasen anymore. "Well, congratulations on that."

"Thanks."

"I guess five years is a long time?"

"Honestly, Marley, five years is a lifetime. And a lot can happen in a lifetime. That's kind of why I wanted to meet up." He scraped a hand through his hair. "I don't want to dump things on you when we've only just started talking again. But you need to know that I've changed my mind about a lot of stuff. Realized things I'd like to tell you. If you'll let me."

Eyeing his face, I dragged my gaze along the three freckles on his left cheek—the place I'd laid my first tentative kisses at age fifteen. I'd been wrong a moment ago. I did know Kasen. Not talking didn't erase the knowing, the history. The eyes that had watched me drive away from Portland had been unsure. The ones looking at me now shone with regret.

But did he want to apologize? Or did he want to take back his decision?

There was no way.

"Kase—"

"Let's not get into specifics right now, if that's okay. I was just hoping to have a nice meal and learn about what you've been up to. I'm...grateful to be here with you."

An immediate response eluded me. Time passed, and things changed. Wounds healed. But I liked his idea. Having a meal with Kasen—catching up—and maybe working our way to being friends. I realized I didn't want to forget about him entirely.

The night stretched into dessert and a second round. Then a third. He laughed when I talked to him about work, and especially about the teachers who were still around from our own school days—now my colleagues. Kasen almost spit out his beer when I told him how I sometimes moved old Mr. Bailey's lunch bag from one shelf in the staff fridge to another, just to mess with him. Eventually, we progressed to reminiscing about my mom. Kasen relayed how she'd helped him pick out the corsage he'd given me for our junior formal. For the second time that night, I had misgivings about asking him to stay away from the funeral.

We stayed until almost midnight, and he gave me a quick hug in the parking lot after walking me to my car.

"I know you're away for the weekend, but maybe we can meet up again sometime?" he asked.

"Maybe. Let's play it by ear." I didn't want to make any commitments without knowing how this weekend would go for James. "But you can text me."

"I'll do that. I had a great night."

"Yeah. It was nice catching up." He opened the driver's side door for me, and I slid onto the pleather seat. In the rearview, I noticed him still standing there, watching intently as I drove away.

ON FRIDAY MORNING, we dropped the dogs off with Travis and Vivienne for the weekend before heading to Seattle and the reunion. James played deejay the whole way. He loved early 2000s indie bands, and I enjoyed the musical education as we traveled west along I-90.

Nerves were coming off him in waves, but he did his best to maintain steady conversation, including filling me in about his family.

"My parents are great people and we're close. I'm sure they knew how things were for me in high school. Even though I tried to fool them and put on a brave face. Looking back as an adult, I can see that the situation was tough on all of us. They did their best to compensate by making our home life as good as they could. They didn't embarrass me with questions about why I had nothing to do on the weekends, or why I didn't bring friends over. I cooked food with my mom and fixed small machines with my dad. We always had in-progress games of Monopoly or Risk on the dining room table. My brother Leo is five years older, so he was away at college while I was at Seattle Elite. But he'd been the same as me—the scholarship kid at our school—so he understood some of what I was going through. Even though it wasn't as bad for him. Whenever he came home to visit, we always hung out together. He was probably my best friend."

My heart squeezed again for teenage James.

We arrived in Seattle before the sun set and pulled into the driveway of a cream-colored split-level home in the north end of the city. The small structure looked slightly out of place between the larger modern houses on either side of it.

James explained the incongruity. "Mom and Dad got the house in the eighties, before Leo was born. But most of the neighbors came in the past few decades. They bought up the little houses like ours and knocked them down to put up huge ones." He pointed toward a small walkway between his parents' lot and the one to the left of it. "It's hard to blame them for building up. Much better view."

I followed to where his finger pointed and saw we were on top of a hill, the steel blue water of Puget Sound visible in the distance.

We'd barely pulled our suitcases from the trunk when the door opened and a man who could only be James's father filled the entrance. His beard mirrored James's, except tinted gray. He was large in the middle and, well, everywhere. And maybe it was just the season, but his wide smile and kind eyes gave off distinct Santa Claus energy.

"Son!" he called, arms open. James only made it a few steps before being enveloped in a bear hug that made me wistful. I missed getting hugs from my mom.

Once James let go and took a step back, he turned to me. "Marley, this is my dad, Chris."

I extended my hand. "Nice to meet you."

He reached out to shake it. The warmth in his eyes put me immediately at ease. "Likewise. We are so happy James brought you home to us."

Interesting phrasing. I realized I hadn't asked James what he'd told his parents about me. Did they think I was his girlfriend?

In the kitchen, James introduced me to his mother, Deanna, a petite woman who paused in her task of assembling a casserole to greet me enthusiastically. James's face broke into a surprised grin when he noticed a large man with long blond hair and a beard sitting at the small breakfast table.

"Hey, I didn't know you'd be here," James said, as the man stood up and gave him a back-slapping hug.

"I wasn't going to miss this," the Viking replied, keeping an arm draped over James's shoulders. Looking at me, he grinned. "I'm Leo, James's brother."

"Marley."

"It's great to meet you finally." Leo had the same easy affability as his dad, his expression so genuine and approachable, it made me think of the dogs. "My brother has talked about you a lot these past few months."

I glanced at James. I knew he and his family held regular video calls, but I didn't know he'd mentioned me. He shrugged, cheeks reddening beneath his beard.

"All good, I hope?" I asked Leo.

Leo snort-huffed. "He's been singing your praises nonstop. So, obviously I had to come see for myself—"

"Leo." James's voice held a warning.

"Dude, I'm just saying. After everything you said about how much she's helped you in your new town, how you guys hang out a lot, and how awesome she is, of course I wanted to meet her."

"Stop. Talking." Embarrassment laced James's voice.

"It's okay," I said to James with half a smirk. Of course he'd said nice things about me to his family. I'd done the same speaking to Maureen and Miranda. "I would've been disappointed if you hadn't mentioned me." Turning to Leo, I stated gravely, "I shall endeavor to live up to the hype."

Leo barked a laugh, and James relaxed his shoulders. Deanna came over to lightly smack her older son on his shoulder. "Stop making your brother squirm, Leo. And leave Marley alone. She just met us." Leo raised his hands in surrender, while somehow still giving me a thumbs up.

James's mom put the casserole in the oven, and we sat at the table with mugs of coffee. I felt immediately at ease with the Wymacks. Their down-to-earth dynamic reminded me of the family I'd grown up in. Chris repaired HVAC systems for a living and enjoyed tinkering with old electronics in his spare time, pointing to a shelf in the living room filled with ancient radios, walkie-talkies, and some kind of tape recorder. Deanna worked as a librarian and told me her primary hobby was cooking. She had a goal of preparing at least one recipe from every cookbook in the library.

"I'll probably never get there," she said. "We just have too many and are adding more all the time. But it sure is fun to try."

For dinner, she'd made a delicious old-fashioned tater tot casserole, one of my own mother's specialties. As the five of us chatted over the meal, I learned Leo lived and worked as a contractor in Tacoma, which was either forty minutes or five hours away, depending on traffic. He loved giving his brother a hard time—in a playfully fond way, of course. He relayed stories about how toddler James insisted on wearing underwear on his head, and how Leo had once convinced third-grade James that their neighbor was an alien. It was uncanny how the brothers were the same, but different. Both thoughtful and kind, but where James was all soft smiles and laid-back contentment, Leo practically glowed with cheerfulness.

The conversation eventually turned to the reunion. Unsurprisingly, James's family seemed...concerned.

At one point, Leo spoke to me directly from his seat across the table. "When James told us a few weeks ago he'd decided to go to his reunion, to be honest, I didn't think it was the greatest idea. I don't know what he's said to you about Seattle Elite but—"

"Leo." James growled.

"Relax, man. I wasn't going to give away the game." Leo glared at his brother before continuing. "Anyhoo, this guy gets on our call a few weeks ago and he's all, 'My high school is having a reunion and I'm going. Marley's agreed to go with me, and I think it'll be okay.' Of course, Mom and Dad and I are like, 'sure, James, you do you.' But it was still a shock. Not his usual MO at all."

James narrowed his eyes. "What do you mean 'not my usual MO?'"

"No shade, bro. I just mean you're not usually one to tackle problems head-on. You're a lover, not a fighter, ya know? So I figured you'd skip the reunion. You facing those fuckers from high school? It's unexpected. But cool."

James scoffed, contemplating his brother's assessment. "You realize I'm not going to fight anyone, right?"

"You know what I mean."

Leo addressed me again. "You must have put some kind of spell on my brother. In a good way, I mean. That's why I wanted to meet you. Like I said, I don't know what he's told you, but hopefully, you know what you're getting into tomorrow night."

Chris and Deanna seemed content to let this conversation play out, watching the three of us from opposite ends of the table as we volleyed across the middle of it. And even though they'd been warm and welcoming toward me, their apprehension for James hung heavily in the air. I felt a keen desire to ease their minds. It was a little odd to be in this position, considering I'd only known James since August, but I had the impression they understood the strong connection I'd forged with their son.

"You don't need to say anything," James whispered to me.

"It's okay," I replied, then turned my eyes to Leo. "James *has* been honest with me about his experience in high school. At this point, I'm ready for anything tomorrow. I'm trying to be optimistic that we might even have a good time." I looked unflinchingly at James's brother. "But make no mistake. If anyone does anything that makes either of us uncomfortable, I'm not afraid to give someone a poinsettia to the face, if the situation warrants. Do not be fooled by the sweet little kittens on my sweater."

Leo looked like he might smile, but James's brow furrowed. "Marley, I don't need you to protect me. That's not what you coming here was about."

"I know that. Just like I didn't *need* you to help me unpack my mom's boxes. I could have done that myself. But having you next to me made it easier. Made it better." I reached out and grabbed James's hand, not caring about the three pairs of eyes on us. "I want to make your reunion a little easier and better for you. Not just out of kindness. But because I'm proud to stand next to you. *That's* why I'm here."

I followed up with a definitive nod, hoping James's family imbibed my sincerity. Deanna rested a cheek on her husband's arm as Chris and Leo both angled their chins in approval.

James laced our fingers together tightly as he leaned into my neck and said, "I'm so glad you're here."

"Me too."

Around eleven, after a marathon game of Settlers of Catan, Leo declared himself exhausted and headed out to his truck to drive home. James and I said goodnight and made our way to the converted basement, as James's old bedroom was now Deanna's home library. Once we were alone, I asked him the question that had been on my mind since we'd arrived.

"So, what exactly did you tell your parents about our relationship? Do they know we're in this undefined limbo-friend state?"

"I haven't really clarified, but I'm guessing by this room situation they think we're together. Sorry."

"It's fine." I looked down at the pull-out couch with its queen-sized mattress, the only bed in the room. "Don't even think about offering to sleep on the floor or something stupid like that. We're adults. I'm pretty sure we can manage it."

"Yeah. Okay." He ran a hand over his head, pulling off the beanie to reveal a looped ponytail underneath.

"It's wild that they never asked you point-blank if I was your girlfriend. On any of your calls."

"Honestly, they were probably afraid to ask. Worried that if they got too invasive, I'd get spooked and maybe not bring you. I haven't really dated since my divorce and they hated Cindy with a capital H. My love life, or lack thereof, has been an off-limits topic for a while."

"Ah. Well, I'm happy to play any part you want me to with your family," I said. "They clearly think we're a couple if they're sticking us on this ancient couch bed together. Nothing says sexy times like dusty cushions next to the forgotten board games shelf." I waggled my eyebrows at him.

He laughed and shook his head. "How about we don't offer any details? I doubt they'll ask."

There was a bathroom in the basement, so James and I could perform our nighttime routines without needing to go up and down the stairs. I watched him wash his face and rub in fancy beard oil. He saw me apply my night cream and remarked on how good it smelled.

After brushing my teeth, I came out of the bathroom to find him standing next to the pull-out. Seeing him in gray sweatpants and a white t-shirt, hair down and dusting his shoulders, caused a shiver of awareness to race through me. No matter our conviction to go slow for now, my reaction was a good reminder of my incredible attraction to this man. I balled my fists as a persistent desire to touch him threatened to override my best intentions. James was clearly in a similar state. While my Christmas thermals covered everything, they also provided a full outline of every curve and dip of my body. He raked his gaze over me, swallowing audibly before catching himself.

I launched myself underneath the covers.

"Do you need me to build a blanket wall down the middle of the bed?" he teased, breaking the tension.

I threw a pillow at his head. "We've had a long day, and I know you're nervous about tomorrow. Let's not add unnecessary worries about this bed situation to the mix." I pulled back the blanket and turned away from him. "Try to get some sleep if you can."

For a long moment, I waited to feel him slide onto the mattress, but the expected movement never came. I rolled over to peer up at him. "Everything okay?"

James released a heavy breath and glanced at the ceiling, shifting his weight from one foot to the other before looking down at me. "I hope you know this isn't a move or anything, but can I—" He paused, exhaling heavily. "Can I just...hold you?"

He was adorable. So much difficulty simply asking for what he needed. Especially when it was easy for me to give it to him.

"I'd like that."

Less than twenty-four hours later, it was time to leave for the reunion. James came out of the bathroom and my mouth literally dropped open.

The invitation said the event would be casual. He wore close-fitting dark jeans and a tailored gray-green button-down with the sleeves rolled up. His one nod to the holiday theme was a deep red bow tie with a silver snowflake pattern. Dark boots and a thick black belt completed the outfit.

His shiny hair was down, with a level of volume I could only accomplish with hot rollers, hairspray, and the exact right amount of humidity. He'd also taken the time to trim his facial hair. It was closer to his skin now, more like long stubble than an actual beard.

I shook my head at the way my blood heated, forcing my reaction to the back burner. In this moment, we needed to keep our minds on the big, scary thing he needed to do.

But it was difficult to stay focused when the memory of his erection poking against me this morning remained fresh in my mind. Not to mention it had been the best night of sleep I'd had in years, cocooned in his massive arms. Combine that with how gorgeous he was. I was only human.

His biceps flexed as he ran a hand along his jawline, the strong sinews of his forearms standing out like ropes. I'd felt those arms while they'd held me as a friend. What would they feel like if we were more?

"Did I do okay?" he asked, holding his arms out at his sides.

"Yeah, you look good."

Good. He was the sexiest thing I'd ever seen. Sleeping next to him last night had clearly flipped some sort of switch in me. And I couldn't seem to flip it back to *just friends* mode. Waking up with a man's morning wood stabbing you in the butt does that to a girl, I guess.

His whole look was a vibe. A hot, big, pick-you-up-and-throw-you-around-while-still-being-a-giant-teddy-bear vibe.

"You sure? I mean, I feel like this belt is kinda tight. Do you think it makes my stomach hang over my pants too much?"

Except that. Him feeling self-conscious. That was not a vibe. James's lack of confidence in his body wasn't something I could solve for him in ten minutes. But at least I could leave him with no doubts about where I stood on the matter. And maybe it would help him face his classmates.

"James, your pants are fantastic. Real talk, they make your butt look amazing. And that little extra padding you're so worried about—don't be. You look strong and capable and sexy. No one cares if you have a dad bod. You're very on-trend."

He scoffed but relaxed a little.

"Thanks for saying that. You look fantastic yourself. I don't think I've seen you in heels before."

I looked down at my feet, encased in three-inch black stilettos. "Fun fact about me—these are my only pair. So take a mental picture because you probably won't see them again." I slipped into what I felt was a very respectable Gollum impression when I continued, "Because we hates them."

He chuckled. "I'm honored."

Truth be told, I'd given it my best effort to look good for him. Even with my admittedly basic starting point, there was a range, and tonight I aimed to be at the top of it. I'd braided my hair and coiled it into an elaborate updo—something my mom had taught me—and shot it through with red and green ribbons. I thought I'd hit the right balance between milkmaid and sophistication. The style also showed off my long neck and the heart shape of my face, two features I liked.

I'd adhered to the holiday theme with a scooped-neck dark plaid dress that flared before ending just above the knees, leaving my arsenal of jingle bell necklaces and ugly Christmas sweaters at home. Tonight, understatement seemed called for. I wanted to play whatever part I could to help James shine at his reunion. Not be his kitschy, holiday-loving co-worker. Because that didn't always need to be me. Some nights I could be this—a high-heels and lipstick wearing sophisticate. At least, I thought I could. James made me want to step outside my box a little.

"Well, you look amazing," James said. "Even if your feet hurt."

We left for the venue, a ballroom at a downtown hotel. The invitation had advised coming anytime between six and eight p.m., and we'd erred on the later side. James told me he didn't want to be put in the awkward situation of standing around with only a few people. That he could potentially fade into a larger crowd provided some comfort.

His demeanor shifted as we drove to the hotel. He'd seemed okay-ish at the house, but the closer we got to actually seeing his classmates, the more withdrawn he became.

When we arrived, after turning off the engine and unbuckling his seatbelt, James didn't make a move to open the driver's side door. Finally, he said, "This is going to be hard. Doing this for real, not just imagining it." He turned toward me, and I could see the tendons standing out in his neck. "Have I told you how grateful I am that you came?"

I tilted my head to the side and smiled softly. "You have, but there's no way it's more grateful than I am to be here."

He reached over and cupped my cheek. "Thank you," he murmured.

We exited the car, our steps echoing across the cavernous hotel parking garage. After shaking some energy out of his hands, James rolled his shoulders and twisted his neck from side to side as we waited for the elevator.

Looping my arm around his elbow as we went up to the main building, I sent up a silent prayer that his old classmates had grown up, that we weren't walking into *James in High School, The Sequel*.

Chapter Twelve

James

Marley held my elbow as we stepped into the lobby. A gigantic sign reading *"This Way to High School Memories"* greeted us.

I couldn't think of a single memory I was interested in resurrecting.

My bravado deflated further as I stepped closer to the reunion entrance. I didn't feel like James, the student-favorite teacher with friends and a job he loved. In an instant, I felt like James, the guy who'd once had four cartons of chocolate pudding scraped into his backpack along with a note. *To James. Our favorite puddin' pie. Did you really think you'd make the team? Loser.* That had been ninth grade, after my one attempt to fit in by joining volleyball. I hadn't made the cut, and the girls watching tryouts had pointed and laughed at my belly where my shirt had ridden up.

Would my old classmates remember me? How they'd made fun of me? Or had it meant nothing to them, dropping casual pain like napalm?

A couple on their way into the reunion walked by. I recognized the woman as Nora Pensley, neither tormentor nor friend in high school. After a quizzical glance, she gave up trying to place me, pulling her companion toward the ballroom.

The relief I felt at her lack of recognition registered. If indifference felt like this, how would I react if faced with one of my former bullies?

Maybe this wasn't a good idea.

"You okay?"

Marley. I'd almost forgotten. My eyes had been so fixed on the entrance ahead. She squeezed my hand and broke the trance, forcing me to meet her gaze as she stepped directly in front of me.

"What do you need, James? A pep talk or permission to leave? Both are okay, and I can knock out a top-notch speech in favor of either right now." Her warm hands traveled up my forearms, stopping to rest gently on my elbows, and her cheeks lifted in a reassuring smile.

She looked lovely in her plaid dress and pretty hairstyle. I liked the heels, not because I cared about her shoes, but because the extra height brought her all the way to my chin, so I didn't feel like such a big oafish beast the way I usually did.

Her expression grounded me as she raised a palm to my shoulder. "Hey, you've got this."

Closing my eyes, I leaned into her touch. "I want to stay, to go in there," I said. "I just needed a minute."

"Take all the time you need." Her eyebrow raised. "We can even pop into the hotel bar if you'd rather pay twenty bucks for a drink instead of getting a free one in the ballroom."

I huffed. "Are you trying to convince me to walk into a potential minefield by pointing out the reunion has an open bar?"

"Is it working?"

I managed a grin for the first time that night. "I think so."

"Great. So, we'll go into the ballroom. We can do a lap, so everyone sees how awesome and brilliant and amazing you are. We'll stay just long enough to make sure they feel like total dumb-dumbs for ever being mean to you. Then we can grab our free drinks and leave."

"Sounds like a plan."

Marley would make this bearable for me. I could already tell. Another group walked by, and this time I got a solid wave from Will Yardley, one of my misfit-sorta-friends from high school. I smiled at him.

THERE WERE NAME BADGES lined up alphabetically on a table. I groaned when I noticed they had our yearbook pictures printed on them.

Our *freshman* yearbook pictures.

Good lord. Seventeen-year-old me would have been bad enough, but the picture of fourteen-year-old James presented a cautionary tale on all the things that could go horribly wrong during the early teen years. The camera angle had been awkward to begin with, so my round moon of a face, covered in angry red acne, looked even more enormous. Also, what the hell was I smiling at? I had taken that yearbook picture at freshman orientation. That grinning, squinty, pimply-faced kid had no idea what he was getting into.

Marley must have heard me groan. She grabbed my badge off the table and pinned it on me like a medal. Reaching up to pull my head down, her warm breath tickled my ear as she whispered, "Absolutely adorable."

"Thank you." I exhaled.

She winked before grabbing one of the blank name stickers and writing her name in artful script—calligraphy skills on point—and adding a smiley face to it.

"A smiley?"

"I'm putting good juju into the universe for you."

We walked into the larger room and were confronted with a scene that could have played out at a high school dance, rather than a party for late twentysomethings.

An enthusiastic middle-aged deejay holding an oversized headset to his ear held court in the corner. He bopped along to an EDM remix of some eighties hip hop. The song had a passable beat, but the dance floor in the center of the room remained mostly empty. A few brave souls along the sides played at moving around, but even they kept stopping to talk in groups.

I hadn't been expecting fake snow and Santa in the corner, but other than four large Christmas trees, it didn't seem like there was much to the theming. The blandness of the nondescript hotel ballroom soothed me.

There were 125 people in my graduating class, and at least ninety-five of them were in the room right now, huddled and chatting softly. Naturally, the largest gaggle was at the bar.

"Let's get this party started!" the deejay shouted into his microphone, switching the music to another EDM mix, this time of Billy Idol's "Rebel Yell." The people who had been half-heartedly dancing gave up and left the floor.

I assumed that, thanks to social media, my old classmates weren't complete strangers to one another, but most had probably lost touch. Coming out of our wealthy private school in Seattle, almost everyone went on to college. While some had stayed to attend the University of Washington, the majority had possessed the means and desire to go out of state.

"This reminds me of my middle school dances," Marley said softly as we moved to stand at an unoccupied tall table. "Except instead of boys on one side and girls on the other pretending not to look across, it's full-grown adults who don't know how to act."

I surveyed the room as inconspicuously as I could. Apparently, high school never truly ended, as everyone sectioned off into the safety of their former friend groups.

Ten years had demonstrably passed. I noticed receding hairlines and a few shaved skulls, feeling thankful for my still-thick head of hair. And I didn't want to be a dick about it—since I was so conscious of my weight—but I took perverse pleasure from the fact that, while I'd been the largest teen in my high school, I'd thinned out a bit. There were at least two dozen guys here tonight with bigger bellies than mine.

Marley unwrapped a piece of candy from a dish in the middle of the table. "How do you want to play this?" she asked, popping the hard peppermint into her mouth. "At my reunion last year, we just went to The Landslide and took over the back room. A lot of us had stayed in Coleman Creek, so it wasn't exactly a big deal. Mainly just catching up with the few folks who had moved away after graduation. I want to be a good wingman for you, James, but I'm not sure what to do. Do we just wait for people to come over and make small talk? Or find the people who were mean to you and start throwing punches?"

I laughed. "How about we get a drink?"

"Always a good idea," Marley agreed. "It seems like a lot of folks in this room need a little liquid courage. This atmosphere is intense."

She wasn't wrong. Nervous faces littered the crowd. Men darting anxious glances, fidgeting with their ties. Women in picture perfect makeup and dresses, running palms across their mommy bellies.

These people had grown up wealthy, many of them from very prominent families. I imagined they were under enormous pressure to perform and produce in their adulthoods. There was a sense of power shifting in the room as it became clear who had "made it" in life and who hadn't lived up to those expectations.

I had an epiphany.

As a teenager, I'd been an outsider, yearning to belong. But now, I felt only a deep sense of gratitude that I'd never been included in their world. Because it meant I wasn't included in their competition now. The furtive glances and whispered gossip had nothing to do with me. I could not care less about scorekeeping and how I stacked up against people I'd never liked anyway.

"Hey, Marley," I said, grinning at her like the Joker.

She cocked her head to the side, registering my expression. "Yes, James?" she asked archly.

"I just realized that I don't give a fuck what these people think of me." A lengthy breath spilled out from my lungs. "I don't have a little group to talk to here. Not really. Because I was never part of this. And I'm not part of it now. It doesn't matter."

"Well, it's funny you should mention that." She tapped her index finger on her chin. "Because I don't care what these people think of you either."

It got easier after that. I'd accomplished my mission of holding my head up in this room. Anything else that happened would be gravy.

Marley and I went to the bar and grabbed two glasses of merlot. At the appetizer table, we filled a plate to share. I received a few more puzzled looks as we circled the room, similar to the one Nora had given me in the hallway. Once we'd returned to our table, Marley clinked our glasses together. "Cheers to you, James, for having zero figs to give about any of these folks."

We each took a sip. It was excellent, and I had a fuzzy recollection of someone in my class whose family owned a winery. I glanced around again to discover more eyes on me, people turning their heads away quickly when I caught them staring.

Connor O'Malley and the rest of the jocks made up the largest group in the room, soft laughter coming from their corner. Someone in their pack—Jonas Wright, our football team's star running back—looked over at me. I refused to turn away, forcing him to glance down first. This group had most likely been behind the puddin' pie incident, but I meant what I'd said to Marley. I had no interest in re-litigating the past.

It took a few minutes to recognize Darby O'Hanlon at another table. I'd had a crush on the cute brunette who'd starred in all our school plays sophomore year. I'd thought I'd hidden it well, but someone had clued her in, and she'd shouted at me brutally across the crowded cafeteria, "Eww, James! Gross! Not in a million years!" That had been my last crush in high school. Now, Darby looked like a cookie-cutter bottle blonde, arm hooked around the attractive guy next to her with his nose buried in his phone. Like Jonas, she peered at me, and I met her gaze until she turned away.

"Do you think they want to say something to me?" I asked Marley. "Now that I'm here, I'm realizing it would be awkward as fuck for them to apologize. I don't need it."

Marley actually laughed out loud. "James—" she started, then chortled again, shaking her head.

"What?"

"These idiots have no idea."

I glanced around again at the people in the room. A woman by the windows squinted at me. Another had her forehead scrunched as she tried not to stare. "What do you mean?"

"That's why they're all looking at you, champ. They're wondering who the hell you are. Or maybe who I am."

I gaped at her. "Not possible."

"Not only is it possible, it's happening." She giggled as she shook her head. "You're crooking your elbow to hold your glass so they can't clock your badge. But they are absolutely trying to. They all want to know who this hot, dad-bod Jason Momoa-looking dude is who wandered into their reunion."

Studying the room again, I acknowledged the truth of her assertion with astonishment. A man I recognized as our senior class president cast a furtive glance my way, gesturing toward me as he spoke to his tablemates. A woman who'd sat next to me every day in geometry for a year smiled shyly from the corner.

Jesus Christ. I'd been worried these people might be mean to me. Or embarrass me.

They didn't even recognize me.

Marley's eyes danced. "I love this for you," she said. "Should you grab the microphone from the deejay and tell them who you are, followed by an 'eff you very much?' Or maybe we should just leave and they can wonder forever."

I honestly didn't know how to proceed. Women were eyeing me with appreciation. That had happened since high school, but never once during.

The re-appearance of Will saved me from deciding. Marley's features remained amiable as he came near. She must have remembered him as the person who'd smiled and waved at me earlier in the hallway.

Will approached with arm outstretched, shaking my right hand and slapping his left against my shoulder. "James, how ya been, man? I wasn't sure you'd come after the way these assholes treated you back in the day."

I felt a fondness I hadn't expected to feel tonight, as I recalled the Will of my youth—feisty, bold, the obligatory goth kid in our class. It didn't surprise me he'd cut to the chase. He'd been the closest thing I'd had to a real friend at Seattle Elite. We hadn't spent much time together outside school, but we'd been constant companions inside, providing a measure of protection.

"I needed to come put a period on things," I said, leaving it there. "But I could also ask the same of you. You weren't exactly bro-ing down with any of these guys."

Will nodded, shaking the same mane of blue-black hair he'd sported in high school. Back then, he'd been a short, skinny teen, drowning in tight black jeans and band t-shirts. He was still on the shorter side, but he'd filled out some, and his uniform tonight was a sleek charcoal Tom Ford suit with a vee neck tee underneath. Nothing Christmasy about it.

He didn't mince words. "I came because I made some smart investments right out of college. Not to be crass, but I'm even richer than my parents now. And probably most of the folks in this room. I'll admit I wanted to rub it in these assholes' faces a little. I spent my whole life going to the same country club as these guys, the same stupid fundraisers. My dad played golf with their dads, stuff like that. But they never stopped making me feel like shit. I'd like to return the favor." He turned to Marley and stuck out his arm. "Will."

"Marley," she said. "It's nice to meet a friend of James's." She looked around and did a quick sweep of the room, not hiding the disdain on her face. "And I'm sorry to hear these bums were awful to you, too."

Will took a sip of his beer. "I take it James told you how it was for him back then?"

"Um hmm. And I was prepared to fight for his honor, but so far, I haven't had to. Mostly, I've just been trying not to laugh at how oblivious he is to all the ladies looking at him like he's dinner."

"Gotta protect your man."

"Oh, he's not my man—" Marley started.

"It's not like that," I finished.

"Ah," Will said, darting his eyes between us.

"We're friends," Marley clarified. "Very good friends." She put her hand in mine and I immediately felt the sense of rightness come over me I'd only ever felt with her. I needed to stop taking it for granted. What she gave me. Space to open up. Air to breathe. I would have missed out on getting this closure if she hadn't supported me. If she hadn't known exactly what I needed.

Marley and Will continued making small talk. I learned Will was single and currently made his living as a venture capitalist. He liked the money, but not the job. He played first base in an adult softball league and owned a condo in Bellevue, across the lake from Seattle.

Although I appreciated Will's friendly face, I only heard him with half an ear. Marley held my attention. The way she ran her fingers absently along my forearm sent shivers down my spine. Her joyful, throaty laugh sent a shot straight into my heart. I longed to place a kiss on the elegant line of her exposed neck.

I felt more than ready to move this *situationship* forward. The instinct to put my arm around Marley and claim her—to let everyone know she was mine—gripped me like a vise. Everything in my life had been better since she'd come into it.

The appearance of Jonas at our table interrupted my thoughts. He swept in on Will's right side, catching me off guard. He may not have recognized me, but he evidently knew my old friend.

"Hey bro." He threw an arm around Will's shoulders. I folded my arms across my chest, once again obscuring my name badge.

"Hello, Jonas," Will replied, giving the other man a sardonic smile. "What brings you over to our table?"

Jonas observed Marley first, then me, hinting at an introduction. Will clearly took subversive pleasure in remaining silent. Jonas shrugged and addressed him directly.

"We were supposed to have lunch a few weeks ago before you had to cancel," he complained. "I called your office on Monday and then again on Wednesday, but your admin said you didn't have a free day until February."

"Sorry. I am very busy." Will's face was the opposite of sorry.

"I know, but, dude, we're old friends."

Will raised an eyebrow. "We are?"

"I mean, we went to the same high school." Jonas scratched his forehead. "That's something, right?"

"It's definitely something." Bemusement crossed Will's features as he explained to us, "Jonas would like me to invest in his new company. He has wonderful ideas."

I held back a giggle. Oh my.

Jonas made a face. His inebriated state revealed itself when he shook his head and whined, "Look, Will, I'm just asking to get on your calendar. Whatever our history is or isn't, I have a good pitch."

Will seemed to have had his fun. "Fine, Jonas. Call Nancy next week and I'll make sure you get in." To me and Marley, he mouthed *he won't get in.*

Satisfied with that resolution, Jonas turned to me and stuck out a shaky hand, "Jonas."

I unfolded my arms and watched his eyes grow big as he saw my badge. "James," I said, reaching out my palm.

But Jonas left me hanging as his mouth gaped. "Oh my God! Jubbs?! Jesus, man. I never would have pegged you for a glow-up." He leaned back and shouted over to his original table. "Hey, Connor, guys, check it out. The dude we were wondering about is Jubbs!"

His shout attracted the attention of not only his friends, but also the rest of the room as I felt all eyes turn to me. Marley stepped closer and wrapped her arm around my elbow as a low murmuring began around the room. *Oh my God, it's James? Is that really Jubbs? Seriously, James Wymack?*

I waited to feel uncomfortable, but the epiphany I'd had earlier, along with the presence of Marley on one side and Will on the other, fortified me.

Leaning to Marley's ear, I whispered, "Jubbs was the nickname Jonas gave me in ninth. It's a mix of James and Chubby. He thought of that himself. He's very clever."

If Marley had been concerned about my reaction to Jonas's rudeness, my words reassured her, although her hold on me remained close and firm.

A few of the folks from Jonas's table started drifting to ours.

"Oh, man, Jubbs. I can't believe it's you," Connor said. "You look great!" His words rang with sincerity, and I realized he'd approached out of curiosity, not to inflict any damage. "Is this beautiful lady your wife?" He reached his hand to Marley. "Connor."

Before I could reply, Marley did. Unmoved by his flattery. "I'm Marley. Not his wife. But I am here with him. And you should call him James."

Connor blinked at the feisty woman at my side.

"Oh, shit. Of course." He turned back to me. "Didn't mean anything by it, dude. Uh, James. Sorry."

"It's cool," I said.

I sensed Connor was about to launch into small talk when Jonas interjected himself into the conversation. "For fuck's sake, do we need to have apologies over *that?*" He slurred his words as he slapped his thigh. "It's just a stupid nickname. Who cares about a stupid nickname?"

"Jonas—" Connor tried to cut off his former teammate.

"No, seriously, bro," Jonas pushed Connor away and stumbled into the table. "We're not allowed to mention how insane it is that fuckin' Jubbs turned out to be all—" He waved his arm up and down in my direction. "This."

Will directed an icy glare in Jonas's direction. "What's your point? Are you mad James is better looking than you now? Or is it just the reminder that the rest of us would like to move on from high school that has you drunk and making absolutely no sense at all?"

"I'm saying it's just a nickname," Jonas sneered.

Darby came over, leaving her companion to his phone.

"It's a horrible nickname," she said. "One that we should be ashamed of ever having used. The only excuse is that we were teenagers. There's no excuse now." Looking over at me, she continued. "I'm very glad you came tonight, James. And it's fantastic to see you looking so well."

"Jesus!" Jonas said. "We're kissing Jubbs's ass now?"

"Don't call him that," Connor said.

"It's just a nickname!"

Marley and I stood silently, becoming a popcorn-eating meme as we watched my former classmates argue about whether it was a big deal for them to still call me by an insulting nickname. Code for how much they did or did not regret the past. Even though it was me being discussed, I had no place in this conversation. The teenager inside me thrilled at this further confirmation that their behavior a decade ago was a *them* problem, not a *me* problem.

Will got the final word in with Jonas. "You're just mad because you have a failing business and a fresh divorce. You only came here tonight to remind yourself of being a superstar in high school. To feel big and important again. That's why you're pissed that the kids you picked on can't be kicked around anymore. Grow up."

As a divorced, first-year high school teacher living in a run-down apartment with my dog, I wasn't necessarily someone to inspire envy. But as I saw Jonas cowering under the judgement of his former friend group, I reveled in my little, authentic life.

Jonas held his hands up. "Okay. Geesh. I won't use the nickname."

"It's fine," I piped in. "You don't need to worry about what to call me because Marley and I actually have to leave." I turned to Will. "I'll be in touch. So glad we re-connected."

"Likewise."

I'd more than achieved what I'd intended by coming tonight. Connor gave me a wave and a "nice to see you" as we walked away. I doubted I'd ever run into him again, but it heartened me he wanted to act right. It gave me hope for Fel, that not all kids who were little dicks at age sixteen remained that way.

We were almost in the hallway when I heard, "James. Wait!"

Panting at having to move quickly within the confines of her long, fitted dress, Darby came up behind us. I laced my fingers with Marley's as I turned to her.

Darby had been so cruel to me once, ruthlessly shutting down my crush and embarrassing me in front of the entire school. I could no longer see any of the drama geek she'd once been, just the woman she'd grown into. I'd dismissed her earlier in the evening as a run-of-the-mill trophy wife type. But maybe there was more there. Her eyes grew stormy.

Nodding slightly at Marley, she said, "I'd hoped you'd come tonight, James. I feel terrible about what happened in high school. How everyone was to you then. Including me." Her sincere regret radiated from her. "Anyway, that's why I sent all those texts. I'm on the organizing committee and I got your number from my husband. He does IT security and knows how to find these things—well, I guess that's not important. But I wanted you to know. I'm glad you came. It probably doesn't mean much to get an apology now, but I really want to say I'm sorry. I wish I had done things differently. And you can tell me to fuck off or whatever you need to do, because I get that it's not about making me feel better. But I just wanted to say sorry."

I sighed, feeling Marley give me a fortifying grip. "I'm not going to tell you to fuck off. I accept your apology."

"Thank you."

"Can I ask why this was so important to you? To get me here? Just to apologize?"

She paused for a moment, and I saw a flash of pain across her features before she stepped back. "My husband and I had our second about a year ago. He was born with a huge strawberry mark covering one side of his face." She smoothed down the front of her dress. "I worry about him, about what...might happen. And it made me think about things."

"Ah." I tried not to grimace. Unless her son was extremely lucky, or the world became a very different place, she was right to be concerned. But it didn't have to mean everything. "Darby, things were bad for me in high school. You said it yourself. But I have a great life now." I raised Marley's hand, kissing the back of it. "Understand?"

"I do," she said. "I'm so glad you came."

"So am I."

Chapter Thirteen

Marley

James emanated subdued joy all the way to the car. Nights like this didn't happen very often. He'd won. It had gone better than he could have possibly hoped for. And I'd been by his side for all of it. I felt giddy picturing the women ogling James, the dumbfounded men, and the look of pure satisfaction on his face once he'd recognized how little their opinions mattered. Watching Will tell off Jonas and getting Darby's apology were simply frosting.

As we headed north on I-5, James reached across the console to grab my hand.

"I don't even know how to thank you, Marley. And before you tell me, 'No thanks necessary,' I'm cutting you off. I won't let you underplay how much this meant. What an amazing thing you did by standing by me for this."

My neck heated at his effusiveness. He was right that I would have told him not to thank me. "It was my pleasure. Truly. I'm sure I enjoyed tonight almost as much as you did. Maybe it's the teacher in me, but it's nice to see a little justice in the world when it comes to bullies."

He let go of my hand, drumming his fingers against the steering wheel. The excited energy in the compact car enveloped me.

We were almost at his parents' house when he spoke again. "I realized something, Marley. When we were talking to Will." He turned up the heater to fight the fog on the windows as he blew out his own heavy breath. "Everything in my life has been better since I met you. It felt risky coming to this reunion, and four months ago, I wouldn't have even considered it."

"That's a really sweet thing to say."

"I mean it. I've been thinking about what Leo said yesterday. That I've never been a fighter. But tonight, I faced my past head-on. I wouldn't have been able to do that without your encouragement."

I thought he might be overstating my influence. I'd just been his friend.

"What are you thinking?" he asked.

"Honestly? That I didn't really *do* anything for you. Not intentionally anyway. You're giving me this tremendous compliment to say I've made such an impact on your life. Is it nice to hear? Sure. Who wouldn't be flattered? But it doesn't feel earned, you know?"

"That's just it, Marley. Don't you see? You didn't have to do anything. Work at it. Just you being you, and letting me be in your life—it's enough. Enough to make a difference."

"Oh," I said dumbly, trying to reconcile his words.

We pulled into his parents' driveway as he declared, "This conversation is to be continued. For now, I'm betting my mom and dad will want to know how tonight went."

James was right about his parents.

The hesitant smiles Chris and Deanna greeted us with grew wider as we relayed the events of the reunion. James opened up about his high school days more than he ever had before, so they might fully appreciate how monumental the night had been. They'd known, of course, but it was one thing to have a vague awareness and another to hear the details of how their son had once been pantsed in front of the girls' cross-country team during P.E.

"Little shits," Chris snarled.

His mom attempted diplomacy. "We are so sad that we couldn't help you more in high school, sweetheart. Your dad and I love you so much. And we would have been proud of you no matter what happened tonight. But it's nice to hear that you got the best of those—"

"Little shits," James's dad offered again.

"Yes dear, those little shits."

I laughed out loud as Deanna grinned at me.

James smoothed circles on my lower back as the four of us sat at the small breakfast table. We drank decaf and ate freshly baked sugar cookies—the perfect way to celebrate an evening that felt like Christmas morning.

Chris and Deanna had been friendly yesterday. But the look they'd given me when James and I eventually said our goodnights and headed downstairs had been downright admiring.

They think I love their son.

I cared deeply for James, had been fascinated by him since the beginning, but how had it gotten so intense so quickly? *He said I'd made a real difference in his life.* It was ironic that in helping James not to be afraid to face his past, I'd become the one who was scared...of falling too hard, too fast.

No matter how much I liked him, I couldn't help that nagging feeling that James wasn't for me. That our relationship—whatever it was—was fleeting. The thought of being with him exhilarated me, while at the same time, I was terrified of getting hurt.

But as he took my hand in his to lead me down to the basement, those doubts quieted.

At least for the moment.

AFTER PUTTING ON our pajamas, James and I collapsed into bed and immediately assumed yesterday's position—him as the big spoon curled behind me. I fell into a dreamless sleep almost as soon as I hit the mattress, his warm breath against my neck.

I woke up in the middle of the night to find the blankets pushed down below our waists. Cool December air penetrated the cave-like space of the basement, but James's body, pressed to mine, provided all the heat I required. His insistent fingers dancing along my torso woke me gently.

Dazed, I roused slowly as his hand traveled a path down my arm. The room remained dark and silent, offering no direction. A glance at the old-fashioned clock radio informed me of the time. Just after two o'clock.

"Marley?" James whispered into the crown of my hair.

"Umph," I mumbled, still waking up.

"I can't sleep," he murmured, speaking into my neck. The vibrations from his voice crawled across my skin. "I've been awake for hours. Thinking. I couldn't wait until the sun came up to tell you again. The reunion. Everything you did. You mean so much to me."

"Thank you," I replied sleepily, half convinced I was still dreaming.

His breathing grew labored. I sensed the tension coiled in his body as his hand clenched into a fist next to my wrist.

"I want—" He exhaled huskily, practically groaning. I came fully awake at the sound, the evidence of his desire stabbing into my hip. Still, when the hesitant touch of his lips to the exposed flesh beneath my ear finally came, it shocked me. "Is this okay?" he whispered, pressing one kiss and then another into the sensitive skin.

I held my breath for a silent beat. Wanting James scared me. But I still wanted him.

I shuddered, breathing out a "yes" in the darkness.

Yes. For however long it lasts.

Even with permission, his movements remained tentative at first. He unclasped his hand slowly and ran it up and down my arm again, then brought it around my belly to pull us close. I felt the firm press of his erection on my backside, and I arched and pushed against him, wordlessly asking for more. He pulled my back against his chest as his hand continued its exploration up my midsection, underneath my thermal as he reached further to lay a rough palm against my breasts. I hadn't bothered with a bra for sleeping, so his touch had my nipples hardening instantly. I writhed torturously, and his lips against my neck grew more urgent, his mouth moving along my nape to place an intense, bruising kiss at the top of my shoulder.

"Want you," I said distinctly, words echoing throughout the room. I lifted my arms, signaling James to pull my top off. He did so quickly, removing his own undershirt at the same time.

I rolled over to face him, barely able to make out his shape in the darkness as we both lay on our sides. I leaned in toward him as he did the same.

And then James and I were kissing.

An indescribable wellspring of emotion lit up inside my chest. Like I had been waiting my entire life to feel this sense of rightness, of being cherished fully. As James's soft lips explored mine and his tongue made a confident foray into my mouth, the impression of everything being in its proper place for the first time ever flooded me.

I ran my palms over his pecs and around to his back, pulling him closer. Wanting to feel all of him. My mouth left his lips to travel down along the thick stubble on his jaw, the rough exterior of his neck. I felt frantic with the need to touch him everywhere, to feel his thick hands on me.

My world tilted sideways when he took my breast into his mouth, licking and sucking on me like a popsicle.

It was too much, and then—all the sudden—not enough.

I leaned back to reach for the side table.

"What are you doing?" James asked.

"The light. I want to see you touching me."

James made a noise that might have been a protest, but I was too turned on to register it. I fumbled for a moment and then flicked the lamp on. The weak beams did little other than cast shadows around the room. Better than nothing, I supposed.

But for James, it was too much.

A ray of lamplight streaked across his center, and I saw the moment he tensed up, reaching an automatic hand to cover his chest. He inhaled as though to suck in his stomach.

I'd forgotten about his insecurities. Everything had been going so well. But of course, one good night couldn't erase a lifetime of negative self-talk.

On his shirtless body, I recognized the imperfections that likely bothered him. His belly was undeniably round, the amount of hair on his chest and stomach above average. Severe acne scars scattered across his collarbone, and I knew they were worse on his back. I'd felt as much with my fingers when we'd been kissing. A few silvery pink stretch marks spread along his sides and under his pecs.

I wished more than anything that he could see himself the way I did. Head to happy trail, I found his hair deliciously sexy. And the size of him, from his height to his belly, turned me on. Made him seem solid and powerful. The line of his erection clearly visible in his sweatpants seemed proportionally large as well, and I couldn't wait to get my hands on it. Maybe my mouth too.

To me, his *flaws* were perfect, and I had the same impression I'd gotten a moment ago when we'd kissed. James and I fit together. Faults and shortcomings and imperfections and all. Because we gave each other what we needed.

Which is why I reached behind myself to turn the light back off.

"That's actually too bright," I said. "I just want to focus on feeling right now." I reached forward and grabbed his face between my palms as I pressed our foreheads together. "Touch me, James. Make me feel you."

A strangled sound came out of his throat and his lips crashed down on mine. He nudged me to my back and rolled on top of me. At first, he held himself up, like he was doing a push-up. But I was having none of that. I reached up to pull him down on me, sighing with deep satisfaction at the full weight of his body on mine.

He kept our naked chests touching as he came up on his elbows. My vision slowly adjusted to the light. I could see the glassy shine of his eyes in the darkness, staring down at me before taking my mouth again in a slow, sensual, tongue-dueling kiss.

"I can't get enough," he said when he finally pulled away, continuing to pepper my face with tiny kisses. "I want to make it so good for you."

"Being here with you is amazing." I whispered hoarsely. "Just keep touching me."

"Whatever you want."

"And James?"

"Mmm?"

"I can't get enough of you either. You are the sexiest, most beautiful man I have ever met. Everything about you. Your mind and your body. It's all mine, and I mean to have my way with you, baby." I hummed, kissing my way across his neck and chest.

"I like when you call me baby."

He pressed further into me, slotting his heavy cock perfectly into my center. He rocked gently, creating a teasing friction, and I moved my fingers down to tug at his waistband.

"Take these off."

He placed more soft kisses, first to one nipple and then the other, before rising to stand next to the couch bed. He reached for his wallet and produced a condom, tossing it onto the end table.

My eyes had almost entirely acclimated to the dimness, and I made out his features as he stood in the moonlight's path. It snuck in from the small basement window, drenching him in a glimmer of silver. I sat up on my elbows, biting my lip in anticipation as I watched him pull down his bottoms, along with his boxer briefs, in one motion.

His erection sprang free from a dark nest of curls to slap his stomach. He gripped himself, slowly moving his palm up and down along the reddish-purple length, running a thumb over the head on each upstroke to catch the drops of pre-cum, smoothing them over the shaft. I hadn't seen many penises in my life—I could count the number on one hand—but James's was certainly the only one that made me understand why the shorthand for them in the modern world was the eggplant emoji.

He stroked himself languidly, clearly emboldened by the darkness, before he finally said, "Your turn."

I reached down to tug my own bottoms off, but unlike him, I left my underwear on, opening my thighs in invitation. "You take them off."

James put one knee on the couch and I felt the old springs groan under his weight. It thrilled me how imposing he was. How he could tower above me and yet his every action teemed with care. He crawled to me and straddled my hips, hooking his thumbs into the sides of my panties.

He pulled the scrap of red silk down in one motion. His eyes raked hungrily over my body. The heat in his inspection acted like a stun gun, paralyzing me as I reveled in his perusal.

James leaned down to place soft kisses on my thighs, inching toward my core. His words hushed as he asked, "Can I put my mouth on you?"

I wanted his mouth on me. Eventually. But right now, there was something else I wanted more.

"Actually, James—I'm burning to have you inside me. I need it. As soon as possible."

His breath hitched as he nodded. He leaned down to press one kiss between my thighs before sitting back on his haunches to sheath himself in the condom.

He stretched out over me, one knee holding his body aloft, as his fingers dipped down beneath my belly to explore between my folds. My clit stood at rigid attention, my preparedness for his entry more than evident.

"You're ready for me?" he asked, as though astonished I'd gotten aroused so quickly.

"I've never wanted anyone as much as I want you," I said truthfully, reaching my hands behind my knees to hold my legs apart and open for him. "Please."

"Goddamn," he breathed out, positioning the tip of his erection at my center. He pushed inside me in one sure stroke and we both cried out at the fullness.

Before I could even process the intense pleasure, his mouth was back on mine. He kissed me repeatedly, shifting to press his lips along my face and jaw, as he rocked his body into mine, murmuring soft words I was too pleasure-drunk to hear.

A few minutes passed as I felt my orgasm building. I hooked my feet around his waist, digging my heels into his round backside as I urged him to move faster. Harder. He lifted a hand from the mattress to reach between us, rubbing the nub of my clit frantically with his index and middle fingers. I came almost without knowing it was happening. One moment we were striving together and the next I was bursting into flames around his thickness, digging my fingers into his back as I surrendered to the waves of the most intense orgasm I'd ever experienced.

"James—" I cried out, legs shaking as I came down from the high.

His breaths became frantic pants as he rutted into me, snapping his hips rhythmically as he chased his own release. Finally, he came with a muffled cry, repeating my name over and over again into my neck before collapsing on top of me.

He paused a moment before getting up to dispose of the condom in the bathroom, coming back to the bed hurriedly before pulling me into his arms and throwing the blankets over both of us.

"Thank you," he whispered so softly I wasn't sure if he'd meant me to hear it.

"I'm glad that happened," I said.

"Me too." He kissed the crown of my head lightly. "And I know there's still a lot up in the air, especially if Coleman Creek cuts me out of the budget. But I realized tonight how I felt about you. What I want. I couldn't wait anymore."

"Baby?"

"God, I love that. Um hmm?"

"What we said before still stands. Even if we changed the game a bit. We don't have to figure it all out tonight."

I snuggled into his arms, letting the blackness steal the worries away. He'd mentioned the teaching job at the school, but there was so much more at play here.

No matter how good it felt in the moment, I couldn't escape the feeling that James and I were very different people. Cool versus basic, interesting versus mid. I believed him when he said he needed me. James was the most mercurial person I'd ever met, a gifted actor. I was the opposite. Steady, straightforward. We helped balance one another.

But as perfectly as I fit with James now, I knew how deceptive that feeling could be. Because I'd felt it before, with Kasen. I'd thought we fit together just right. But what I'd learned is that even perfection doesn't equal permanence.

Chapter Fourteen

James

I woke up with Marley in my arms, cupping her firm breasts over the top of her thermals. She'd insisted on getting dressed in the early morning hours, reasoning that my parents might come to the basement for a laundry emergency. It amused me I'd never once snuck around with a girl in high school, but the experience of having sex in my parents' basement still felt disconcerting as a grown man.

Marley's even breaths showed deep slumber, but even though I'd barely slept, I couldn't stay in bed any longer. My body thrummed with energy. Questions and possibilities.

I tiptoed up the stairs and found my dad sitting at the kitchen table, brow furrowed over the crossword in *The New York Times*. I had fond memories of working the *Seattle Post-Intelligencer* crossword with him as a child, before that paper folded. Since I'd been sixteen, my annual Christmas present to my parents was a subscription to the *Times*.

He looked up at me and smiled, gesturing to indicate fresh coffee.

"Morning, pops," I said, shuffling the mugs in the cabinet to locate the Britney Spears one Leo had given me as a joke on my twelfth birthday.

"You know you can take that with you."

"Nah. I like knowing it's here."

I poured coffee into the chipped ceramic, lamenting that the cartoon bubble extending from Britney's face that read, "*Hit Me Baby, One More Time...With Caffeine*," appeared to be fading. Leaning a hip against the counter, I studied the familiar decorations in the living room. My parents had switched to an artificial tree years ago, but it was still covered in the handmade ornaments Leo and I had made with our mother every year as kids.

"What's an eleven-letter word for 'Denzel's drama?'" Dad piped up.

"*St. Elsewhere*."

"Darn. I should have gotten that."

"You always say that, and yet, you always ask."

"Alright, smartass, just help me finish this."

We worked side-by-side for a few moments. This family love of puzzles and games had been one of the few highlights of my adolescence. Even if he couldn't fix all the problems I had in school, he was always willing to sit with me and do a crossword, play Battleship, or my personal favorite, Mastermind.

It sucked that what had happened with The Game Place somewhat tainted the memory of our shared hobby. That sudden grim thought must have showed on my face because Dad asked, "Everything okay?"

"Yeah. All the shit that went down with Oliver just popped into my head for some reason."

"Hmm. I guess that makes sense, with you being back in town. Dredges things up. At least your reunion went well."

"I almost still can't believe it." I thought about Marley asleep downstairs. "Last night was something I'll never forget."

Dad smirked and glanced at the entrance to the basement. "That good, huh?"

"Dad, jeez," I choked out.

He released a good-natured cackle. "I'm just happy for you, son. Don't mind my nonsense. Can I ask you something, though?"

"Okay."

"You told Marley about high school, obviously. Have you told her about Oliver?"

"No. Just that I had a business once. I haven't told her much about Cindy, either. This whole being more open about stuff is a recent phenomenon. I'm still getting there."

"Seems like she really brings out the best in you."

"She really does."

"Then maybe you should tell her. I mean, since it's still bothering you."

"I'll think about it."

The appearance of Marley cut short our conversation. She smiled at me and blushed when my dad said good morning. Dressed in a long red sweater and leggings, she took my breath away. I couldn't believe I'd been inside her last night. And when she'd called me sexy and beautiful, I'd believed her.

She clearly understood I had reservations about my body. The bullied teenager known as Jubbs would always live inside me somewhere. But in the split second before she'd switched the lamp off, I'd seen the naked desire on her face. Seen the way her hungry gaze had taken in my naked chest, my belly, and my hard cock. Nothing forced or fake about it.

It had filled me with a confidence I'd never felt in the bedroom. Jubbs stayed quiet. The man who'd made love to Marley last night, the one who had touched her and answered her plea to go hard and fast—that had been James. I'd been with other women, of course, but the man who had been with Marley last night had felt brand new.

A HALF HOUR LATER, after pouring our second coffees into to-go mugs, I told Marley we should hurry and get packed up. We'd made a plan to have lunch with her sister Maureen before getting on the road to Coleman Creek, but after talking to Dad that morning, there was somewhere I wanted to show her first.

On our way, we drove by the large complex that housed Seattle Elite. Marley made a face when I pointed it out to her.

"After everything that happened to you there, it's kind of a bummer to see," she said. "The educator in me wonders how much the administration knew and ignored."

I thought about Daniel and Fel. How powerless I felt sometimes to help the students. "You know how it is. It's hard to step in. It wasn't like I was making formal complaints. Hell, I didn't even tell my parents."

She nodded. Both of us were resigned to doing what we could, knowing it would never feel like enough. At least after last night, I knew I'd have less trouble keeping a professional distance from bullying situations. Sometimes I'd been in danger of seriously going off on the students for being mean.

"I don't want to make it a downer morning, especially after last night." I grinned wickedly as I trailed my eyes over her body. "But there's something I want to show you."

I maneuvered the car off 125th Street into the Lake City neighborhood. Luckily, street parking was easy to find. I beckoned Marley to follow me as we walked along the retail avenue lined with little shops, bars, and restaurants. I stopped in front of a Korean BBQ place and pointed across the road.

"You see that bar there, the one called The Place?"

"Yes."

"Well, that bar used to be called The Game Place, and I used to own it with my former best friend, Oliver."

Marley placed a wrist above her eyes, blocking the glare, peeking up at me from underneath. "I think you mentioned that once."

I pulled her aside to a little bench along the sidewalk, doing a careful pre-check for anything sticky or otherwise disgusting. It seemed safe enough, so we sat down.

"Oliver and I went to college together. Friends since freshman year. He studied business. I studied to be a teacher, got my degree, and was scheduled to start student teaching the fall after I graduated. Instead, Oliver came to me with this idea of running a game shop in Seattle. He's a video game guy, and super into card games as well. He had this vision of a store where people could buy all types of games and it could also be a sort of coffee shop where they would sit and play. There could be tournaments and tutorials. Consoles set up for customers to test drive. It would be a place for people who loved games to buy things and hang out. Maybe meet like-minded people.

"He wanted me to go into business with him and his friend Steve. It flattered me he'd asked. Like I told you before, I had friends in college, but I think there was always a part of me looking for proof that people *really* liked me. Oliver asking me to help get The Game Place off the ground felt like that validation. I also had such great memories of playing games with my parents and brother. In my mind, our shop could be a space for families to gather."

"It sounds like a great idea."

"We had to spend a lot to get it going, but it seemed to be a success right away. The neighborhood liked it, and there were tons of people coming in and out. The income from game sales and the coffee shop side was enough for the three of us to earn a steady paycheck. We had to bust our asses, but it worked. I was happy."

I paused there, wondering if this would be a good time to bring up Cindy. We'd met that first year of the shop. I'd been so blinded by her beauty, so seduced by the idea that my life was finally coming together, that I'd missed all the red flags. With her and with Oliver.

I decided the story of my marriage could wait.

"What happened?" Marley prompted gently.

"It was good for a few years, but Oliver and Steve started getting annoyed that we weren't making more money. I hadn't known at first, but they had much higher expectations for the shop than just getting by financially and being a popular spot in the neighborhood. In college, I remembered Oliver being ambitious, but it was nothing compared to how he acted once we'd opened.

"He and Steve became ruthless about pulling under-selling games off the shelf. When families would linger in the coffee shop to play without making more purchases, he'd start hinting for them to leave. Our reviews started tanking. We'd been seen as a family place, but that changed. We started doing more tournaments, sometimes all weekend long, and let's just say some of the players they attracted were not the best humans. Some gamer stereotypes are true, apparently, because we had more than a few incel types coming in and out. Not the majority, but enough to sour the punch. I tried talking to Oliver and Steve, pointing out when the players were out of control—some comments these guys made were truly disgusting. Our late-night tournaments developed a reputation for being unfriendly to women. But my partners didn't care because the money was rolling in.

"The worst part was, I thought Oliver and I were tight. Except he wouldn't listen to me. Didn't care what I thought at all. Kept saying I was overreacting. When I insisted, he made a half-hearted attempt to fix things. Put up a few signs. I felt like he was just managing me. We'd talk around each other and fight, and the guy who had been one of my first true friends in college became a stranger.

"The last straw came when Steve applied for a liquor license and the cute little coffee shop side of the building that served tea and muffins to families playing Monopoly on the weekends became a bar. The bar side swallowed up the game side until it was unrecognizable from our original vision. By the time I left, The Game Place was essentially a bar with board games on the shelves that held weekend tournaments."

"Goodness. I'm sorry. That must have been awful, to watch it change like that."

"Yeah. I finally came to realize that the money wasn't worth it. It wasn't something I wanted to be a part of anymore. I asked them to buy me out. Steve didn't protest, but Oliver acted genuinely hurt. To this day, I don't know if that was real or not. I explained that this wasn't our agreement and questioned why he'd even asked me to help. He insisted it was a natural progression, that all businesses changed, and that he'd wanted me to be part of it because we were friends. When I told him I felt like he'd betrayed me, he accused me of being weak and hysterical. Like somehow, I was the problem because I didn't want a bunch of misogynists coming into our business.

"Obviously, the situation had gone too far to repair. So, he accepted my decision. To his credit, he did the one thing I asked him to do and changed the name. The Game Place became The Place. I haven't spoken to Oliver since the day we signed the papers."

There were details I didn't offer Marley. Long nights when I felt my friendship with Oliver dying along with the business. Oliver making an appeal to Cindy to get me to see things his way. Cindy screaming at me that I was unambitious, that I had an obligation to our marriage to make as much money as possible, and why couldn't I be more like Oliver?

"That sounds intense," Marley said. "I don't even know what to say."

"It ended up being okay. I went back to my original plan of teaching, resolved to put the whole mess behind me." I took a deep breath, delving into the rest of the story. "My marriage didn't last too long after that. Cindy thought she was marrying an entrepreneur, not a student teacher. A few evenings in a row of coming home to find me grading papers was enough to send her packing. That, and the fact she was screwing someone else."

Marley sucked in a breath before leaning into me and tilting her head against my shoulder. I wrapped an arm around her and pulled her to me, kissing the top of her head. Dad had been right. Her silent support meant everything.

"James, I'm glad you told me, and that you showed me this place, but I'm curious why. I hope you understand you don't owe me anything because we slept together. I know you've gotten burned opening yourself up to people in the past. We can move at your pace."

"After last night, it felt weird that you only knew about the bad stuff from high school." My cheeks lifted as I continued, "If we're going to be together, it's important you understand I've had the shit kicked out of me *multiple* times."

She barked out a laugh. The sound carried even on the busy street, and several nearby pedestrians glanced at us. Marley waved at them as she pressed further into me. "Well, I'm grateful that your teaching career brought you to Coleman Creek."

"There weren't many positions out there for me. Principal Nadal got that funding so last minute, it was more like being in the right place at the right time. Lucky me."

She breathed into my chest. "No, James. Lucky me."

I smiled.

"It's been a good fit for me, small-town life. After my marriage, after Oliver turned into someone I didn't recognize, I started questioning my ability to know what was real. I thought Cindy and I were happy, but apparently not. I thought I was making the right choices with my career, but it turns out I should have just stuck with the dream I had when I was eight, to be a teacher. Coleman Creek feels real. The people are real. Main street is real. The way the town celebrates the holidays is real. So many times in life I've tried to remake myself, and all that happened was I ended up exhausted from hiding. Pretending to be the person I wished I was. Even now, I'm not sure I know where my image ends and the real me begins. But from the minute I got to Coleman Creek, it seemed like the place to find out. And now, I know that you're the one I want to be with when I do. If you'll have me."

"Dang, James. That's the nicest thing anyone has ever said to me."

"I mean every word, Marley, I—" I stopped short as my eyes lasered in on the door to The Place as it opened quickly.

And Oliver raced out to the sidewalk.

Holy shit. He was there. I hadn't seen him in almost two years, yet somehow, he was sixty feet away. Same ash brown hair with a gentleman's cut. Same signature tapered navy slacks and scoop neck tee. He'd come out like a dart, as though noticing me from inside, but now he stood paralyzed on the sidewalk.

Across four lanes of traffic, he stared, and I saw the moment register when he became certain it was me sitting on the bench, that I wasn't some apparition he'd dreamed up.

A huge grin lit up his face, and he raised his hand in a wave. His eyes darted back and forth, apparently deciding whether he wanted to risk running into traffic to reach me.

I didn't wave back. I shot him a glare and shook my head back and forth, making sure he understood I hadn't come to say hello. My arm around Marley stiffened and I tugged on her sleeve to communicate that we should get up. I didn't want to talk to Oliver. I'd never dreamed he might be here on a Sunday morning.

The smile on his face died. His steps stuttered in indecision before I narrowed my eyes at him, hastening his retreat. He gave me one last wave before turning back toward the bar.

"Let's get out of here," I said to Marley.

She hadn't missed the tension that had ripped through my body. It was easy enough to put two and two together.

"That was him? Oliver?"

"Yes."

She nodded, eyeing the bar's exterior. "You sure you don't want to go across the street? I'm not pushing it one way or the other, especially after everything you've just told me, but he looked like he wanted to talk to you."

"No. This isn't like the reunion. There's no unfinished business. When it comes to him, I've said all I had to say."

Chapter Fifteen

Marley

James stayed quiet on the way to the restaurant where we were meeting Maureen. It had been wonderful having him open up to me. But Oliver's appearance putting a halt to our conversation felt surreal. James declaring he'd said everything he needed to say reminded me an awful lot of myself five years ago, when I'd split from Kasen.

I'd begun to believe that, in every relationship, there was always something more to say.

By the time we reached Las Espuelas, James had returned to his usual self. As much as he'd admitted this chill, jovial persona could be a mask, I understood him well enough at this point to know he was genuinely okay. Even seeing Oliver couldn't derail our amazing weekend. Tacos would only make things better.

My sister already had a margarita in front of her when we arrived, although the chips and salsa on the table remained untouched.

Maureen had dyed her hair a dark auburn since Thanksgiving, complimenting the elegant appearance of her plum-colored sheath dress. She gave James's tapered utility pants and three-quarter sleeve flannel tunic an admiring glance while smiling indulgently at my boring sweater and leggings. I'd barely introduced them before she launched into a monologue about the foibles of working upscale retail during the holiday shopping season.

James sat next to me, holding my hand underneath the table, running his thumb back and forth over my wrist. We hadn't put a new label on our friendship this morning, but there was an unspoken understanding that we were a couple and weren't hiding it.

"Miranda owes me twenty bucks." Maureen smirked.

"What do you mean?" I said innocently as James moved his palm to my knee, drawing slow circles on my leggings.

"After the way you were talking about your *friend* James, she said you'd probably be with the guy by Valentine's Day, but I knew it would be before New Year's, since you're so crazy about Christmas and the magic of the season and all that. Blah blah blah." Maureen waved her wrist around dismissively, but her gaze was fond. She turned to James. "I hope you're planning on being good to my sister. She deserves the best."

"Completely agree," James said, leaning over to kiss my cheek.

The look in my sister's eyes reminded me of Mrs. Allen and Coach Hurley, which was strange since Maureen was generally something of a cynic. It unnerved me she wasn't cynical about this. I was happy to be with James, but I needed to stay realistic.

The sensation that our time together had a ticking clock persisted.

After attending the reunion, meeting his old friend Will, seeing how close James was with his family, and hearing about Oliver, I had a new perspective on James moving to Coleman Creek. He'd said he liked my little town because it felt "real," and yet by so many measures, James's real life was here, in Seattle. He'd just run away from it.

Tomorrow he could wake up and realize how different we were, how much he had waiting for him here. He could be like Kasen and decide that a relationship with me wasn't exciting enough to commit to long term. He could make me love him and then walk away.

After we'd finished eating, James handed his credit card to the server and excused himself to go outside to take a phone call from Leo, who'd been texting all morning.

"I really like him," Maureen said after he'd gone. "Well done."

"He is pretty great. But don't get too excited. It's just casual."

She raised her forehead at me, but didn't comment, seeming to weigh her next words.

"Not to change the subject, but I've been wanting to find out. Did you ever end up communicating with Kasen? You never said, and I didn't want to ask in front of your new guy."

I ignored her reference to James as my guy. "That's because me and Kasen are none of your business. I don't need you and Miranda gossiping. Yes, we texted. And a few days ago we met up at The Landslide."

"You saw him? How was it? What did he want? Does James know?"

I frowned at Maureen's barrage of questions. "It was fine. Just catching up. Sorta weird but not really. He didn't seem to want anything specific. And I told James beforehand so it wouldn't seem like I was keeping anything from him."

"Of course you did." She huffed. "Well, I'm glad it wasn't too weird. It's probably good you can be friends with Kasen now. You two were together a long time."

I knew she was curious about my ex, but my focus was entirely on the man in front of the restaurant windows, smiling as he spoke on the phone. "Um hmm," I said absently. "I hope James and I will always be friends."

Maureen's eyebrows knitted together. "That's a seriously bizarre thing to say, sis. Along with calling it 'casual' before. James seems super into you. Why are you acting like you two already have an expiration date? What are you not telling me?"

"Can you stop with the interrogation, please? That's not what I meant." I sighed heavily. "I'm just saying that James and me being short term is the inevitable outcome here. James's whole life is in Seattle. The only thing he has in Coleman Creek is his job, and there are some budget cuts on the table, so he might not even have that."

"What about you?"

"What about me?"

"Duh. I mean, he has you in Coleman Creek."

I scoffed. "C'mon, Maureen."

My sister's eyes widened as she deduced my reasoning. "Jesus, Marley, I know Kasen left you, but that's no reason to assume James is going to do the same thing."

"It's not about that," I hissed. "I'm just taking care of myself!" I paused for a few seconds, running my hands over my thighs as I worked to get my tone under control. "Look, I'll own that there's a part of me that would love for James to stay, to give up his career and remain hundreds of miles away from the family he loves, and declare that nothing is more important than what we have. But just saying those words out loud reminds me how foolish that scenario is. I can't allow myself to get too wrapped up in this thing with James."

"Marley, Kasen being an idiot doesn't mean everyone is. Just because you live in Coleman Creek and wear unfortunate clothes doesn't mean you don't deserve something amazing."

"You know, I'm not nearly as self-loathing as you're implying. I'm enjoying something amazing with James *right now*. I'm just not trying to delude myself that it's going to stay that way!" I'd opened up and let him in, but only by degrees I could manage. It would be idiotic to give him too much of my heart. And I wasn't an idiot.

Maureen disagreed. "So, you're just going to talk yourself out of falling in love?"

"That's a bit much, don't you think? We've been officially together for less than a day."

"Maybe. But, Marley, I can see how he looks at you. Like you're precious. If you just sit around waiting for the other shoe to drop, you're not even giving it a chance. You can't insulate yourself from pain by not investing in your relationship."

"That's not fair."

"Marley, I love you so much, but sometimes I feel like Miranda and I did you dirty by letting you step in and handle everything with mom. I think you got so used to being thought of as dependable—practical—that you won't allow yourself to crack even a little. It's okay to get upset. And putting yourself out there can be a good thing, even if you end up getting your heart broken."

Maureen looked so earnest, but history undermined her words.

I thought about my mom's last year. Neither of my sisters had made a compelling case for allowing yourself to be overcome by emotion. Maureen had barely visited. Every time she'd gone into Mom's room, she'd come out red-faced and snotty. A few months before the end, she'd declared, "I don't think I can do this anymore," and hadn't come back again until the last day, when we'd gathered to turn off the machines. Miranda had been much the same, with the added bonus of staying near blackout drunk from Mom's passing until after the funeral.

Meanwhile, I'd held myself together. Made the arrangements. Planned the funeral. Worked with the lawyer. Tackled the paperwork. For sure, I'd cried, and I'd grieved—I'd spent almost a year on auto-pilot—but I'd come out okay.

I held no ill will toward my sisters for how any of it had played out. If Miranda had become stoic and calm, or if Maureen hadn't covered her pain by burying herself in work, I would have had to add them to my long list of worries back then.

"Maureen, how I acted after mom died and how I am with James are two different things. Apples and oranges."

"I'm just saying you don't do very well with big, messy feelings and—"

"Enough, okay? I get you're my big sister. And you want to help. But I don't need your psychoanalysis. My relationship with James is not up for debate. For now, we're together, and that's all that matters." She opened her mouth to argue before I cut her off. "I'm serious, Maureen. End of lecture."

She nodded resignedly. "Okay. He just...seems special."

"He's wonderful. And spending these months with him, especially these past few weeks celebrating the holidays, has been one of the best times of my life. That won't change, no matter what happens in the future. Even if it turns out James is too bright for Coleman Creek." *Too bright for me.*

"I think you're wrong, Marley. Dead wrong. I wish you could see yourself the way I do. The way I'm pretty sure James does." I glared at her, and she averted her eyes. "Fine. I won't bring it up again." She took a sip from her glass. "But you can't stop me from hoping.

Or to put it in terms you'd understand, wishing on a Christmas star."

My lips flattened as James made a timely return to the table.

"Everything okay?" I asked him.

"Yeah. Leo heard from our parents that the reunion went well and he wanted the details. He kept threatening to blow up my phone with more texts, so I figured I'd better just take his call. Hope that was okay."

"Totally fine," I said, moving to get up from the table as I eyeballed Maureen. "It's time for us to head back to Coleman Creek anyway."

AS WE DROVE HOME, I forced the conversation with Maureen from my mind. Her opinion meant very little in the long run—how could she know anything when she lived on the other side of the state? We made good time to Travis's house. Oscar and Bambi came rushing out the front door as soon as it opened, jumping on us like we were returning from a Middle East deployment rather than a long weekend.

Travis and Vivienne came outside with their kids, who'd apparently fallen in love with our dogs. Their youngest even threw a small tantrum, throwing her arms around Bambi and wailing as we attempted to get him into the car.

"We'd love to dog sit again sometime," Travis deadpanned, peeling his daughter off the labradoodle's fur. "It's a wonderful experience for the kids."

Vivienne smacked her husband on the arm. "Don't listen to him. We loved having them, and we appreciate the test run. I think the kids might be old enough now for us to consider getting a pet." Her eyes dropped to James's hand on the small of my back. I felt a momentary panic, realizing the whole town would probably know James and I were a couple by tomorrow. But there wasn't any help for it. This was Coleman Creek, after all.

"Want to come to my place for dinner?" I asked once we were back in his car. I still had a full stomach from the Mexican place, but I didn't want the night to end, and I doubted he did either.

"Maybe something small," he replied.

"We should drop by your place first, though."

"Why?"

"To get your stuff so you can stay over. Maybe grab enough for a few nights. Whatever you need for you and Bambi." I didn't have to believe James and I had a future to want to make the most of right now.

He smirked. "A sleepover, huh? I know I've told you this before, but let me reiterate how much I love how zero bullshit you are."

"James, last night barely scratched the surface. Weren't you were the one who mentioned wanting to put your mouth somewhere? And I've been waiting all day to get my hands on that huge tool of yours again." I reached my arm out so I could stroke the back of his neck. "I'm not done with you yet. Not by a longshot."

"You know, Marley, for someone who doesn't curse, you sure can talk dirty when you want to."

I laughed, dropping my voice comically low, "You like it, baby?"

"You know I do."

James didn't laugh back. The heated look he gave me rivaled the air coming through the vents. He reached across the console to knead my thigh over my leggings. We pulled up in front of his apartment, and I went inside with him. He brought in his duffel from our weekend, exchanging the clothes inside it for fresh ones, grabbing more toiletries from the bathroom, and a bag of dog food from the kitchen.

This was only the second time I'd been to his place. Very little furniture filled the living room, only a couch and a dog bed. Nothing on the walls. The kitchen appeared similarly bare. Another reminder that James hadn't exactly put down roots here.

On the bright side, there was a cheerful wreath on the front door and another hanging above the faux fireplace. James saw me noticing. "I bought two at the lot when we were there last weekend—to support the school."

James might not have a bookshelf or a suitable set of knives yet, but he was connected to the town in other ways. Maybe I could be more hopeful?

Ugh. I needed to squash that.

By the time James drove up my driveway, we were already kissing. The dogs barked and yipped around us as we continued touching one another, carrying our bags into the house. Once inside, I kicked the front door closed and immediately felt James's large body pushing me up against it. His fingers journeyed underneath my sweater to touch the bare skin of my torso, creating goosebumps along my spine.

I pulled myself away from him just long enough to feed the dogs and get them settled for the night.

In my bedroom, I found James lying against the headboard in nothing but his boxer briefs. Soft light from two candles shadowed across the white walls, and he seemed okay with the fact I could see his features clearly. It wasn't a spotlight, but it was something.

As I quickly divested myself of my clothes, he did the same with his boxers. Undressed, his rock-hard erection beckoned me across the room. I approached him from the foot of the bed, crawling my way up as I ran my lips and tongue along his calves, his knees, his quads. My fingernails raked through the wiry hair of his inner thighs before I leaned down to take him in my mouth. I moaned in appreciation of his thickness, and he responded by arching half a foot and shuddering.

"Not gonna last," he gritted out.

I pulled off for a moment and winked. "S'okay. I'll take that as a compliment."

Licking a stripe from the root of his shaft to the tip, I engulfed him again. Deep throating was not a particular skill of mine, so I positioned my grip around the bottom to jerk him while I focused my attention on the head. James placed a hand on my hair to help guide me into the rhythm he needed. A minute later, he came down my throat with a shout.

I flopped down next to him, running a finger through his chest hair. He bent his elbow and threw an arm over his eyes. "Just gimme a sec to recover and then I'm definitely returning the favor."

"Yeah you are," I said with a grin.

He breathed out roughly. "I don't know why I'm so surprised by how amazing this is with us. In the bedroom. I don't have a ton of experience, Marley, but this is next level. Like, the best I've ever had."

"Did you think I'd be bad in bed?" I said indignantly.

"No. You're sweet and adorable, and I thought you'd be like that. And you definitely are. But Marley, you're also so goddamn sexy. I knew it would be good, but I don't think I was prepared for this level of epic. And fuck me for that, because you never cease to amaze me. Surprise me."

I could forgive James for assuming I'd be "sweet" and "adorable" in bed. After all, I was the woman who'd spent the entire month in fashion-forward-grandma holiday sweaters. I imagined many people would make that mistake. But I also liked being in control, even if being with James had me on the edge of losing my mind. In more ways than one.

"Maybe because we've been friends all these months, you got used to seeing me as not bedroom material. I'm glad that, with this, the transition has been seamless."

"Marley, seamless doesn't even begin to describe it. When you put your hands on me, it's like I'm being touched for the first time."

I chuckled. "Okay, Madonna."

He didn't laugh back. Instead, he positioned himself on his side, head resting on his fist. He reached out two fingers to run them softly along my cheek, following the line of my body down my neck and chest, before coming to rest on my hip. His eyes blazed with intensity, and I realized with alarm what was about to happen.

"I'm being serious. When we're together, skin to skin, it's like I'm more aware of myself—in a good way—than I've ever been. I really think I might lo—"

"James," I interrupted. "I believe you promised me a return of favors."

He flinched at my obvious shutdown of his words but recovered quickly, seeming to understand I wasn't ready to hear them. Rolling on top of me to deliver an absolutely filthy kiss, he then started working his way down my body.

He did, in fact, return the favor. Payment in full. One hundred percent satisfaction for all parties involved.

Chapter Sixteen

James

The dogs had worked their way into the bedroom during the night, and I woke up to Bambi's wet nose nudging my hand while Oscar gave Marley similar treatment on the other side of the mattress.

"I guess our long weekend is over," she muttered, stumbling down the hall to the bathroom completely naked. It would be nice getting her moved into her mom's old bedroom, since it had the ensuite.

After taking a moment to enjoy the view of her bare ass, I pulled on pajama bottoms and went into the kitchen to start coffee. Looking across the counter, I saw two additions to the living room I hadn't noticed last night in our haste to get to the bedroom. We never had come out for dinner.

On the bookshelf, I discovered a brand-new holiday picture frame containing the photo Marley and I had taken at the #colemancreekholiday selfie wall. The evidence that she'd made room for me here, among priceless objects that told her family's history, humbled me. The second thing I saw was a seven-foot noble fir in the corner. It seemed impossible I'd missed it, considering it dominated the space.

"Coach brought it by Thursday," Marley said, walking into the room dressed in the sweater and leggings she'd worn yesterday. "Since this would have been the weekend I'd normally purchase trees, he did me a solid. There's another one downstairs."

"It's unfortunate we had to miss the tree lot and chaperoning the dance. I wonder how everything went."

"I'm sure we'll find out in an hour when we get to work."

"It would have been nice to go to the dance with you. For obvious reasons, I never went to any of mine in high school."

"Hmm. Well, it's a little different when you're a teacher. It's mostly attempting to keep the kids from grinding up on one another. Funny story—Mr. Bailey used to go around sticking his arm in between the couples and telling them to 'leave room for Jesus.' Principal Nadal gave up on getting him to understand why we don't say that in a public school, and eventually just banned him from chaperoning altogether."

I smiled and shook my head.

"It's a shame you never got to go to a dance," she said, grabbing her phone off the counter. A minute later, Leona Lewis's "Kiss Me It's Christmas" came through the sound bar on the bookshelf and Marley stood in front of me with her hand out.

"What are you doing?"

"I'm asking you to dance."

"Now?"

"James, if there's a better time to dance than six a.m. on a Monday when we're half-dressed and haven't even brushed our teeth yet, I don't know when it is."

Her eyes brimmed with amusement, and I couldn't resist saying yes. We danced cheek-to-chest next to the Christmas tree.

Feeling her against me was a revelation. Cindy used to shy away from my extra flesh when we'd touch. She rarely said anything outright rude, but I always had this knowledge that I disappointed her. In so many ways. She'd always been a fit person, but while I'd been working fifteen-hour days to make The Game Place a success, she'd taken on fitness as a hobby. That I hadn't shared her enthusiasm had taken its toll on the physical side of our relationship. She'd ended up leaving me for one of her workout buddies.

It made sense. She and I had been a terrible match from the start.

As opposed to Marley, who slotted in perfectly. She shut her eyes and nuzzled into my pecs, getting as close as possible. Her hands around my middle played above the waistband of my pajama bottoms—keeping things decidedly PG while still enjoying the tease. I held her to me firmly with one hand around her back and another buried in her hair as we swayed to the romantic song.

The music ended and I leaned her back into a dip with a flourish, causing her to squeak.

The reality of needing to get ready to leave for work invaded the moment. I kissed her softly before letting go.

"Thank you, James. I'm going to remember that forever," Marley said, calling dibs on the first shower.

At first, her words didn't entirely register, but then I blinked. She sounded so detached from the amazing dance we'd just shared. It wasn't possible that Marley wasn't in this the way I was, was it?

I thought about last night. When she hadn't let me tell her I loved her.

Suddenly, that photo of us on her bookshelf took on a new tone. Was I up there because this Christmas season was the start of us? Or was our picture another object providing happy memories of Christmases past?

I LOOKED FOR clues as to Marley's true feelings as we drove to work in her truck. I'd been so busy admiring how open and honest she was, but maybe she'd been holding herself back more than I'd thought? There was a vast difference between putting herself out there and letting me in.

Then again, we'd had an amazing weekend together, and last night had been transformative. Whether Marley was second-guessing us, or simply trying to be cautious, I still had plenty to work with.

"What do you want to tell people?" I asked. "About us?"

"Nothing. I'm pretty sure Vivienne and Travis figured it out last night. We don't need to advertise. It will just get around. Trust me." She grinned.

We arrived at school and walked through the student parking lot into the main building. Daniel stood near the bike rack talking to some other sophomores. They were including him in their conversation, joking around. I caught his eye, and he gave me a reserved upnod.

Marley noticed too. "That's a positive sign. I haven't seen him since that incident with Fel at the tree lot, since I don't have him this semester."

The mystery of Daniel's improved social standing was solved during my first period class. The juniors seemed perfectly happy to put off our discussion on the Magna Carta to fill me in on all the gossip from the weekend.

It sounded like the #colemancreekholiday selfie idea had taken off, with some folks coming from as far as Spokane to get a picture. At the dance, not only had Nan Tourman made a point of dancing with Daniel, she'd also told everyone that the selfie wall had been Daniel's idea, that he'd asked her to bring the proposal to the student council but had been too shy to take the credit.

I didn't know if that was true, or if she was just doing Daniel a solid. I only knew that—with a snap of Nan's magical, manicured fingernails—Daniel was no longer a pariah. He'd been smiling this morning by the bike rack. I couldn't recall ever having seen him smile before.

During our planning period, I went to Marley's classroom and found out she'd gotten the same story from her seniors.

"It's the magic of Christmas," she said.

"It's the magic of popularity," I retorted. "But whatever it is, I'll take it."

In the teachers' lounge at lunchtime, several of the other faculty members looked conspiratorially at us. Marley had been correct that no one would say anything directly about our relationship, but word had definitely spread.

Coach Hurley came in and sat at our table, pulling a vinegary-smelling tuna sandwich from his cooler. The appearance of Principal Nadal spared me from watching him eat it. My boss motioned for me to follow him into his office.

Without Marley.

His down-turned expression was the first sign our run of Christmas magic had hit a speed bump.

"WHAT DID HE SAY?" Marley asked when I came out fifteen minutes later.

I looked at her dazedly. There was no way to sugarcoat it. "He said they cut the funding. I won't have a job after June."

A momentary panic crossed her face, but then she steeled herself. "Did he mention the tree lot money? Everyone said the selfie wall is bringing in a ton of folks and we've sold almost double what we normally would by this time."

"Marley, c'mon. You knew that was an incredible longshot as much as I did. They're completely different budgets. The PTSA can help fund certain positions, but not ones like mine. You know that." It had been a nice fantasy, but even in smaller districts like ours where it might be a little easier to bend the rules, some things could simply not be done.

She let out a weighty exhale. "Maybe we can appeal? The kids really love you. And you're great with them."

I fiddled with the ring on my thumb. "We need to be realistic. Enrollment is lower than expected. If they don't need me, it doesn't make sense for me to stay and take up budget space that could be better utilized elsewhere. Just because I love teaching here doesn't mean it's responsible to keep me."

"But—"

"Hey." I leaned over to kiss the top of her head, making sure no one could see us. "I just got this news. I haven't even had a minute to process. Let's just take it slow. We don't have to have it all figured out this second, right? Isn't that our motto?"

I gave her a smile, but inside, my emotions mirrored the dejection I saw in her eyes. There were no other high schools around for miles, and even if I'd been willing to make a massive commute, open positions were scarce. None of the teachers at Coleman Creek were planning to retire in the next few years—Principal Nadal had asked. He'd been adamant I'd been doing an excellent job and he wished he could keep me. I'd thanked him for the opportunity, because I knew this knife to the gut wasn't his fault.

I liked Coleman Creek. I wanted to stay. But I also felt like I'd found my calling as a teacher. I couldn't envision living here and working at, say, The Landslide. Or one of the warehouses nearby. I had zero interest in running my own business again after The Game Place. Then again, it was hard to imagine not seeing how far Marley and I could take what we'd started this weekend. The thought of giving her up after I'd just found her made me physically ill.

Both of us made our way back to our classrooms, and I managed to keep my focus on the students for the last two periods. Marley had a parent meeting she needed to stay late for. She gave me a key so I could head to her place and let the dogs out.

Leaving my classroom, I got stopped in my tracks by Mr. Bailey.

"Mr. Wymack, do you have a minute?"

"Sure." I smiled at him. "Are you here to complain about my piercing again? Or tell me I need a haircut?"

Against his will, one side of his mouth raised. "Don't be fresh, young man. And while you certainly need a trim, and while I am disappointed that you seem to have switched out the small gold stud for that hideous hoop through your nostril, I've come to discuss something else."

I leaned back against one of the student desks, intrigued. "I'm listening."

He cleared his throat. "I heard about the budget cuts and how they affect your position here."

"Good Lord. It's been five minutes. Can't anyone keep a lid on anything around here?"

"No, city boy. If you want secrets and to be treated like a stranger, you're in the wrong town. Especially during the holidays."

"I guess it's fine then." I huffed. "But anyway, yes, it looks like I'm out at the end of the school year."

"Hmm. Well, I just came by to say that we'll miss you around here. It's a damn shame."

My eyes popped. Even though I'd gotten on Mr. Bailey's good side, I thought I'd only moved that needle from open hostility to mild tolerance. But he was acting as though he genuinely liked me.

"I like you," he asserted, as though reading my thoughts. "The students respond well to you and you...care about them. You're an excellent teacher."

"Mr. Bailey, I appreciate you taking the time to come and tell me that. It means a lot."

"Call me Fred, please." He took a step back and cleared his throat. "I just wanted to make sure you knew that this doesn't have to be the end of everything. When I heard about the budget, it reminded me I was about your age when I came to a similar crossroads." I watched his eyes glaze a bit as he delved into his memories. "I haven't always been a teacher. When I was thirty, I was working as a government analyst. I found out I was being transferred to the West Coast, a major promotion. I'd been seeing a young lady, Ellen. We'd only been dating for a few weeks, but I was already crazy about her. When I found out about the transfer,

I had a wild hair to ask her to marry me. But I let my logical side drown out that impulse. We attempted to date long distance. This was before the days of texts and emails. We used letters and phone calls. My new assignments grew more difficult, and eventually, we stopped communicating. I convinced myself it was for the best, that I was holding her back. In hindsight, I was just afraid. I reached out a year later to beg her forgiveness, but by then it was too late. She was engaged to someone else."

Funny to think that Mr. Bailey was as human as the rest of us. But I wasn't entirely clear why he thought I needed to hear this story. "With all due respect, Fred, I'm not sure how this relates to what I'm going through."

"The day I met you, you told me that teaching was your dream job. I've heard you say that to other folks, too. Something kept you from it until you were almost thirty years old, but now it's finally in your grasp."

"Are you saying I shouldn't give up on teaching?"

"That transfer was my dream promotion. I'm saying things get in the way of our dreams sometimes. The trick is figuring out if those things are worth it."

"You think Ellen would have been worth it?"

"Absolutely." He gave me a pointed look and then turned and walked away.

I got to my car, dizzy from our conversation. My mind kept going back to the idea that when two dreams conflicted, with no way to reconcile them, you had to figure out which one you wanted more.

Staying in Coleman Creek was one path. I could explore a relationship with Marley, go out for beers with Travis, and continue to ingratiate myself within the town I was growing to love. I wouldn't be able to teach anymore, but I could keep myself busy, find another job until, hopefully, something opened up at the high school.

The other choice, to leave and remain a teacher elsewhere, loomed as an option. There were so many schools in the greater Seattle area. I could live close to my parents and Leo again. Reignite my friendship with Will. Or I could go somewhere completely new. But where did that leave Marley? Had Fred been telling me to stay or to be better than he'd been at handling distance?

I opened Marley's front door and the undecorated Christmas tree filled my vision. When we'd danced next to it this morning, I'd felt that first inkling of reality intruding. Had our long weekend been the beginning of something, or had we just been making memories? Our selfie mocked me from its place on the shelf. Could I risk my entire future, my career, on someone who might not be as invested in me as I was in her?

Three texts came through in rapid succession. Stealing my breath.

OLIVER: Hey dude. Hope you see this. I saw you outside The Place yesterday. I debated calling but wanted to give you space. Texting splits the difference I hope. I still feel awful about the way things went down. I realize we didn't see eye-to-eye on the business but I didn't know about everything else.

OLIVER: I wish you would have told me how bad things were with Cindy. I didn't know you felt so strongly you'd just stop talking to me forever. I figured you just needed time to calm down and then we'd go back to being friends. That's why I bought you out. Changed the name when you asked me to. But then you just split.

OLIVER: I want to connect with you again, brother. I'm sorry business got in the way of that, but I never meant for it to be the end of all of it.

I leaned against the wall, stunned.

What. The. Actual. Hell?

Was he serious? My legs grew shaky as a cold shot of adrenaline coursed through my veins. I felt like everything I knew about those final months going back and forth with him had just been upended. My chest tightened. Could it be possible? Did I have a completely skewed perspective about the situation with The Game Place? I pictured the look on Oliver's face yesterday morning. The undeniable happiness in his expression when he first saw me.

My understanding of what I'd perceived as Oliver's betrayal became cloudier. A new awareness of how quick I was to run away from conflict, how little I trusted people, made me wonder.

Businesses changed, and Oliver and Steve wanted to make money. They'd never wavered in that. Had I been too stubbornly attached to my idea? Too unwilling to compromise? Or so full of self-doubt that I'd taken their pushback too personally?

Had I lost a friend unnecessarily?

Another text moved me from leaning against the wall to actively slumping against it, unsteady on my feet.

OLIVER: I love you man. Always. I hope you'll pick up the phone and call me sometime.

If my friendship with Oliver had been genuine, then my old life in Seattle had been more "real" than I wanted to admit. The problem hadn't been the city I lived in, or the people surrounding me. It was me. My head. Always assuming the worst, or not crediting that other people could truly respect—or love—me. I hadn't been happy because I'd never allowed myself to have faith in any happiness I felt.

Marley hadn't been the first person in my life who'd believed in me. But she was the first person who made me trust that belief. The first person to work their way past my defenses. Just by being herself.

I trusted the desire in her eyes when she ran her hand over my soft belly. Trusted that she'd been proud to stand next to me at my reunion, no matter what happened. Trusted the authenticity of her laughter and the kindness of her smile when she looked at me.

And now that I believed it about her, the possibility of truly having faith in the good intentions of other people blossomed. My parents. Leo. Will. Travis. Perhaps even Oliver.

The door opened and Marley walked in, carrying several Walmart bags.

"I know I already have so many ornaments, but I want to do the trees tonight and I saw these on sale and I couldn't resist—"

Stalking across the room, I cupped her face with my large palms. I dusted my thumbs lovingly across her cheekbones, gazing down before kissing her firmly. She let out a small sound of surprise. After a few moments, I relaxed and ran a hand down along her neck, moving my mouth reverently against hers. Her arms dropped to her sides, and the bags slipped from her fingers onto the floor.

Pulling back, I leveled her with a lava-hot stare.

"What was that for?" she breathed out, bemused and blinking, lips swollen from the press of my mouth.

"You changed my life, Marley."

"What?"

"You changed my life. The way I think about things. It's like I told you the night of my reunion. Everything is different—better—since I met you."

"I'm not sure—"

"And you're not going to stop me from saying it, because I know it's true."

"James—"

"I love you, Marley."

Her mouth opened as my words hung in the air between us. An expression of intense joy flashed momentarily across her face before she schooled her features to a more sedate smile. She closed her eyes and reached for me, leaning her forehead into my chest as she gripped the edges of the coat I still wore. "Thank you for saying that, James. You mean so much to me."

I exhaled, holding her in my arms for a few minutes. Waiting. But she didn't say anything more.

The familiar creep of insecurity invaded me. Did she not feel the same way? Maybe she didn't believe me?

Then I recalled the flicker of happiness she'd tamped down but had been unable to completely conceal. I hadn't imagined it. Something had stopped her from letting my words sink in. Perhaps she needed time, or more evidence of my sincerity. We'd only been an official couple for three days, even if our friendship felt like a lifetime. I recognized my self-doubts for the horrible little joy thieves they'd been my entire life. No more.

Marley had told me a million times she believed in holiday magic. But we didn't need magic.

We only needed what was real. And for the first time, I knew exactly what that was.

Chapter Seventeen

Marley

I slid into the booth across from Kasen the next night, thanking him for ordering me a soda.

"Sorry I'm late," I said, removing my coat to reveal a *Where's Waldo?* sweatshirt, Waldo sporting a Santa hat instead of his usual beanie.

"No problem. Katy came by already. We spent a few minutes catching up while I ordered our drinks. It sounds like Mike got his parents settled and will be home soon. Probably a good thing because she seems stressed dealing with the kids on her own."

"Yeah. They're a handful."

I spoke slowly. I'd been in a fog since James told me he loved me yesterday. Everything since then had been swimmy, like moving in slow motion. But I hadn't canceled my agreed-upon meet-up with Kasen. I wanted to keep things as normal as possible until I could figure out what the heck to do next.

You changed my life, Marley.

I love you.

I thought I'd done a decent job in the moment of not letting on to James that his declaration had caused mild panic. He'd seemed to understand I wasn't prepared to dissect our next steps. As a subject change, he'd given me the surprising information that Oliver had texted, that there might be the possibility of salvaging that friendship. We'd then spent the evening playing with the dogs in the backyard, enjoying the relatively mild weather. I'd pleaded with him to reveal what he'd be doing for the talent show on Friday. We'd discussed our classroom plans for the last week before break. Benign stuff. Just a new couple enjoying a night together talking about their lives—even as I low-key freaked out inside.

The knowledge that James wouldn't have a teaching job come June added an unnerving urgency to the situation.

I looked at Kasen across the table. Talking about something he'd watched on TV last night. With him, the progression of our relationship had been so simple, almost automatic. One minute, we'd been high school sweethearts, the next, we were going to the same college and moving in together.

But then my mom had gotten sick. And he hadn't chosen me.

"Are you okay?" Kasen's concerned voice penetrated my brain.

"Sorry. Yeah. Just a lot on my mind."

He smirked and huffed out a laugh. "Uh huh."

"What's that supposed to mean?"

"Well, since you're bringing it up, when I talked to Katy earlier, she mentioned you were seeing someone, and she might have hinted—and by hinted, I mean drove the point home with a hammer—that you seemed happy, and I ought to not mess things up for you and this other guy."

"James," I said instinctively. "Yes. He's...important to me."

"James," Kasen repeated, drawing out the syllable.

His indecipherable tone pulled me from my head. "What did you have to tell me?" I asked.

"Huh?"

"Last week, when we were here, you said you had something to talk to me about. What was it?"

He shifted uncomfortably in his seat, surveying the room before turning back to me. "I wanted to tell you I was wrong about...well...everything. It wasn't more than a year in Portland after you left before I concluded a big part of the city's charm had been that you were there with me. I missed you. I missed Coleman Creek. But it didn't seem right to reach out at that point. Not without an exit strategy. That's why I left Myerson and struck out on my own." He yanked a paper napkin out of the dispenser and began twisting it. "By the time I woke up determined to move home, maybe beg you to take me back, I got your letter about the funeral. It seemed like a sign to keep trying to make Portland work." He dropped the napkin on the table and stretched his fingers before releasing a thick breath. "But I just can't anymore. I wish it hadn't taken me so much time to realize this is where I belong, but now that I have, I want to come home—as long as it's okay with you. That's what I wanted to ask you. If you really need me to stay away, I will. After what a jerk I was to you, I'd understand."

"Oh, Kasen." I shook my head. It would always sting a little that he hadn't chosen me, but he shouldn't be punished forever. "You weren't a jerk. It hurt, but couples split up. It happens. And I might have overreacted by cutting you so thoroughly out of my life. I told myself it was to make the break-up easier, but a part of me wanted to hurt you, too."

He nodded. "I think we can let it go now, both of us." He cleared his throat. "So, friends?"

"Definitely. And of course you should move home if that's what you want to do. I wish we'd had this conversation sooner."

"Marley, I hope you know I'm not trying to throw a wrench into whatever it is you've got going with this guy—James—but I'm not going to lie. I'd kind of been hoping to shoot my shot here. I remember how it was with us. Solid. Uncomplicated. I could barely even date the women in Portland. Everyone I contacted on the apps was more incomprehensible than the one before. I took for granted how easy it was to be with you. I want to have that again."

The lost puppy expression on his face reminded me so much of the boy I'd fallen in love with at fifteen. "You will, Kasen. I'm sure of it. Just not with me." I spoke gently. Fondly.

"You don't need to say anything else. I'll get over it. Like I said, I'm not trying to mess up your life."

He leaned back in his seat. A part of me felt vindicated by his words. That he regretted not choosing me. It wasn't quite as affirming as if he'd never let me go in the first place, but it was something.

Katy came by with our food. Kasen put a layer of French fries on his cheeseburger before digging in, something I'd watched him do a thousand times.

Being with Kasen again would never be an option. I might not be vibrant enough to hang on to someone like James, but I had enough self-awareness to know I'd never reconcile with my ex. Still, the *idea* of Kasen, the "uncomplicated" relationship we'd had, appealed. Being safe and familiar. It had never been electric with him. But a part of me craved steadiness. The same part that broke into a cold sweat when I thought about how out of control my heart felt with James.

THE CONVERSATION WITH Kasen lingered in my thoughts as I paced my living room the next evening. James had texted to tell me he was staying at his place tonight, his reason being some mysterious preparations he needed to make for the talent show. Unwrapped presents mocked me from the dining table, and sugar cookie ingredients sat out on the kitchen counter. But my restless mind struggled to focus.

Oscar began a noisy growl-bark combo, his method of letting me know someone was walking up to the front door. The scratchy notes of "Rockin' Around the Christmas Tree" rang out as the visitor stepped onto the HO-HO-HO doormat.

I hadn't been expecting anyone, but finding Mrs. Allen at the door didn't surprise me. I waved her inside, out of the stinging wind.

"It's cold tonight," she said, shivering as she unwrapped a ginormous wool scarf from her neck. "I know it's five days away, but maybe we'll get a white Christmas."

"That would be a treat, as long as it doesn't block the roads. Maureen and Miranda are driving out this weekend."

"I'm glad to hear that. Please tell them I said hello." Mrs. Allen lifted the grocery tote she'd been carrying. "I came by to bring you your gift. I have to leave early in the morning to head to my daughter's place in Boise. She's gone into labor."

"Oh, wow. That's early, right?"

"About three weeks. But it should be okay. With her first, it was four."

"Bummer that you'll miss the talent show."

"Yes. But the A/V Club will film it. I am certainly sad to be missing Mr. Wymack's performance." Her eyes lit with mischief and I gave her a light smack on the shoulder.

"Do you know what he's doing?"

"I might."

"Tell me!"

"Would you believe me if I said it was juggling?"

"Nope."

"Well, too bad, because my lips are sealed. Anyway, I'll watch the video when I get back. I might even pop onto YouTube to check it out. Something tells me it'll be there."

Okay, now that was interesting as heck. "Can you give me a hint?"

"Not even a tiny one. And I'm not gonna budge, so just drop it." She smiled at my misery as I pouted. "Like I said, I have your gift."

"Fine. Keep your secrets. I can wait until Friday. And I have your gift, too. Let me go grab it from the bedroom."

I came back with the wrapped box containing the smoked salmon and chocolates I'd purchased in Seattle, along with a set of Kraken potholders I knew she'd like. "Don't open it until Christmas."

"You got it," she replied, handing me a wrapped box that looked just big enough for a sweater, or maybe a hat and gloves. "Same rules apply to you."

"Do you want coffee?"

"That would be lovely, Marley. It's crazy how the older I get, the more I feel it. Maybe all those old folks are onto something retiring in Florida or Arizona."

I laughed. "You would hate both those places."

"I know. What is it about Coleman Creek?"

"Exactly."

I went into the kitchen to start the coffee and came out to find Mrs. Allen standing in front of the bookshelf, studying the picture of my mom and dad from the Christmas party so long ago.

"Did you know I went to high school with Alice? We were pretty good friends in our early twenties, before the burdens of raising young families took over, as they do."

"I remember. She mentioned it when you were my teacher."

"She'd be proud of you."

"I hope so."

"And she'd like James."

I didn't reply, merely gave her a watery smile.

"People thought Alice and Frank were a strange idea, too." She picked up the frame to hold the picture closer, examining it. "Not that you and James together is strange. Mr. Wymack is just very different from most folks around here, and you're not exactly known for stepping outside your comfort zone."

"Yeah, I'm kind of known for being boring." I tried to laugh a little, but Mrs. Allen wasn't having it.

"You are *not* boring. Just because you're honest and can take pleasure in the little things. Not everyone needs to jump out of a proverbial airplane to feel alive. I just worry you think that means you're obligated to end up with someone more—"

"Like Kasen?"

She winced. "I didn't say it. But James is not like Kasen, is he?"

"No, he's not." I smiled wider, trying to picture Kasen with a nose ring or blasting Radiohead from his truck instead of country. Nope. Couldn't even imagine it.

"That's why I think Alice would approve. She was a lot like you. Really happy to simply spend time with family and friends. She dated a lot in high school, could have had her pick of Coleman's men, honestly. But then she met your dad, and that was it. A reason to step off her usual path and take a risk."

"You remember my parents together?"

I had so many memories and had heard lots of stories about my mom. But my dad remained a bit of a mystery. Mom hadn't spoken of him too often, just enough so we'd understood our parents had been blissfully in love. She'd never dated after he'd passed away, loving Frank Davis until the day she died.

"I remember them," Mrs. Allen answered. "They were incredibly happy. The kind of couple who held hands and checked in on each other, always sneaking into dark corners at parties. And once the town got over the scandal of him being twenty-five years older, everyone recognized their relationship for what it was. True love. They were 'hashtag couple goals,' as the students would say."

I chuckled. "I wish I could remember him more."

"Me too."

I retreated to the kitchen to grab the coffee, thinking about that photo of my parents.

Even if Mrs. Allen was correct about it being true love, had it been worth it? My mom had had my dad for fifteen years, then spent the rest of her life alone. Did she ever regret not making a different, safer choice? One that could have provided decades more of—if not explosive love—at least companionship. I hugged my arms around myself, snuggling into my mother's "Deck the Halls" musical notes sweater, wishing she was here so I could ask.

The ache of missing her flared.

James had captivated me from the beginning, but I had insisted to my heart it was only an inevitable infatuation with the fascinating new man in town. Then an effortless friendship I could easily manage. When he'd agreed to help me move my mom's things, and when I'd stood by him at the reunion, I'd convinced myself we could support each other without developing a deeper attachment. And even though being with him in bed had been mind-blowing, I still hoped I'd held myself apart enough to protect my heart. But my ability to maintain this conviction was slipping away a little more each day.

Mrs. Allen was correct that I'd diverted from my usual path because someone extraordinary enough to warrant doing so had come into my life. But James belonged to an uncertain future. Letting myself fall in love with him would mean giving up control, losing the ability to narrate my story.

Chapter Eighteen

James

Marley held herself at a distance. She said all the right things, but I could feel her pulling away.

I understood her well enough to know that the lack of a clear path forward in our relationship disturbed her. She was aware of my history of walking away from difficult situations. Ending our attachment because I'd lost my job provided certainty, but I didn't believe for a minute it was what she wanted. I wished I had the words to convince her we could make this work.

Hopefully, my concept for the talent show would do the trick. I'd run my idea by Mrs. Allen after the last bell. She'd dropped by my classroom to inform me she would be leaving early tomorrow for the birth of her grandchild. Coincidentally, she planned to stop in at Marley's that evening to bring her a Christmas present.

Mrs. Allen had enthusiastically endorsed my plan and agreed to be part of it, lamenting that she wouldn't be there on the big night. I'd given her more details, and she'd addressed my worries about Marley's hesitance.

"It's never easy at the beginning of relationships, James. Especially when you've been friends for a while. And this budget nonsense just adds to the pressure. But I'm confident you and Marley will work it out."

"That's pretty much all I want at this point."

"Then tell her. But don't be surprised if she fights you on it," she cautioned. "Marley likes things orderly. She likes to be in control."

I snorted. "You don't say?"

Guffawing, she continued, "She comes by it honestly. She's great at making things okay for other people and terrible at demanding more for herself."

"I think I understand."

"Loving you gives you the power to hurt her. After her mom—and Kasen—She might not be ready for that just yet."

"For the first time in my life, I trust how I feel. I can be patient."

"That's beautiful, James."

I reached an arm out to Mrs. Allen. "I know this isn't very professional, but can I give you a hug?"

She came to me. "I'd be sad if you didn't." I engulfed her in my arms, imbibing how teeny she actually was. "Good lord, James. I've always wanted to know what it would be like to get a bear hug from an actual grizzly."

"Roar," I deadpanned, feeling large and okay.

TO PROVE TO MYSELF that I'd turned over a new leaf, that not every relationship in my life had to be crippled by doubt, I called Oliver that night.

He picked up on the second ring. "James."

"Uh...hey."

The silence hung heavy on the line. Apparently, my resolve didn't extend beyond an awkward hello.

Finally, Oliver said, "So, I'm guessing you got my texts."

"Yeah." I exhaled heavily, leaning against the cracked surface of my kitchen counter. Bambi peeked up from where he'd been snoozing on the couch and trotted over to me, nuzzling his snout into my hand. "Good boy."

"*Good boy*? Either you called me after two years with the most bizarre opener ever, or you still have Bambi?"

I huffed. "It's the dog."

"Aww. I miss that pooch. Best doggo ever."

My mind recalled the royal blue dog bed where Bambi had spent his days as the unofficial mascot for The Game Place. I ran my fingers between his ears, and he turned around to coax me into scratching his rump. "He still is."

Another loaded silence rose between us.

Oliver broke the stalemate. "I'm guessing you didn't call me to talk about Bambi."

I gave myself a mental kick in the ass. "No. Sorry. I didn't really mean to call and then go mute. This is...maybe a little harder than I thought."

"I get it."

"After Sunday, when I saw you, and then your texts, I needed to get some...clarity."

"Okay?"

"It's only been recently, like literally the past few weeks, that I've been thinking a lot about how some of the shit that happened when I was a kid might have affected how I perceive things."

"With the business?" Oliver asked.

"Yes. Well, sort of. What I mean is that I'm realizing how quick I am to assume the worst about what other people think."

I could practically hear Oliver scratching his head across the line. "James, I really want to understand, but I'm gonna need you to help me connect the dots here."

I paused. "Basically, what it comes down to is that I'm at a place in my life where I'm finally starting to recognize how much I've held myself away from other people. There are reasons, of course. Stuff I'm probably not going to work out until I get my ass to the comfy end of a therapist's couch. But the bottom line is—until recently—I've had trouble believing anyone could truly like me. Not deep down."

"Shit. That's heavy, James." There was silence on Oliver's end before he said, "It tracks, though. I remember freshman year. It took a while to get to know you."

I thought of Oliver's friendly offers to sit with him in the student cafeteria or have coffee together off campus. I'd kept saying no, and he'd never taken offense, had just kept the offers coming until one day I'd given in. He'd been the first friend I'd made since Will.

"That's true. But meeting you and the rest of our crew in college helped."

"So, let me see if I have this straight. You thought me wanting to change the business meant I didn't like you?"

"It's difficult to say. I just know that when you changed your mind and turned our family game place into a gamer bar, it felt like you were stabbing me in the back. And I went shields up, because that's how I roll."

"Until now?"

"Yes. Until now. I'm working on it."

"Ah, dude. Changing things...was just business. Not personal. The first concept didn't make money the way the bar does. And

Steve was up my ass because he thought we were giving you too much leash. Especially after we instituted that code of conduct you insisted on, even if it resulted in fewer assholes coming in. He would have pulled the plug a lot sooner, but I was trying to make it work the way I knew you wanted it to."

"Because we were friends."

"Yeah. And I knew it meant a lot to you. I mean, you never offered the details, but I read between the lines that stuff in your past went tits up, and the puzzle concept was super important to you for sentimental reasons. But in the end, I agreed with Steve. We were barely treading water."

"Cindy told me she talked to you, that you tried to convince her to get me to change my mind."

"Well, that is...inaccurate." He sounded pissed. "After you left, and wouldn't take my calls, I'd hoped Cindy could help you see that I never meant to end our friendship. I suspected she wasn't delivering the message when she came in trying to strategize with me to get you to give up the teaching. I told her I'd never do that. You'd been slapped around enough by what went down, and in the end, I figured I owed it to you to respect your wishes. I stopped calling."

"It hurt me. But not because the business ended. Because I thought my best friend had betrayed me. Turned his back on me. That I'd never really known you."

"It was just business, James. I never wanted to stop being your friend."

"I think I understand that...now."

Oliver and I continued talking. I wasn't delusional that we'd fix our issues overnight, but the friendship we'd had since college was worth preserving. And so, even though I still had a lot to do to prepare for my performance Friday, we spent fifteen minutes catching up.

I didn't want to get my hopes up too high, but it felt like we were on the way to repairing our bond. And in the end, I was happier teaching than I'd ever been running The Game Place, so things had worked out the way they were supposed to.

I SPENT THE NEXT afternoon at my apartment putting the finishing touches on my talent show plan, then went to Marley's for dinner. I needed to reassure myself we were okay. She'd been so in her own head the past few days.

She had two plates of pasta ready when I arrived. The dogs nipped playfully at one another in the corner as we sat down at the table.

"Does Oscar seem weird to you? He's been doing that for the past few days."

I looked over to see Marley's dog sprawled on his back. He rubbed against the living room carpet, satisfied sounds emanating as he mouthed the air. Bambi stood sedately next to him, head tilted as though to say, *will you look at this guy?*

"I think he's fine. You just put up a gigantic, foresty-smelling tree in his living room, not to mention this whole place has smelled like sugar and cinnamon since Monday. He's just living his best life, enjoying all the fresh scents." Oscar startled, bolted upright, then started furiously licking his crotch. I arched an eyebrow as Marley giggled. "See, what'd I tell you—normal dog."

"The cookie smell has been overwhelming," she agreed. "I'm trying to get ahead for the last weekend of the tree lot. All those selfie-takers have been clearing out the treats for sale."

"Good problem to have though."

"True." She swallowed a big bite before she asked, "So what have you been up to the past few days, James? You've been super cagey about this whole talent show performance. I'm mentally preparing myself to either be blown away or experience a serious case of secondhand embarrassment."

I laughed. "Ouch. I sincerely hope the former. Also, I'm not telling."

Her playful smile warmed my heart. This was the woman I loved. The one I wanted to keep. She just had to let me.

"Fine. I guess I can wait until tomorrow."

I felt butterflies—more like angry hornets—in my stomach as I thought about the preparations I'd made over the past few days. Marley was correct that abject embarrassment was a distinct possibility. I changed the subject.

"So...I called Oliver yesterday."

She dropped her fork. "What? How have you been here half an hour and you're just now mentioning this?"

"I dunno. It almost doesn't feel real, but, yeah, we talked."

"Wow. When you mentioned he sent those texts, I didn't realize you were planning on reaching out."

"It was a spur-of-the-moment decision. Something Mrs. Allen said inspired me."

"Ah. That's sweet. She's a good egg." Marley seemed to have recovered, dabbing her mouth with a napkin before inquiring, "So how did it go, with Oliver?"

"Good, I think. As it turns out, I may have been a little harsh with him. It sounds like I probably could have salvaged the friendship. I just wasn't ready to hear him then. I'm not sure where we'll end up, but he was my friend for a long time. It's nice to imagine not ending all that history on such a sour note."

"That's awesome, James." She coughed and gazed away absently.

"Are you okay?"

"Yeah." She shook her head and offered a self-effacing smile. "I'm just thinking it's funny how you and I sort of had the same conversation the past few days."

"What do you mean?"

"Well, I had dinner with Kasen the other night—you remember?" Marley had given me the heads up about having dinner with her ex. I had been trying not to dwell on it, not wanting to pry. I didn't want Marley to think I didn't trust her.

"Um hmm. Everything went okay?"

"We might take a pass at being friends. I want to be honest with you. He did sort of insinuate he'd be open to getting back together, but I made it clear that's not an option, and he was respectful of that."

I blanched. "I'm not sure how I feel about you guys being friends if he secretly wants more."

"Don't worry. As much as it flatters me he said that, he's not burning with desire or unrequited love or anything. He said he likes that I'm familiar and steady. Not exactly a passionate declaration."

"Alright. If you trust him and say he's a good guy, I believe you." I nodded slowly.

"He is a good guy. But talking to Kasen brought up some stuff. That's what I meant when I said we'd had the same conversation. You were harsh with Oliver. I'm realizing that I might have been a little too hard on Kasen. In the end."

I directed a dubious expression her way. "You just did what you had to do during a tough breakup."

"Maybe. That's the story I've been telling myself all these years. But I could have given a little ground and responded to a text. I didn't need to ban him from my mother's funeral. I mean, I made him feel unwelcome in the town where his parents live. Even though I told myself I was doing it to cope with the break-up, deep down, I know at least a part of me meant it to punish him. And it worked."

"Well, I don't think you should be too hard on yourself. He left you when your mom got sick. No one can blame you for wanting to twist the knife a little."

She chortled, then her face turned down in a frown. "Are you alright?" I asked, concerned.

"I was just thinking that if you're getting along with Oliver, it's one more thing to draw you back to Seattle."

"What?"

"I mean, you have your family—who clearly miss you—and now you might have Oliver. And there was that guy Will at the reunion. Seems like he'd like to be friends again."

"So?"

She hmphed. "So—the universe keeps reminding you that you have so much waiting for you there."

My stomach churned at her vague insinuation. "Right," I drawled out. "Guess I'll have a lot of folks to see when I visit."

"But don't you think it's something you should at least consider?"

"Consider what?"

"Moving back, obviously."

"I'm sorry...what?" I somehow kept my boiling gut in check. "Why would you say that?" I attempted to snag her gaze, but she kept her eyes decidedly on her lap. "Marley, you're not even pretending not to push me away. Why? My life is here, in Coleman Creek. We are *together*, right? Where in this scenario does me living in Seattle make any sense?"

"Please don't be upset, James. This is coming out all wrong." She scrubbed a hand across her face and pinched the bridge of her nose. "I just want you to know I understand why you'd need to move on. You shouldn't have to stay here, not being able to do the job you love."

"Move on? Am I in *The Twilight Zone*? Did we break up while I was sleeping or something?"

She made a pfft noise. "You're not going to stay here for me."

"Why the hell not?" My voice raised an octave at her casual assumption that I'd leave. But I also knew—to the core of my being—that this had nothing to do with her not wanting me. I tried a different tack, lowering my voice to a plea. "Marley, I've never fit with anyone the way I fit with you. And that's besides the fact that I meant what I said. I fucking love you. Love. You."

"But for how long, James? How long until you get tired of not being a teacher, of living in a tiny town where everyone knows everyone's business and there's nothing to do but go bowling and hang out at the same bar night after night?"

"Don't do this. Don't push me away. I meant what I said. Coleman Creek is home now, and I'm not planning on leaving. We can be together."

"I'm sure you think that. And it's a nice fantasy. I love that you want me. That you're the sexiest man I've ever met and you like me back—"

"I love you."

"That you love me, then. Okay." She exhaled deeply. "But I also think you're still reeling from what Leo said, that you run away from things. And I don't want you to stay here and make me fall in love with you, just to prove you've changed."

I flinched, my lips flattening into a tight line. "It feels like we're talking in circles, Marley. You keep throwing out more reasons I should leave. So, I guess I need to ask. Do you even want me to stay?"

When we'd met, Marley had thought I was just some cool guy who liked to do puzzles and could French braid his own hair. Now she knew I'd been a scared, bullied kid who'd grown into an uncommunicative, conflict-avoiding adult. A real prize. I knew she liked me, but maybe she wasn't up for all that long term.

"Don't make me ask you to stay, James." She leaned back in her chair and rested her forehead in her hands before whispering down to the table, "I've been okay on my own. Don't make me hope for more."

She peered up, the truth within her glassy eyes all the response I needed.

We stared at each other for a long moment. Even the dogs stayed quiet as the silence picked apart all the secrets between us. But I had my answer. *Throw all the grenades you want, Marley. I'm dodging them this time, not retreating.*

"How about we get started frosting those cookies?" I transitioned awkwardly.

"I'd like that." She smiled. "To be honest, it's four days until Christmas. I'd love to just enjoy being together until then. Decisions can wait until...after."

I let that predictable comment slide. She could keep pretending I hadn't already decided. Normally, I loved how controlled and calm she was in her approach to everything. Unless she was about to control us both right into unhappiness.

There was a lot more riding on the next day than I'd imagined even an hour ago.

And if I really wanted to make it count, I needed to get a hold of a few more people. Including Kasen.

THE DAY OF THE talent show dawned brightly. I hadn't slept at Marley's the night before. After we'd frosted the cookies, I'd left to put the finishing touches on my performance. I'd worked into the early morning hours and, fingers crossed, it was ready.

But before the show that night, I'd have to get through the gauntlet of the school day. Which meant the good intentions of both my colleagues and the students.

By now, everyone possessed the two most pertinent facts—Marley and I were together, and I wouldn't have a job at Coleman Creek High come June. While preparing for the talent show, I'd interacted with a lot of people, and they all seemed to have an opinion about what I should do next.

Unsurprisingly, no one advocated I leave Marley.

No one except Marley, of course.

Mr. Bailey dropped by my classroom in between first and second periods. He hmphed at the Christmas tree scrunchie—from Marley's collection—holding my hair in place, then stood across from my desk, arms folded.

"Everything okay, Fred?" I asked.

"I didn't tell you about Ellen just to hear myself talk, young man. It was my way of reminding you to do the right thing."

Jeez. Sir, yes sir, I thought. But before I could reply, he turned on his heel and walked out of my classroom. "Good talk," I whispered into the empty air.

Diane Montoya and Nan Tourman sat next to each other in my second period class.

"I really hope you figure it out with Ms. Davis," Diane offered, twirling her pencil like a baton. "It's, like, tragic how you just got together and then this happened."

"Yeah," Nan agreed. "You guys are so cute. Plus, Ms. Davis is the best. She's been my favorite teacher since ninth."

I sighed. "First, it is completely inappropriate for you two to speculate about the personal lives of teachers. Full stop. But also, yes, Ms. Davis is the best." I walked over to the whiteboard in an attempt to shut down the conversation. "Let's finish up our discussion on The Reformation. Since you're about to go on break for two weeks."

They weren't having it.

"Seriously," Diane said. "We all know you won't be back at school next year. We're super bummed about that. Nan got the student council to write a protest letter, but that probably won't do much." She switched from twirling her pencil to chewing on the eraser. "What are you going to do? It's hard to picture you working at the plant up the highway like my dad and brother. Pretty sure they'd make you take your nose ring out."

"He's going to let Ms. Davis be his sugar mama!" Gary Spinner piped up from the back row, causing his classmates to chuckle.

I turned around to glare at him. "Children—and I say that with emphasis because you all are certainly acting your age right now—you need to back off. Ms. Davis and I will figure things out on our own. Right now, I'm staying focused on not embarrassing myself at the talent show tonight, and you all need to be focusing on Martin Luther."

They groaned but relented. And even though I made them talk about the politics of sixteenth century Europe for a few minutes, I eventually put on *Spartacus*, because it was the last day before break, and I wasn't a total monster.

Travis came in during my passing period with coffee. I hadn't dared go into the teachers' lounge. By necessity, several of my colleagues were aware of my plan for the talent show. And while I appreciated their discretion in not spilling the beans to Marley, they seemed to have interpreted this as an open invitation to comment on the situation.

"Nervous about tonight?" Travis asked.

"Hell, yes. Marley is not making it easy on me." He nodded thoughtfully as I relayed some of the conversation Marley and I had had the previous evening. "Thanks for giving me Kasen's number, too."

"No problem. But I've gotta be honest. I'm super curious what you needed it for."

I groaned, tugging the scrunchie from my hair. "Do you mind if I don't answer that? At least for now. I'm already halfway ill over the idea that I could end up looking like a total chump tonight." Marley had pulled away when I'd told her I loved her, pushed even harder when we'd spoken yesterday. Tonight could be the reason she shoved me out of her life for good. "Putting myself out there is kind of new for me."

Travis snorted. "Well, you certainly are doing that in a major way."

"If you could have heard Marley talking last night, you'd understand. It's going to take something big to convince her."

"I'm glad you're in this. She really deserves someone to fight for her."

"I know."

"Sometimes, I'm not entirely sure you do. I'll bet she's told you a bit about coming back five years ago, taking care of her mom, but I'm guessing she put a Marley-colored spin on things."

"What does that mean?"

"I mean, it was bad. She came back and had to put up with months of everyone in town asking where Kasen was, their shocked faces when she explained they'd broken up." Travis leaned his hip against a bookshelf. "I didn't know Marley very well as kids. I'm closer in age with her sister Maureen. But I knew enough to know that everyone expected her and Kasen to last. Before you got here, we were the two youngest teachers for the longest, so now and then we'd chat. Everything was so hard for her. Alice dying was one piece—the biggest piece, of course—but having Kasen stay in Portland added this extra layer of something. I dunno. It was almost like she was ashamed that he broke up with her."

"He was such an idiot to let her go."

"Maybe. Probably. Or it's also possible they weren't meant to go the distance. I think she fits better with you. You give her this weird extra sparkle she never had before. It scares the shit out of her, because she spent her whole life thinking she'd end up with someone like Kasen. Someone much less sparkly."

I grinned. Travis wasn't telling me anything I didn't already know. Diagnosing the root of Marley's behavior wasn't the puzzle that needed solving. "How do I get her to surrender to the uncertainty? To trust that I want her? She's so stubborn."

The lilting chimes of my phone ringing saved Travis from having to reply. I looked down at the caller ID. Kasen.

"I have to take this," I said. He nodded as he walked back out, flicking the ornaments on my gigantic second-place Christmas tree on his way into the hall.

Chapter Nineteen

Marley

I came home from work to find Maureen and Miranda hanging out in the living room, picking up photos and decorations and exchanging stories.

"What are you doing here?" I asked, dropping my purse on the counter before rushing over to hug them both. "I thought you weren't coming until Sunday."

"Miranda finished her finals yesterday and flew in last night. Abel agreed to cover me at the store in exchange for the next few weekends. So we came early," Maureen answered.

"We thought we'd check out the talent show tonight," Miranda said, smirking as Maureen smacked her on the shoulder.

It made sense they'd want to attend. Half the town went to the show. We'd all grown up going every year, so the nostalgia factor remained strong.

"Awesome," I said. "And I'm glad you're here because James is actually in the show tonight. Remember, I told you how he lost that bet to me?" I chuckled. "He won't tell me what he's doing—keeps threatening elaborate juggling—but I'm betting it'll be something more interesting."

Maureen and Miranda exchanged glances.

"Um, sure. It'll be great to see him," Maureen said.

"Yeah, we're definitely looking forward to watching James perform." Miranda grinned hugely and Maureen smacked her on the shoulder again. "Ouch. What was that for?"

"You know."

"What? I can't be stoked to see Marley's boyfriend?" Miranda switched her attention to me. "I'm really looking forward to meeting him, Marls. He sounds like a great guy."

My lips flattened. "I've told you it's just casual. Not really a boyfriend thing. I'm happy to introduce you, but you don't need to get all excited."

Miranda rolled her eyes. Maureen made a pained noise before saying, "Didn't we just talk about this at the restaurant last weekend? You don't need to downplay your feelings, Marley."

"I'm not."

"Sure you're not. Just like at Thanksgiving when you told us you guys were just friends," Miranda said.

"That's not fair. I didn't know that things were going to...develop...between us."

My sisters scoffed in unison.

"It doesn't even matter because he doesn't have a teaching job here next year," I insisted.

"So?" Maureen looked at me with genuine confusion.

"Obviously, it means we can't stay together."

"Does James have some rare condition that prevents him from working at any job other than teaching?"

I scowled at her. "Of course he *could* do something else. But he's magical in the classroom, like he was born to it. He loves being a teacher."

"Yeah?" This time it was Miranda who spoke up, raising her perfectly threaded eyebrow at me. "Well, it may turn out that he loves something else more."

"You can't just keep protecting yourself, little sister. You've got to let it go and take a chance sometimes," Maureen said.

"I've taken the chance on James. We're together now. I'm enjoying every moment we have for as long as it lasts."

"You realize you sound ridiculous, right?" Miranda straightened her shoulders as she eyed me pointedly. "Because you keep talking like things between the two of you are going to end any moment. That's not taking a chance. That's hedging your bets."

Maureen walked over to the picture of our parents at the Christmas party. "I know it's been rough for you these past few years. You've always been a planner. You've never had Miranda's wanderlust or my obsessive need to prove myself at work. But you've made a mistake in somehow equating that with being boring or undesirable. And when bad stuff happens, that's the lens you use to logic it away."

I suddenly wished very much that my sisters hadn't arrived early. "What are you getting at, Maureen?"

"When Kasen broke up with you, it was a shitty thing to go through. But you interpreted that as a *you* problem. Like, you weren't exciting enough or good enough to make him want to stay. I knew the breakup hurt you. We all did. But you didn't want to discuss it. You came home and took care of Mom. You never got emotional about Kasen."

"Except for the part where I refused to speak to him and didn't answer any of his texts."

"That's just what you do. You go into robot mode. You did it the whole time Mom was sick. In order to take care of her without falling apart."

I looked over at Miranda. By her expression, she was in firm agreement with Maureen. My hackles rose. "Don't accuse me of being a robot. It's not like I didn't care. I have feelings, you know. Sometimes I cried all day!"

"I don't doubt it. I'm just trying to get you to see the pattern. You're more comfortable with a script. It was like you were a star student going through the five stages of grief. Textbook-perfect."

"Why are you ragging on me for coping with our mother's death? Would it have been better if I had been too overwrought to speak to the mortuary people like you were? Or if I'd stayed drunk for a week like Miranda?"

"Hey!" Miranda cried.

At the distraught look on her face, I softened. "I'm not judging you, baby sis. I know we all did what we had to do when Mom passed."

Maureen wasn't done. "I'm not ragging on you. We are so grateful you stepped in back then. I just don't want you to give up something great. Because I've never seen you light up more than when you talk about James. And I know you don't like messy, jumping in without a script or pre-ordained outcome. But I don't want you to have this regret." She put a comforting arm around my waist, plastering me to her side.

"What do you want me to do?" I mumbled into her shoulder.

"I want you to be damn sure before you shove him away. Fighting for him is an option. Recognizing that he's fighting for you is another." Maureen straightened. "I know it's hard for you to demand anything for yourself. So, I'm asking plainly, do you want James to stay?"

The question was so reminiscent of the one James had asked last night, almost verbatim. Except this time, I had an answer.

"Yes."

"Then tell him. Be with him."

My heart leaped at the prospect, while also clenching in absolute terror.

"What if we can't make it work?"

"I doubt that will happen, but if it does, we'll be here. With rum-laced eggnog and whatever else you need. And it'll be okay even if you cry and scream and don't handle everything perfectly. No matter what happens, you'll be alright. Even if James does break your heart, he won't break *you*. I promise. And you'll be better for having taken a chance."

I loved my sisters so much. "I think I understand. I want to."

"But Marley?" Miranda piped in.

"Hmm?"

"Let's go watch James juggle first."

Chapter Twenty

James

By six thirty, it was standing room only in the school's massive auditorium. When Marley and I had planned the scavenger hunt back in October, she'd told me the story of how one of the town's wealthier citizens had gifted the money to the district to build it thirty years ago. Gordon Mumford had loved attending the talent show when it had been a cramped affair in the gym. He'd gone every year, even after his own kids graduated, and had wanted to ensure there was a space large enough where everyone who wanted to go could do so.

Knowing that bit of history gave me courage. I was learning about this town. Becoming a part of it. I might be the only guy over the age of twenty-five who wore skinny jeans, and I would definitely need to tone down the cursing, but I felt like I belonged here.

Principal Nadal came to the microphone. "Please disengage from your current conversations and take your seats. We are delighted to commence our entertainment and ask that you give our performers the respectful attention they deserve."

The audience quieted and faced the front of the room in cheerful unison.

Mr. Bailey stood onstage in a Santa hat and snowflake sweatshirt. That image had not been on my Coleman Creek Bingo card, but I didn't hate it. The background music for "Snow" came through the speakers and he walked up to the microphone, body stiff and unyielding. A moment later, his arms rose, and he projected the first notes of the song into the audience.

Good lord.

While I'd heard that Mr. Bailey always performed in the show, everyone had failed to mention that the man possessed the voice of an angel. An angel that sounded like Christmas—like Bing Crosby and Nat King Cole and Elvis and Andy Williams all rolled into one. The song traditionally had a four-part harmony, but he somehow sang his own version in a low baritone that captured both the joy and the yearning in the melody.

When he finished, he removed the Santa hat—glaring at it as though wondering how it had landed on his head—and made a stilted bow in the general direction of the packed seats. Applause erupted from the crowd.

Hopefully, his phenomenal opening number boded well for the rest of the acts. I'd previously spoken to Principal Nadal about going toward the end of the program. He'd informed me less than an hour ago that my performance would actually close the show.

Winking at me, he'd added, "I am truly sorry, Mr. Wymack, about the budget. You have been a positive and welcome addition to our teaching community. This feels like the least I can do to thank you. And even though what you have orchestrated is rather unorthodox, especially with students in attendance, what better time to believe in the power of love than Christmas? I'll be keeping my fingers crossed that you get your holiday wish."

Jeez. Thanks man. No pressure or anything. But he had a point about the power of the season. I'd take all the Christmas mojo I could get.

I pulled my phone out of my pocket and glanced at it for the millionth time that evening. Still nothing from Kasen. I'd been hoping he'd come through, but I supposed it had been a long shot. No matter. I felt satisfied with what I'd come up with. Kasen would have been a cherry on the sundae, but I understood.

Fel Torres and some guys from the football team were doing what looked like a choreographed gymnastics routine to Chuck Berry's "Run Rudolph Run." It was mainly an opportunity for them to show off their ability to do flips and one-armed push-ups in unison. Still, the crowd seemed into it. A loud chorus of cheers followed them as they came off the stage.

Fel caught my gaze as he exited the side stairwell, upnodding me. I had to admit he'd been cool to Daniel since the tree lot incident, and not just because Nan had taken the younger teen under her wing. I chose to believe Fel had listened to at least some of what I'd said to him and taken it to heart. It was good to realize that even though my time at Coleman Creek would be short, I'd been able to make some small impact. Travis had already assured me he'd be the advisor for the student groups I'd sponsored this year—D&D Club was up to twenty members—and I knew Marley would keep an eye on Daniel and some of the other struggling students.

I looked out into the audience from behind the curtain and saw Marley sitting near the front with her sisters. Thank goodness Maureen and I had exchanged phone numbers last weekend. Clearly, she'd gotten my text from a few hours ago because they were in the perfect position for viewing the projector screen. I pulled out my phone to message her.

ME: I see where you are sitting. Glad that worked out *thumbs up emoji*

MAUREEN: I had to push some teenagers out of the way, so you better make it worth the trouble.

ME: That's the plan.

MAUREEN: *red heart emoji*

My attention drew back to the stage. I startled at seeing Daniel sitting on a stool, holding an acoustic guitar. Nan, Penny, and a few of the other senior girls, wearing short dresses with candy canes on them, made a horseshoe shape around him. He glanced back nervously at Nan.

She whispered to him, "You're so talented. They'll love it."

Daniel nodded and turned back toward the crowd. Steeling himself, he lifted the guitar to his knee and began playing a gorgeous medley of classic carols. The familiar notes of "Greensleeves" were followed by those of "Good King Wenceslas," and then "God Rest Ye Merry Gentlemen." During the songs, Nan and her friends occasionally harmonized with "oohs" and "mmms," but it was Daniel's elegant playing that caused a hush to fall over the crowd. Shockingly, he played almost the entire piece with his eyes shut, dealing with his obvious nerves by surrendering to the music.

When he was done, he pulled the stool to the side while the girls stayed on stage and did a dance routine to Mariah Carey's "All I Want for Christmas is You." Not an unexpected choice, but still enjoyable. Especially with Daniel adding to the soundtrack with his guitar from stage right.

"That number turned out great," I complimented them as they left the stage.

Nan stopped to tell me, "I overheard Daniel playing in the music room one day. I didn't know he was so amazing on the guitar. No one did. I'm just glad I convinced him." She glanced over to where Daniel cautiously accepted a fist bump from one of the other students. "I think he'll be okay here, after I graduate."

"I think so too. Hey, Nan—"

"Yeah, Mr. Wymack?"

"I've enjoyed being your teacher. You're a good egg."

She laughed. "That's what Ms. Davis always says."

"So she does."

Her smile positively glowed. "Good luck tonight, Mr. Wymack."

AN HOUR LATER, it was go time. The other performances had gone well and the audience still seemed engaged. There would be a big post-show party in the gym following the event, and I hoped I'd be in a celebratory mood.

I peeked out into the crowd and caught Katy's gaze—The Landslide had shut down for the show tonight—and she gave me a thumbs up. My eyes drifted to the darkened section at the back of the auditorium. It seemed more packed compared to when the show had begun. A spotlight circled and I saw the crowd clearly for a moment. *Wait. What the hell? That almost looked like...* The light dipped around the room again, and... *It had to be a trick of the eye, right?*

I pulled out my phone.

ME: Are you here? In Coleman Creek?

No reply. But I couldn't stop to worry about it. I had to keep my head in the game.

My fingers tingled as I smoothed out the lapels on the red velvet suit I'd ordered for the occasion. I'd thought about adding a bow tie, but in the end decided on a white button-down with the top three buttons undone. I knew Marley appreciated my furry chest, and frankly, I'd take all the help I could get. My hair hung full around my shoulders, the same way I'd worn it to the reunion.

Once I reached center stage, I took the microphone out of the stand to hold. I needed to project confidence, and bending down to the mic would not be a good look. Since I didn't carry juggling balls or an instrument, it had to be apparent to Marley by this point that I'd be singing.

I gripped the mic tightly, my limbs almost numb with anticipation.

Taking a deep breath, I pointed a finger at Travis, his signal to start the slideshow on the giant projection screen behind me. A moment later, the first piano notes of Kelly Clarkson's "Underneath the Tree" rang out across the auditorium, and at the appropriate place, I began to sing.

I'd chosen the song for its lyrics, but a beefy six-foot-three man singing an upbeat soprano pop song was objectively attention grabbing. I imagined every pair of eyes in the room locked on the stage. Not that it mattered. As far as I was concerned, I had an audience of exactly one.

A trained vocalist I was not. Even my best efforts sounded only a step above drunk karaoke. But I carried on despite the burn of embarrassment, reminding myself it didn't matter whether I completely mucked up the high notes. The only thing of true concern was the crowd pointing at the slideshow behind me.

I kept glancing in Marley's direction. She was close enough that I could see her clearly. When I'd begun, she'd appeared to be stifling laughter—likely as horrified by my warbling as the rest of the crowd—but I saw her features shift as she noted the images flashing on the screen.

At first, they were just pictures of me around Coleman Creek. I'd taken selfies at the tree lot and the dog park, multiple locations around the school, in the corner booth at The Landslide, and standing in the bakery aisle at Walmart—all places I'd been to with Marley.

The audience seemed slightly confused by this first medley of photos. I didn't care. I only wanted Marley to see that I belonged in this town. Diving into the chorus, I stared directly at her as the lyrics explained she was the only thing I needed for Christmas.

The next shot was of me holding a posterboard with big block letters—reminiscent of Bob Dylan's "Subterranean Homesick Blues" video, or the famous scene in *Love Actually*, depending on audience member age. The sign read: I CHOOSE YOU, MARLEY. NO MATTER WHAT ELSE IS IN STORE FOR ME, I CHOOSE YOU.

I knew the second it flashed up behind me because Marley's hands raised to her face as her mouth dropped open. Maureen squeezed her sister's shoulder and gave me a huge thumbs up while Miranda laid her head against Marley's other side and grinned from ear to ear.

A collective gasp came up from the audience when the next picture appeared on the screen. Me, holding another sign, this one reading: MERRY CHRISTMAS, MARLEY. I LOVE YOU.

Multiple heads in the crowd whipped around to get a glimpse of Marley as she sat stunned in her seat. Somehow, I kept singing as the next set of photos came up. I'd been gathering these all week, and had just received the last few this morning while throwing the final version of the slideshow together.

- Pictures of the bowling alley owner, the general manager at Walmart, and a broker at the insurance office, all holding poster boards reading: JAMES CAN WORK HERE.

- Katy, playacting, looking dead on her feet at work, holding a sign: THE LANDSLIDE ALWAYS NEEDS MORE SERVERS.

- Travis and Vivienne: WE NEED COUPLE FRIENDS (THAT COMES WITH FREE BABYSITTING, RIGHT?).

- Bambi had one looped around his neck: MARLEY IS MY MOMMY.

- Mrs. Allen: SOME THINGS ARE WORTH STEPPING OFF SCRIPT FOR. HE'S YOUR FRANK. #COUPLEGOALS.

- Nan and Penny: THE WHOLE SCHOOL HAS BEEN SHIPPING YOU FOREVER! DON'T LET US DOWN.

- Coach Hurley: THE BEST MEN CLIMB LADDERS TO MAKE SURE EVERYTHING IS JUST RIGHT

- Principal Nadal: NORMALLY, I WOULDN'T CONDONE FRATERNIZATION, BUT YOU TWO BELONG TOGETHER.

- The D&D Club: MR. WYMACK NEEDS SOMEONE WHO THINKS ALL THE WEIRD THINGS HE DOES ARE COOL.

- Mr. Bailey: HE MAY NEVER FIND ANYONE WHO LIKES HIS JEWELRY, OUTLANDISH OUTFITS, AND RIDICULOUS HAIR AS MUCH AS YOU DO.

- Daniel: IT'S NOT ALWAYS EASY TO BE HAPPY. YOU MAKE MR. WYMACK HAPPY.

- Will: YOU REALIZE HE NEVER WOULD HAVE MADE IT TO THE REUNION WITHOUT YOU, RIGHT?

- Oliver: THANKS FOR HELPING ME GET MY FRIEND BACK.

I'd stopped singing a few moments ago and the last of the background music faded away, but the slideshow continued. Evidently, in my bid to add a few last-minute pictures, I'd messed up the timing. The slides rolled on in silence. The audience remained deathly still as I breathed loudly up on the stage, staring hard at Marley as the last images came on the screen.

- Leo: I'VE NEVER SEEN MY LITTLE BROTHER AS HAPPY AS HE'S BEEN SINCE HE MET YOU.

- Maureen: YOU DESERVE EVERYTHING. I BELIEVE

JAMES LOVES YOU WITH HIS WHOLE HEART.

- Miranda: NOTHING BASIC ABOUT IT, SIS. HE'S
  YOUR TEN. YOU'RE HIS TEN.

The last slide was my mom and dad, sitting at their kitchen
table: YOU MEAN EVERYTHING TO JAMES. WE HOPE
HE VISITS SEATTLE, BUT OUR SON BELONGS IN
COLEMAN CREEK WITH YOU.

The projection screen faded to black. The entire crowd let
out a collective breath before the room erupted into cheers and
clapping. I could hear the whispered words of the students and
some other folks as they clued in audience members who weren't
familiar with our situation. But the din of the people in the
auditorium sounded like distant noise, something I barely heard
above the whooshing in my ears and the thumping in my chest.
Only Marley mattered.

Marley, who remained paralyzed in her chair.

I wasn't sure if I should get off the stage or make another
declaration into the microphone. I felt the weight of hundreds of
pairs of eyes as they volleyed between me and the woman I loved,
seeking some kind of resolution.

Finally, someone in the crowd—probably Coach—called out,
"Go get her, you lug nut!"

That gave me the push I needed. I went down the stairs directly
in front of the stage and into the audience. Everyone parted,
clearing a path to Marley. She was only about five rows back, but
it felt like a million miles. *Did she like the presentation? Or was she
embarrassed? Would she accept my love? Or keep pushing me away?*
How would she respond, other than staying frozen in her chair?

I reached Marley's row, and Maureen moved out of her seat so I could sit down next to her.

She turned to me. The silence was deafening before she said, "That was really something, James."

Her expression was maddeningly indecipherable. "I hope it wasn't too mu—"

"I love you too."

The words sounded like an alien language at first, and it took me a beat to process what she'd said. "You love me?"

"So much. It scares the stuffing out of me, but I do." She reached out to cup my face. "I can't believe you did that. And managed to keep it a secret. No one's ever done something like that for me before."

"Marley, you have to know by now—" I pulled her hands from my face and brought them to my chest. "I'd do anything for you."

Miranda couldn't hold back a high-pitched squeal. Marley looked at her younger sister with an exasperated expression before asking me, "What about teaching? What will you do?"

"I don't know. We'll figure it out. The bowling alley seems like a fun gig."

She laughed, lacing her fingers around my neck across the armrest. I stood up, taking Marley with me, lifting her feet off the ground as I gave her a big kiss right in the middle of the auditorium. Dozens of approving glances were directed our way as people began filtering out.

"Merry Christmas, baby," Marley whispered in my ear as we separated. No need to put on even more of a show for our colleagues and students.

We hugged one more time as folks exited the auditorium, heading to the reception. A sixth sense compelled me to look to the right, and I discovered that what I'd seen before my performance hadn't been a mirage.

Will, Leo, and my parents all stood there grinning at me.

"I thought that was you earlier," I said to Leo. "I texted."

"I didn't want to ruin the surprise by replying. After you made us take those pictures and send them, we felt like we needed to be here. We actually ran into Will outside."

I had been texting steadily with Will since the reunion, excited that we'd reconnected. When I'd asked him to send me a picture for what I'd been calling "Project Make Marley See the Light," I'd had no idea he'd show up for my performance.

Will reached out to clap me on the back. "I didn't have any plans for this weekend, and after you explained what you were doing, it seemed worth the drive to witness it in person."

"What if Marley had turned me down?"

He scoffed. "Dude, I saw you two at our reunion. The way she showed up for you. If that's not love, I don't know what is."

My parents had been quiet to this point, per usual, but my mom looked over at Marley and said, "We don't want to overwhelm you, dear, by being here. I hope you don't mind that we've intruded on your moment."

Marley grinned and waved her arm around at all the people pretending not to stare at us. "It's okay. Half of Coleman Creek is intruding on this moment. Just like they've been butting into our relationship for months. It's sort of how this town rolls."

Dad laughed. "Yes. James keeps telling us charming stories. It sounds like a great place."

"That's true," my mom agreed. Turning her attention back to Marley, she continued, "We're sorry if having us here is a bit much, but you'll understand when you're a parent. We've waited James's whole adult life for him to be truly happy, and now that it's finally in his grasp, we just wanted to see it. Being here is sort of a Christmas present to ourselves."

Marley took an unconscious step toward my parents. It was tentative at first, but then they pulled her into a double-sided hug. "You're part of the family now," Dad told her.

I looked up at the circle of family and friends surrounding us and felt nothing but joy and contentment. I'd miss teaching, sure, but being with Marley in Coleman Creek more than made up for it. And hopefully, I'd get back to the classroom down the road. At least a few of the teachers were in their late fifties. They'd have to retire at some point. In the meantime, there was always substituting.

Our group headed into the reception, where well-wishers greeted us. Maureen and Miranda melted into the crowd, saying hello to old friends they hadn't seen in a while. After fifteen minutes, Will, Leo, and my parents excused themselves to go back to their hotel. We agreed to meet for lunch the next day before Will had to drive back to Seattle. My family said they'd like to stay until after Christmas, if that was okay with us, and Marley practically leaped out of her skin to say yes.

Once we'd waved them off in their rental cars, we went back into the reception to say goodnight to our colleagues.

As we entered, Nan, Penny and Daniel pulled away from the group they'd been with to come talk to us.

"It's so cool you're in love," Daniel said quietly. "You're my favorite teachers."

"For sure," Nan concurred.

Penny scrunched her forehead. "But what I don't understand exactly is why Mr. Wymack had to do this big, huge thing at the talent show. I mean, it was cool and all, but why did the performance make it seem like he was fighting for Ms. Davis? You're already a couple."

I started to answer when Marley beat me to the punch. "It's because I didn't know what kind of couple James and I were until he showed me."

"What do you mean?" Nan asked.

Marley searched for the right words, clearly concerned with being appropriate with our students. "You know how this time of year everything is so fun and magical, with all the lights and decorations and presents, and then things feel kind of dull for a while after New Year's?"

"Uh huh." The teens answered in unison.

"Well, Mr. Wymack makes me feel the way the holidays do. Like there's another layer over my life." I squeezed Marley's waist, reveling in her words as she continued, "It's a little intimidating to realize that being with the right person makes you look at the world in a whole different way. I found out it's possible for relationships to feel full of surprises and new adventures *all* the time. Being with Mr. Wymack is like having Christmas year-round."

"That's really sweet," Nan said.

"You should, like, put that on a coffee mug or something," Penny agreed.

Daniel offered a shy smile before the three of them headed back to their friends.

We stayed a few minutes longer than planned, getting our fill of apple cider and cinnamon cookies. It felt amazing to put my arm around Marley's shoulders and know this would be our new normal, that there weren't any more questions about what we were to each other. We were each other's top priority.

Chapter Twenty-One

Marley

After waving goodbye to the last of the crowd, we got into our respective cars with a plan to meet back at my place. James needed to stop at his apartment to pick up Bambi and pack some clothes for the next few days. I made it clear I wanted him in my home and in my bed at least through Christmas morning.

My sisters did me a solid by grabbing a room at the Hampton Inn near the highway, giving us privacy for tonight. I had enough time to straighten up before James arrived. When I stopped to put some carols on in the living room, the image of him singing Kelly Clarkson flashed in my mind. I hadn't had the ability to focus on the stage during his song—I'd been so keyed in on the messages flashing in the slideshow behind him. But there had been plenty of folks recording. I'd already received texts from friends containing links to James's performance. Maybe it would go viral. A burly bearded guy in a red suit, long hair flowing, doing his best to channel his inner diva. I giggled, thinking of James's voice breaking on the high notes and—oh my goodness—the image of him making the heart shape with his fingers, pumping them against his chest as he sang. Priceless.

And he'd done it all for me. By the time he finally knocked on my door, I was ready for a proper celebration.

Once we got the dogs settled, James and I retreated to the bedroom. It wasn't my usual mode to play pillow princess, but he immediately had me on my back, coaxing me to "relax and enjoy it," as he put his hands and mouth on me, drawing two orgasms from my overheated body before finally slipping inside.

As he moved himself slowly and methodically above me, I realized how much more confident he seemed compared to the first time we'd been together, especially considering the brightness of the moonlight through the window. But if he believed I loved him, then he must have understood that meant his sweet, grabbable love handles too.

We'd built so much trust between us in such a short time. The chemistry had always been there, waiting to ignite, but it had taken the magic of the season to fan the flames.

The next morning, James and I relaxed on the couch in our pajamas as we drank coffee and munched on toast, teasing the dogs with ribbons. From opposite end tables, our phones vibrated at the same time. I looked down with a frown to see James and I had been included in messages on a group text. From Kasen.

KASEN: I know I probably should have sent this yesterday. But in my defense, I wasn't there yet. It's hard when you realize the girl you once loved is actually the perfect person...

KASEN: For someone else.

KASEN: Just so you know, this next part is a copy/paste. These words took a minute.

KASEN: Marley, when James reached out to me explaining his position and telling me what he wanted to do, it really hit home how much I'd failed you during our years together. He's known you less than half a year and he's ready to do whatever it takes to make you love him. I picked our college. I picked Portland. Our apartment. And you went along with it because that's what you do. You take care of people. You did everything to make me happy. Then the one time you asked me to do something, you asked me to come home with you while you took care of your dying mother who we both loved. And like a ginormous dick, I said no. I justified it at the time. But you were right to drive away and never look back.

"You contacted Kasen?" I asked James.

"Um...yes. After our last conversation, I kind of freaked out—you were pushing me away pretty hard—and Travis had his number. I figured it was a longshot, but I was willing to try anything."

I smiled at him in understanding as a picture came through our phones. Kasen, standing in front of his parents' house, holding a sign: MARLEY—IT'S OKAY TO CHOOSE HIM. HE SEEMS LIKE A GOOD GUY.

"Wow," James breathed out.

I thought about the earnest way Kasen had asked for my friendship only a few days ago, hinting that he'd be open to something more. Deep down, he must have known our ship had sailed. "That must have been hard for him."

I'd already made my decision about James. Kasen's gesture was just a bonus. An unexpected, beautiful bonus. I opened my private text chain with him and sent just two words.

ME: Thanks, friend.

A moment passed. Three dots appeared and disappeared a few times before his message came through.

KASEN: Anytime, pal.

I showed the texts to James. He was probably a ways away from being totally comfortable with mine and Kasen's friendship, but I imagined it would be okay, eventually. And, of course, it didn't need to be figured out right this minute.

Just after noon, my sisters came back, followed closely by Will and James's family. We ate an easy lunch of sandwiches and chips as they exclaimed over the decorations in my neighborhood and my house. Deanna and Chris had been charmed by everything they'd seen in Coleman Creek. I laughed when Leo leaned over to show me something on his phone, a picture of his parents with their arms around the Hawaiian-shirted Santa in front of the bowling alley.

I explained to everyone how James had helped with my decorations. There were several instances where James picked up a photo or knick-knack and could competently deliver its origin story. He'd clearly been listening when I'd relayed some of my family history. My sisters stood next to me as James held a photo of our mom from twenty years ago. He was telling his family about how Oscar had kept my mother company in her last days.

"I want that. One like him," Miranda whispered in my ear.

I put my arm around her shoulders. "You will. You just have to stay in one place long enough to get it."

Maureen murmured even lower, "I thought I had that once. But I was wrong."

"What?" Miranda and I asked as one.

"Nothing." Maureen said. "It was a long time ago, and it's not up for discussion." I thought I caught her eyes narrowing at Will, but it might have been annoyance with herself over the shocking piece of intel she'd just unwittingly given up.

I knew Maureen dated, but to the best of my knowledge, nothing had ever been serious. But judging by the rigidity of her shoulders and her pursed lips, she wasn't going to be offering that story anytime soon. I settled for slinging my other arm around her, making myself the filling in our sister sandwich, and watching with a full heart as the Wymacks showered Oscar with attention. And for good measure, Bambi too.

Will left just after one o'clock. We saw him off from the driveway. Maureen held back in the living room, still in a bit of a mood, but it seemed to improve as the afternoon went on.

In keeping with my resolution to be more flexible, I changed my mind about waiting until after New Year's to switch bedrooms. I'd never felt more like I was at the beginning of something than I did today. Besides, with so many family members in town, we could complete the move to the master suite quickly. And it would eliminate the need for James and me to share the hall bathroom with my sisters while they stayed in the house.

Deanna and Miranda took charge of cleaning and airing out the master while I boxed up the last of my mom's things and labeled them for a charity pickup. Leo helped me move her dresser and the remaining nightstand out to the covered carport. I didn't want any of my mom's old furniture. James and Leo then began moving some of the larger pieces across the hallway while Chris got to work disassembling the bed. James and I shared a glance as he tipped up the mattress. Hopefully, Chris didn't think too hard about the fact I'd done some very naughty things to his son on that bed twelve hours ago.

Once we'd reassembled the bed in the master suite, we began walking everything across the hall. My long mirror and small lamps, the framed posters on the walls, Oscar's dog bed, James's duffel bag. The master bedroom, empty for well over a year, now looked lived in. Maureen brought in the bulk of my toiletries from the hall bathroom and put them in the ensuite. James rushed to open his bag and grab his toothbrush, placing it next to mine in the holder.

James and I had one last obligation to Coleman Creek High School for the season. We'd agreed weeks ago—which felt like millennia—to be on shift at the tree lot for its final night. While it would be slim pickings for tree shoppers, the #colemancreekholiday selfie wall remained a community hot spot, so the baked goods and cider would likely sell out.

Even though the success of the tree lot and the talent show tickets hadn't resulted in job security for James—that had always been a pipe dream anyway—it meant that we could look forward to lots of fun extras for the kids next year. A discretionary budget for field trips, supplies, and new equipment.

James's family and my sisters went out to dinner together at The Landslide. I texted Katy to let her know to charge their first round to my tab. She sent back a thumbs up emoji, and also a longer text letting me know Kasen was there having dinner with his parents, and he seemed in good spirits—just in case I was curious.

At the tree lot, we arrived to discover everyone's tongues still wagging over James's performance.

"We were taking bets on whether you'd show up," Coach said as we walked up the path.

"Why wouldn't we? We're signed up. Even if there isn't much to do." I glanced around, trying to figure out where James and I could be most useful.

"That's not it. It's just that everyone is still gossiping about you two. I wasn't sure you'd want even more attention."

"Let them talk," James said, smiling. He came up behind me and wrapped his arms around my waist. "I got the girl. I don't care what people say beyond that."

From over at the selfie wall, some students snickered. Diane Montoya came over with a posterboard. She turned it around to reveal: MS. DAVIS AND MR. WYMACK 4-EVA.

"Very nice," James said. "I can see by your grammar that Ms. Davis's English courses have been very instructive."

I tapped him lightly on the arm. "Hey!"

"Come on, you two," Diane cajoled us. "Come take a picture with the sign in front of the selfie wall."

We took the picture. Then we took a few more. One with Diane. One with Coach. A few with other student volunteers. Even Fel wanted in on the action.

"Why are you taking these pictures, exactly?" I asked Diane.

She looked up from her phone, where she was busy posting on Instagram. Instead of responding to my question, she looked over at Fel and said, "I think I'm going to stick with #colemancreekholiday. I thought about starting a new one just for Ms. Davis and Mr. Wymack, but it might be better to keep it simple."

"Probably a good idea," he drawled, opening up the app on his phone.

"What are you doing?" I asked.

"Obviously, we're trying to get you two to go viral. That video of Mr. Wymack singing already has a bunch of views. You need to capitalize. Maybe this could even get the district to change its decision about his job."

"That's a thoughtful idea, Diane, but I doubt the school board members pay attention to viral videos. Ms. Davis and I don't want to 'capitalize,'" James asserted. "We just want to finish our shift at the lot and go home to enjoy the rest of the school break."

Over the course of our two-hour shift, we realized Diane hadn't exaggerated how many people had viewed James's performance online. Multiple tree lot customers we didn't know asked to take a picture with us, holding Diane's sign. They all told us they'd been moved by the video, several even saying it had made them cry. I agreed with James that I didn't mind if people talked about us, but I preferred our moment to be kept somewhat private. Just me, James, and the five thousand residents of Coleman Creek.

"Don't worry about it too much. People always move on quickly from these Internet things," James assured me. "They're just noise."

A moment later, my phone, James's phone, and Coach's phone all vibrated with the same incoming picture. Mrs. Allen, seated in a rocking chair holding her brand-new grandson.

"Aww, he's so cute." I hearted the picture.

"See? That's what I mean about the Internet being full of noise. This is all that really matters. Family and friends. And of course, spending as much time as possible with the love of your life." James kissed the top of my head. Turning to Coach, he said, "I hope you have a wonderful Christmas. Marley and I are going to leave if that's okay."

"Fine, fine." Coach waved us away. "You lovebirds have fun."

As we headed out, Fel trotted to catch up with us in the parking lot. Stopping a foot away, he eyed James. "Uh, Mr. Wymack, I just want to say that it was pretty cool what you did last night." He rocked back on his heels. "I know you didn't ask me to hold a sign or take a picture for your little slideshow, and I totally get it. But

I just want you to know that, if you had asked, I would have said yes, you know? And that shi—um, the stuff that happened with Daniel. I want you to know that, like, I heard you. Okay?"

James studied the teenager in front of us before angling his chin in acknowledgement. "I appreciate that, Fel. And if I ever make Ms. Davis another video, you're the first one I'll call to help."

"Okay. Sure." Fel allowed himself a hint of a smile before shoving his hands in his pockets and returning to his friends.

"Jeez." James shook his head. "How many more Christmas miracles are we getting this year?"

I laughed lightly. "It doesn't matter. The only one I care about is that you're here with me."

"James and Marley forever—I mean, *'for-evah.'*" James's impression of Diane was spot-on.

"How did I ever think you were cool when you are clearly the corniest guy on the planet?"

"Says the woman wearing the sweater of Santa doing the Macarena."

"Sorry. No take-backsies. I'm yours."

"You're mine."

Epilogue

James

The next few days were magical as my family meshed with Marley's. The house seemed a lot smaller and cozier with so many people coming and going, not to mention two overexcited dogs. Watching Marley cook in the kitchen with Leo and my mom filled my heart with peace. They laughed while trading stories and recipes, chatting like they hadn't met less than two weeks ago.

My dad ventured down to the rec room to investigate the shelves of books and games gathering dust there. He was in heaven, having enough people in the house to play epic games of Risk and Scrabble. For a moment, watching my dad and Maureen argue over the legitimacy of a high-scoring word, I felt a brief flash of sadness over the demise of The Game Place. It had been a good idea, bringing people together to play games. I still thought it could work, but I wasn't the one to execute it. Somehow, I would find my way back to teaching.

On Christmas Eve, Marley and I were the last to go to bed. She had on full-zip footie pajamas that made her look like The Grinch. I wore flannel ones. We'd both agreed that sexy times could wait until this house—with its very thin walls—wasn't crammed with family.

I caught her staring out the window into the backyard, reaching down to scratch Oscar's head.

"No snow this Christmas, I guess," she said.

I came up behind her and ran my hands up and down her arms, bending to rest my chin on her shoulder. "Maybe for the New Year."

"Maybe." Her voice sounded distant.

"Everything okay?"

She sniffed, just a little, but I still heard. "My mom would have loved this," she said. "Having a full house at Christmas. Seeing this home filled with so much joy again."

I moved my arms to tighten around her. "You're missing her tonight?"

"More like remembering."

"We'll always do that. C'mon. Let's get under the covers. I need you to keep my feet warm."

She smiled, but her mood stayed serious. "I'm probably always going to be sad about her." She turned away from the window and crawled into bed with me. "Just like there's always going to be a little part of me that worries you're going to stop loving me."

I rolled to my side and ran my palm along her cheek. "Marley, there's always going to be a part of me that wonders if you think I'm a loser. And I'll never understand how you can find my belly and muffin top sexy—"

"I do."

"I know. And every time you say it, I believe it a little more. Just remember, anytime you're sad about your mom, I'll be there for you." The mattress jostled as both dogs jumped on the bed. But James wasn't finished. "And if that scared little part of you ever rears its head, just ask me, and I'll tell you again. I love you, Marley. Always."

WE'D JUST FINISHED opening presents and were in a post-Christmas brunch coma when the doorbell chimed.

I knew Marley hadn't been expecting anyone, so I went with her to answer the door. It surprised us to see Mr. Bailey on the other side. He stood in his usual attire of crisp button down and pressed slacks underneath a wool winter coat, old-fashioned camel fedora on his head. Even Christmas Day could not mitigate the stern look on his face.

"Hey, Mr. Bailey." Marley furrowed her brow. "Is everything okay?"

"I came to give you some information. Some news that is also a Christmas present of sorts."

Marley and I looked at each other in confusion as Mr. Bailey removed his hat.

"Okay," I said. "Would you like to come in?"

"No, thank you. I won't be long." He addressed me directly. "Mr. Wymack—James—I want to tell you that your little stunt on Friday night inspired me. When you asked me to take that photo, I wasn't sure how it would all come together, but seeing that public display...Well, it humbled me. I doubt I could have been so brazen."

"Um, thank you," I replied. "But you get at least some of the credit. When you told me the story about Ellen, it made me see the truth. At some point, Marley had gone from being my friend to being my dream."

Marley gave me a hot look at that, one that promised some very fun times once we were alone again.

Mr. Bailey coughed. "Yes. That's very nice. But my point is that you made me see that a real dream doesn't have an expiration date. I am sure you would fight for Ms. Davis forever."

"That's true." I spoke without hesitation.

"Which is why I finally gathered up my courage to reach out and get a hold of Ellen. It wasn't hard. She's on Facebook. I just had to let go of my pride and reach out. I imbibed two fingers of bourbon and sent her a message. She replied the next day. Turns out she's widowed and spends her time working on veterans' charities in Maryland. We've been talking on the phone nonstop for the past few days."

"Wow. That's amazing," Marley said, and I agreed.

"It feels like no time has passed. And this go-round, for her, I'm not going to be afraid to make the big overture. We could keep talking on the phone, and I could visit. *Or* I can show Ellen that she's still my dream." Mr. Bailey finally looked less rigid—almost gleeful—when he continued, "Which is why I emailed my resignation to Principal Nadal and let him know I'll be moving to Maryland at the end of the school year."

"What!?" Marley exclaimed. "You're leaving Coleman Creek?"

"Yes. I just said I'm moving to the east coast. Young lady, focus." He spoke stiffly, but his eyes danced with merriment. "Principal Nadal made it very clear that the next available opening belonged to Mr. Wymack."

At first, I didn't register what he was telling us, but then it sank in. "Oh my God!" I leaned forward to hug Mr. Bailey, but he put out an arm to stop me, offering a firm handshake instead.

"Merry Christmas, Mr. Wymack, Ms. Davis." He put his hat back on. "I'm off to call my ladylove and work through some logistics. I have a big adventure waiting for me." With that, he turned and headed to his car.

After a moment of stunned silence, I pulled Marley into my arms. "I can still teach," I whispered into her hair. "I get to have you and my job."

My performance hadn't gone viral the way Diane had hoped it would. I'd been correct in my assessment that the Internet moved on quickly. Especially during a time when most people were paying attention to their real lives and all the demands of the season. But apparently my performance had had a tremendous impact on Mr. Bailey. And the end result was the same—I could keep my job at Coleman Creek High.

Marley and I went into the living room to share the good news with our families, but judging by the grins on their faces, they'd overheard. Even the dogs looked happy.

"Congratulations, little brother," Leo was the first to speak up.

"Yeah," Miranda concurred, adding impishly, "Although I had been looking forward to getting discounts on bowling."

Everyone laughed, and I couldn't help but marvel at how much my life had changed in just the past few weeks. It was like being with Marley had permitted all the other pieces of my life to slot into place. I'd just needed that foundation. The real me and the real her—flaws and all—facing the world and our fears together.

Living the dream.

Acknowledgements

This book is the product of me needing to write something a little sweeter. In the middle of researching some heavy topics for a different story, I decided to take a breather. I love holidays, and Christmas in particular, so this seemed like a good fit. I've also been missing my mom a lot recently, and wanted to honor how much she loved this time of year. Along the way, I started binge watching *Sons of Anarchy* (I know, I know, I'm ten years late to the party). I was inspired to give Opie a better, happier ending, so that was some of my inspiration for James in *Christmas Chemistry*.

As I was writing, I fell in love with Coleman Creek, so keep an eye out for more books in this series!

First and foremost, I want to thank my critique groups, who remind me that the secret to a soul-filling writing community isn't big words and correct use of ellipses. It's trust.

To the GLA—the OG, bestest book cheerleaders—who come to my house and don't mind if my dog jumps all over them: Aviva, Chun, Erin, Leann, Madison and Woody. You continue to be a source of inspiration, humor and joy.

To the Monday Night Bros, who always challenge me on re-writes and provide thoughtful feedback, along with occasionally making me laugh so hard I cry: Alexander, Alicia, Judy, Marc, Russ and Veronica. Thank you!

Thanks to Stephanie at Alt 19 Creative for the adorable cover. I liked it so much, I added a scene to the book.

To my alpha readers, beta readers, and friends who let me bounce ideas off of them and read bits along the way – thank you!

And, of course, to my husband and son, who continue to have to live with me during this author journey. This one didn't result in nearly as many late nights and questionable Internet searches as the last one, but I realize that meeting those deadlines in the home stretch made things rough. I'm grateful to you both for many reasons, but chief among them is that you love and support me during crunch time.

Lastly, I want to thank all the ARC readers, Instagram followers, and other folks that reached out to me to let me know how much they enjoyed *The Outline*. It truly meant the world to me, and I can never thank you enough for taking time out of your day to show kindness to a new author.

About the Author

Rory London is a writer of contemporary romance who lives in the delightfully gray Pacific Northwest. Rory is way too into football and holidays, and would write a lot more if there weren't so many books to read. When not engaged in something book-related, Rory is likely drinking large quantities of coffee and diet soda, or taking long walks around the neighborhood dreaming up more HEAs.

Other interests include outdoorsy things—as long as there is a real bathroom nearby—and indoorsy things—especially the kind that include good friends hanging out.

Rory lives with two other humans who bring laughter and joy into each and every day, as well as the world's most lovable dog, and three cats who are secretly plotting their revenge.

Connect with Me:
Email: rorylondonauthor@gmail.com
Website: www.rorylondonauthor.com
Instagram: @rory_london_author
Facebook: Rory London, Author

Also By Rory London

Printed in Great Britain
by Amazon